Marry for Money

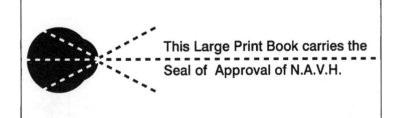

Marry for Money

Faith Baldwin

Thorndike Press • Thorndike, Maine

Published in 2001 by arrangement with
Harold Ober Associates, Inc.

Thorndike Press Large Print Romance Series.

The tree indicium is a trademark of Thorndike Press.

The text of this Large Print edition is unabridged.
Other aspects of the book may vary from the original edition.

Set in 16 pt. Plantin by Minnie B. Raven.

Printed in the United States on permanent paper.

Library of Congress Cataloging-in-Publication Data

Baldwin, Faith, 1893–
    Marry for money / by Faith Baldwin.
      p. cm.
    ISBN 0-7862-3211-0 (lg. print : hc : alk. paper)
    1. Married women — Fiction. 2. First loves — Fiction.
    3. Large type books. I. Title.
    PS3505.U97 M34   2001
    813′.52—dc21   00-068286

TO

DOROTHY AND ED MCKEOWN
with love and with constant gratitude
to our mutual friend
MISS OLDING

Cast of Characters

GAIL (RUSTY) ROGERS was the golden girl whose picture appeared on countless magazine covers.

SAM MEREDITH, newspaper reporter, was irresponsible, but fascinating.

BRAD SPENCER, scientist, had twenty million dollars and felt Gail was worth every bit of it.

ALEXANDRIA, Spencer's grandmother, was a domineering old tyrant.

MISS MILLICENT ELLIS was Alexandria's companion and yes-woman.

HELENA STURM worked with Brad, thought nothing was too good for him.

ERICH STURM, crippled and cynical, had little faith in his wife.

I

They had dined early at the Italian place around the corner from Gail's. The two rooms were, as usual, crowded, and people, waiting for tables, looked at the tall man and pretty girl with acute, impersonal dislike. Anyone could see that they had finished eating long ago and were just sitting there, talking. Even at some distance you could see the ashtray overflowing with stubs, the empty wineglasses; and from these could deduce that the coffeepot had been drained and what was left of the spumone reduced to a sickly soup.

A fat man, whose feet hurt and whose wife bored him, clutched a hurrying waiter and spoke, irritably, "Hey, Jack," he demanded, "what's with the couple at the corner table? Why don't they go to a movie, or something?"

The waiter, who had never seen the gentleman before, looked at him coolly. He suggested, "Maybe they don't like movies."

"Well, we do," said the fat man, shifting from one foot to another, as his wife wailed thinly, "Let's go somewhere else, for goodness' sake!"

"This place was recommended." He kept his grip on the waiter's sleeve, and put his other in a pocket. "Would this get us a table, Jack?" he inquired.

The waiter shuddered. His name was not Jack. But he took the offering and said, "I'll see what I can do . . ."

They watched him approach the corner table and speak to the tall man, and presently they saw results. The man rose, the girl slid into her short fur coat, her escort dropped a bill on the little tray and they went out, brushing past the fat man, who, with a bellow of indignation, perceived another couple sliding hurriedly into the vacated places.

"Why, that damned double-crossing . . . !"

His wife poked him. She said, "That girl . . . I've seen her somewhere . . ."

"Who cares?" said the fat man. "I'm starved."

The waiter came back, with becks and nods and wreathed smiles. He said, soothingly, "In the next room, a very good table . . ."

"Probably," said the fat man, following fussily, "it was there all along." And added as they entered the other room, "Good Lord, it's the kitchen!"

Copper utensils, chefs with towering

white caps, great ranges, and considerable noise. Their table was close to one of the ranges and hotter than the hinges. And his wife went on worrying her mental bone, as the waiter drew out her chair. "That young woman who just went out . . . Is she on the stage? I'm sure I've seen her before . . ."

"She's a model," said the waiter, "she gets her pictures on magazine covers . . ."

The fat man wasn't interested. He had long since lost interest in pretty girls, because what good did interest do you when your wife had the settled income and you had no way in which to make up for your lack of physical charm? Therefore, being frustrated, he found his greatest pleasure in eating. He said, with anticipation, "Bring us a menu, Jack, and make it snappy . . . also, two Manhattans."

The tall man and the pretty girl exchanged some badinage with the hat-check girl and went out. The autumn night was cool and dark and a small wind whispered. On the East River a boat spoke in a deep, warning voice. There was fog obscuring the high stars.

"Movie?" he asked.

Gail shook her head. And Sam continued, "Shall we go back to your place and fight it out?"

"Why not?" she agreed, after a moment.

The flat was two flights up, in a converted brownstone house. They climbed the stairs in silence, Sam took the key from her hand and opened the door. The miniature hall contained a chair, a mirror and a table. Roses bloomed on the table in a squat blue vase. Sam dropped his coat on the chair, and slung his hat on the table.

"Come in," said Gail, from the living room.

It was very like a million other living rooms. The two girls with whom she shared the apartment had gone out and not returned. Gail went into the smaller bedroom, which she occupied alone, and looked around her. A bureau drawer was half open, and she deduced, without rancor, that Evie had been hunting for nylons. She put her coat on the bed, and unslung her shoulder strap handbag. She called, "Find cigarettes and amuse yourself while I re-do my face."

She sat down at the mirror. Her hair was in disorder, and she never wore a hat. For a moment she looked at herself, with impersonal criticism. Her hair was wonderful, a deep pure gold just washed with copper. It was shoulder length, and curled naturally, she could do anything with it; pageboy, upsweep, the works. She leaned forward and deepened the curves of her flexible mouth with a lipstick. Her skin was pale and cool, her eyes gray, under brows darker than her hair.

"Hurry up," said Sam from the other room.

She went out, presently, and sat on the couch, and Sam, standing at the windows, turned, a cigarette burning between his stained fingers.

"Okay," he said, as if their conversation had not been interrupted, "so we'll get married, any time you say. I'll make you a fond husband. Also, a bad one. If you don't believe it, ask Betty."

"I don't have to," Gail said equably, "she's already warned me . . . in detail."

"Women have no decency," said Sam, amused.

He was thin, he carried himself badly, his clothes had an air of having seen better days, but his shoes were polished within an inch of their lives. He had dark hair, a lot of it, and nearly black eyes. His face was lined and sharp, his smile particularly charming.

"Rusty —"

"Don't call me that, you know I hate it."

"Rusty Rogers, Girl Model," he said, grinning. "Okay . . ." He came and sat down on the couch. "You're the stubbornest dame

I ever met," he told her. "Also, you're crazy. You won't live with me, in happy sin; you won't marry me. What else is there?"

She said evenly, "I could be a sister to you."

Sam made disconcerting noises. He said, "I have a sister, thanks, and she disapproves of me."

"So do I."

"Be that as it may, you are in love with me," Sam reminded her. "We've been in love for months. You, first."

A faint color rose in her cheeks but she looked at him steadily. "What of it?" she asked.

"What of it?" he repeated, aghast. "I meet you at a clambake and you go to work on me and then —"

"I'm sorry, Sam."

"You are, like hell. Look, sugar, we're getting nowhere fast. We fight, argue, and hold hands in the movies. That's no life for a beautiful girl and a brilliant journalist. I'm tired of beating my brains out . . . I can't eat, I can't sleep —"

"You eat like a horse," she said, "and if you don't sleep it's because you won't go to bed."

He said pontifically, "I made my position clear tonight, didn't I? All the cards on the table, including the joker. I don't *like* being married, baby. I tried it once. It was strictly from horror. Of course, you might argue that, at the time, I was married to Betty."

"I won't. I like Betty."

"She's a half-wit."

"Pete doesn't think so. And he's married to her now."

"Pete isn't even a half-wit," said Sam. "Gail, I might not even like being married to you."

"You'll never know," said Gail. "It's the crackpot question. Never answered."

"There you go again! I wish," he said in despair, "you'd shut up."

He made a long arm, pulled her toward him and kissed her. She was quiet under his kiss, neither struggling nor responsive. He let her go and asked roughly, "What's got into you? You know damned well you like me to kiss you!"

She thought, Yes, worse luck, and looked at him gravely. She had been looking at him, on and off, for more than a year. Sometimes she thought she would never tire, and at other times she wished she might never see him again. I'm tired, she told herself, edgy and all mixed up.

"It's no use, Sam," she said, "my mind's made up."

"Your what?" he demanded. He added, "Look, I'm resigned to a fate worse than death. What's the percentage in playing hard to get?"

"I'm not." Her voice, usually low and a little husky, sharpened. "I appreciate your sacrifice," she said, "I know you don't want to marry anyone —"

"Skip it."

She said, "I'm not going to see you any more, Sam."

"Why?"

"You know why."

"You're scared," he said slowly, "scared that I'll wear down your resistance . . . one way or another."

Now he was laughing. He didn't believe her; maybe she didn't believe herself, but she had to . . . she thought drearily. She said with an effort, "Sam, look at me."

"It's a pleasure."

"As if you had never seen me before; as if it were for the first time. What do I look like, to you?"

"Very pretty," he answered promptly, "very desirable."

"Me," she agreed, "and a hundred thousand other girls . . . girls who become a year older on each birthday, and eventually a year less pretty, a year less desirable."

"You've been reading books," he accused her. "What's the gimmick?"

"There's nothing special about me," Gail told him. "A lot of girls are young and have good figures, good legs, and the sort of face now in fashion — you see it everywhere . . . advertisements, fashion magazines, calendars, illustrations. The sort of face that flashes on the screen or sits back of desks. The sort of face that waits on you, in restaurants and shops . . ."

He said, interested, "I've never had a face wait on me."

"You know what I mean. A photogenic face . . . I'm too tall for the screen," she said, "and, moreover, I can't act."

"What's this leading into?"

"Nothing, really. I've been in love with you. In a way, I still am. I don't know why," she added, "but I'm going to get over it. There's no future in it, Sam."

For the first time tonight he was genuinely alarmed and angry. He asked, "What do you mean, no future in it? I offered you a future, didn't I? . . . as legal as a marriage license."

"Oh, sure," she said, "you offered. But you admitted what I've always known. You don't want to be tied down. You've never wanted that, and since you came home you're more restless than ever. You told me

15

so on our first date."

He said, "Look, Gail, discount half of all I say. I'll settle down, one day."

"Possibly, but not with me."

"What in hell do you really want?" he demanded.

"Nothing you can give me. A couple of years ago I knew what I wanted . . . or thought I did. I wanted out, from behind a typewriter. I had two chances, there in the advertising agency. One was a nice boy. No world beater but he'd always make a living. Eventually, a house in the suburbs, a part-time maid, a couple of kids and a station wagon. I didn't want that. Then someone came in and saw me and said I was wasting my time. So I took that chance. I learned to walk, dress and put my face on, properly. I'm a good model, Sam, and I get paid for it. I carry a hatbox and everyone says, aren't you lucky, and, you must meet such interesting people."

"You met me."

"You," she said, "and a lot of other wolves. Sam, I'm sick of it. I'm sick of lights and cameras, of wearing a bathing suit in winter and mink in summer; I'm tired of illustrators' studios and fashion shows. I'm even tired of flying to Arizona to lean against a corral fence in Levi's and a red shirt, talking to wranglers or maybe to a horse. I'm tired of going to the Bahamas to sit on a hunk of coral, looking relaxed, and of standing on the edge of a tiled pool in Arizona with a backdrop of mountains, desert, and cacti. I'd like to start going places without the camera."

Sam said, "Don't be sorry for yourself, baby. That kid in the agency, were you in love with him?"

"I've never been in love with anyone but you."

"That's funny," he said, "considering your temperament."

Her color rose again. She said, "All right, Sam . . . but I wasn't aware, until quite recently, of my temperament, as you call it."

"A euphemism," he agreed.

She said slowly, "I don't really like you, much, Sam. You're careless and inconsiderate. You're unreliable. You drink too much."

"You sound like Betty, or any wife."

"Maybe. You're tough," said Gail. "I suppose you had to be. The war gave you your chance . . . that and the fact that you and Betty were divorced just before the war —"

"You don't like me," he asked, "but you're in love with me? That's a man's angle, Gail, not a woman's. Most men don't like the

17

women they fall in love with . . ."

She smiled, for the first time. She said, "That's right. You don't like *me*, as a matter of fact."

"You're wrong," he said. "I didn't at first. Another good-looking babe, I thought, and on the make. Hard as nails, seen in the right places, keeping her pretty eyes peeled and smarter than most. Not making any errors, even for love. All façade and no emotion. It wasn't a new challenge, but most men fall for it. Most of them say, Maybe I'm the one. Most of them get fooled. I didn't. Plenty of emotion, Gail, and there's no sense denying it."

"I don't deny it."

"If you don't want me," he said, "what do you want?"

"Security."

"Where is anyone going to get that, nowadays?" he demanded. "In the Victorian era, yes. Marry, put on a cap, sit by the fire, wait for the Mr. Big to come home. Kids, as compensation. What compensations are they now? And Mrs. on the calling card. If you'd wanted what passes for, what even might be, if you're lucky, a little security, why didn't you marry the kid in the agency?"

"I didn't want that kind."

"Penthouses," he asked, unbelieving, "a

couple of yachts, a safe-deposit box? Not you, Gail. I might have thought so when I first met you but not now. You can have fun for peanuts: you can ride on a bus, you can go to the movies, you can eat a blue-plate dinner and have fun. You aren't a grabber; buy this, gimme that. I know. I was once married to a girl with an incurable case of the getmes."

"Not incurable," she said. "Betty was just trying to compensate for the things you wouldn't or couldn't give her. Pete doesn't earn any more than you, Sam, and she's happy. She's all over the getmes. She has what she wants."

"Oh, sure," he said, "love. A wonderful invention." He pulled her to him again, and added roughly, "I love you and you know it. What's the use of talking about it? Maybe I'll *like* being married to you, maybe I'll be crazy about it."

"For how long?"

"Who knows? We're adult, we're realistic, and we don't know. Do you suppose the kids know, who haven't grown up, who go to the altar with bells ringing, walking on rosy clouds, accompanied by dreams, cupids, innocence? They take a terrific chance and don't know it. We do."

She said, "Sam, when I marry, I'll marry

19

someone I like . . . someone I — you'll laugh at this, it's pretty corny — someone I respect."

"Someone," he said angrily, "with most of the mint, too?"

"Yes."

"Platinum mink, emerald-cut diamonds, triplex flats. Gail, for God's sake . . . if you even had a chance . . ."

She said evenly, "I think I have. And I don't want money for what it can buy."

"What else is it good for?" he asked helplessly.

She freed herself from his arm. She thought, If we could stop talking . . . but we can't. We have to talk and be bright and — what was it he said? — realistic. If we could stop talking and I could stop thinking. But I can't . . .

She got up and walked to the windows and he made no move to follow. He took out a pack of cigarettes and his lighter and sat there smoking. He thought, Okay. But tomorrow or next day I'll phone and say, What about dinner? and she'll say, All right, Sam . . .

Gail spoke over her shoulder. "Once I made a promise . . . to myself, and to someone else. I'll keep it."

"What sort of promise, and why?"

"I won't tell you . . . and I can't tell you why. In order to know why you would have had to know me since I was born."

He said, after a moment, "All right. But I like my mysteries complete with solution. Someone you like and respect, someone with heavy dough. Would that be Brad Spencer, by any chance?"

"It could be."

"I introduced you to Spencer," he said, "a couple of months ago. I remember. We went to the Cub Room. The regulars were there and Brad wandered in, with Ike Evans. Ike's a regular and any pal of his is okay, particularly someone like Brad who never sets foot in the better boîtes. After that, I went out of town, took a swing around the country to see what was cooking. I got back two weeks ago, I've seen you almost every night since."

"You were away quite a while."

"Do you mean to tell me you've been seeing Brad Spencer?"

"Yes."

"You haven't a prayer," he said harshly; "practically every girl in New York, to say nothing of other places, has been thrown at him by her doting parents. All the rest, given the chance, have thrown themselves."

"I haven't, yet."

Sam went on as if she had not spoken,

"And in addition to being the last of the bachelors — and I do mean bachelor — he's a damned nice guy. Also plenty smart."

"We'll see."

"I like him," said Sam, "and even if I weren't interested . . . I'd hate to see him snapped up with the usual spinner. Not that I think he'll bite. But if he does . . ."

"If he does, what?" asked Gail, turning.

He said, "I'd seen him around town in unlikely places, but I never knew him until we sat together in a dirty little cellar in France and listened to the whiz-bangs. He's quite a person . . . he deserves the best."

"And I wouldn't be?"

"For a man you loved," said Sam, with unusual gentleness, "better than the best. For me, even, unreliable as I am . . . a fact you've pointed out. But not for Brad. Not that I'm worried," he added mendaciously, "he's not likely to fall. But if he should . . ."

She said wearily, "If he should, you'll tell him, I suppose? You have a photographic memory for conversations. You rarely take notes, I believe."

He said stubbornly, "Sure, I'd tell him and he'd hate my guts for it. And you'd try to persuade him I was jealous . . . dog in the manger stuff —"

"Would you be?"

"Yes. But that's not all the reason."

She said, "Don't worry, Sam. If Brad Spencer ever asks me to marry him —"

"Well?"

"I'll say yes, and tell him why." She walked back toward him, carrying her slender height like a banner. She said quietly, "Good-bye, Sam."

He rose, by an unfolding process, and took her by the shoulders. She looked small, in contrast and was forced to look up, which pleased him. He bent his head, kissed, and then released her. He asked, "You mean that, Gail? You still mean it?"

She was white, and so shaken that there was no possible concealment; she could not trust her voice, so nodded mutely.

He said, "I know you too well . . . and maybe too little. You don't make sense, baby. We could make a go of it, we could be happier than most people. Think it over."

"No."

"You love me."

"I can't help myself," she said desperately, watched the little familiar smile twitch at the corners of his mouth, and added, "But I'll learn, I swear it!"

"You don't believe that." He went out to the little hall and she made no move to follow him. He came back presently and said, "You haven't seen the last of me, I don't brush off easily."

She heard the door slam, hard; she heard him running down the stairs. "Sam," she said aloud, "Sam . . . ?"

II

She was not asleep when Evie and Pat came in; they returned late, first Evie, then Pat. Evie looked in on her, opening the door softly, but Gail lay quiet, her eyes closed, until the door shut again. She knew it was Evie, she could tell by her step, not as quick or as light as Pat's. Later, she heard Pat talking, in the room next door . . .

"Gail in?"

"Sound asleep. I opened her door, she didn't budge."

She heard them moving about, opening drawers, shutting them, running the water in the bathroom. She heard Pat's effortless laughter, and heard Evie say, "Hush, you'll wake her."

She might as well get up and go in the other room and ask, What sort of time did you have, you two? But she had no wish to, no wish to learn, just yet, how Evie had made out with the new man, whether or not Pat had set her wedding date, nor to have them ask, How's Sam?

After a while she heard the windows go up next door and the little rustlings that meant they were settling down. She felt very much alone, and the tears crowded back of her eyes, thick and urgent, her throat was tight and swollen. It isn't easy to cry quietly, especially if you are crying with your heart.

Give over, said her heart urgently, take the gamble, what are promises, made a lifetime ago? No one's happy for long, you're entitled to as much happiness as you can get, aren't you? Sam's your guy, you've known that from the first time you set eyes on him.

She wanted Sam Meredith; the crazy jokes they shared, the warmth and excitement . . . she wanted the mounting challenge of their sudden, stormy quarrels, their reconciliations, as sudden and complete. She wanted the easy response of her senses, young, ardent . . . the illusion that, with Sam, she need never again be lonely or afraid. But her mind rejected him, when they were not together. She could not think clearly, with Sam, except on the surface.

Her mind did not want Sam at all; his moods and tempers, his unreliability, his willful restlessness.

She had met his divorced wife before Sam returned from Europe . . . at a party one night, twenty people sitting around a crowded living room . . .

Betty was small, fair, childlike, wearing

new happiness for anyone to see. Her husband was a pleasant, grave young man. Gail had liked them both.

Someone spoke of Sam, of a dispatch over his by-line, and someone else hunted up the paper. And Betty had touched her husband's hand and smiled; it was as if she had said, Don't mind, it's all over.

"Sorry," said the man who had spoken of Sam, "I forgot," and Betty had said, "It doesn't matter."

She had explained matters a little to Gail, sitting beside her on a big couch with sagging springs.

"I was married to Sam Meredith," she said, "for three years . . . we were divorced just before the war . . . I met Peter shortly after . . . people forget, I suppose, because Sam never *seemed* married, to anyone."

Betty had stopped working after her marriage to Peter. She had been on a fashion magazine for young women. The second time Gail saw her they met at a cosmetic counter, around two o'clock on a spring day and neither had lunched. So they had gone into Hicks', found a table and sat there talking for a time, over salads and iced tea.

Gail had asked idly, "Do you miss your job?"

"No," Betty told her, "I never wanted to

work, really. I'm not the type. I'm that peculiar creature, a domestic woman. I like to cook and run a house and raise a family." She was older than Gail, she must have been twenty-eight or so, but she looked very young. She had flushed, a little, and added, smiling, "I've begun . . . that is, in a few months I shall be raising a family . . . I hope it's twins."

Gail remembered laughing and saying she hoped so, too.

"Sam never wanted children," said Betty. "He never wanted a home; he never even wanted a wife."

"He sounds very selfish," said Gail, who didn't much care for the intimate confidences which come so easily to many women.

"You can say that again," Betty had assured her. "I couldn't take it, after a while; never knowing where he was nor what he was doing. I lived in a boardinghouse in Reno and cried steadily for six weeks. What a dope! But then I didn't know I'd meet Peter . . . not in Reno, but back here, at my aunt's, of all places. He was her insurance broker."

"Didn't your husband mind . . . about the divorce, I mean?"

"He asked for it," said Betty. "He wanted to be free . . . as if he had ever behaved as if

28

he were anything else . . . there was a war coming up, he said . . . such an original reason for asking for a divorce."

Now Gail turned on her pillow, and clenched her sopping handkerchief. She had seen Betty . . . since . . . Betty knew about her and Sam; everyone knew. Betty had warned her.

Funny, the excuses you made, the illusions you fostered . . . all so simple, with such clarity. You said, Betty hadn't been the right woman for him. It was as easy as that. You went on from there, excusing, condoning, embroidering . . . With the right woman, Sam would be satisfied to settle down, it was only because he had been unhappy that he had done the things which Betty had told her . . . if he *had* done them . . . it was common sense to discount half of what an ex-wife said . . . three-quarters . . .

If he drank, if there had been other women, it was because he wasn't happy.

That had been a brief illusion, it hadn't lasted long; just until Sam had begun his arguments against marriage . . . which was, he said, as everyone knew now, an entirely artificial institution.

She thought, I'll get up and bathe my eyes and take a bromide or something. But the girls would hear her, Evie was a very light

29

sleeper and would patter in, asking anxiously, Are you ill, Gail, what's the matter?

She forced herself to lie still, but she felt cold, the crazy, chilly sensation starting with her feet, creeping up slowly like a little death, until she was shivering under the blankets.

She closed her hands, taut, tense, experiencing a most bitter loneliness, a forlorn bereavement. And presently slept, without warning, and toward morning, dreamed.

She did not know where she was, the outline was vague, there was only uncertainty. The place could have been anywhere; a dingy hotel bedroom; a room in a boardinghouse; a back bedroom and bath, let to respectable people . . . the smell was there, always the same smell; cooking and dust, face powder, soap . . . it was cold, with a damp, frosty shivering; or perhaps it rained in long gray streaks against unwashed windowpanes, gusty and slashing or in a dispirited, half-hearted way; and now it was hot, with a brassy sun and the feeling that the roof was too close overhead . . . In the dream, discomfort shifted to discomfort, train wheels revolved, and someone said loudly, "It's no use," and someone else said gently, "I am afraid there is very little hope," and in a room which she could not see there was the sound of difficult, loud breathing . . .

Then it changed, and she could feel the hairbrush, brushing ceaselessly through the tangles, brushing the pain out and the shine in, she could hear the voice saying, "You're all I have, honey, you were worth it all." She could hear the voice saying, "Remember, a hundred strokes a day" . . . saying, "Promise me, promise me, promise me" . . . while the hands, strong and inexorable, went on brushing, brushing . . .

She woke, sweating, her heart pounding, and it was morning and she could hear Pat skittering around the kitchen, she smelled coffee, she heard Evie crying wildly, "Dammit, my last pair of nylons . . . that *would* happen today!"

Gail sat up and took her head in her hands. Why do you have to dream, asleep and waking? But your waking dreams are of your own volition, and are sometimes as revealing as those which come by night.

She got out of bed with an effort, put her feet in mules, reached for her robe, and then opened her door. "Hi," she said, and Evie came to stand with the snagged stockings in her hand and say, "I thought you were never going to wake."

Gail asked, "What do you mean, *your* last pair? I don't know what you do with stockings, you'd think you lived in a bramble bush. I can let you have another pair, Evie."

Pat called, "You up, Gail? How about some coffee?"

Evie went into the tiny kitchen and Gail followed. There was a little range, a sink, a table and cupboard, two chairs and a stool. Gail sat on the stool and drank her coffee, clear. She said, "How not to appear with a bright morning face! I haven't even washed!"

Pat looked fourteen in her pajamas. She was twenty but so small she could model for teen-age clothes and usually did. She was thin and cute. She could wear her red hair loose or scrabbled up on top of her head, as now; she could wear her face scrubbed and shining, and, on her, it looked good.

Evie was dressed. She looked always as if she had never known a moment of dishevelment. Her figure was average, a little out of proportion, her legs only fair. But her face was remarkable, and greatly in demand by illustrators and photographers. You could see her face almost every month on magazine covers, in advertisements . . . just the nobly shaped head, the cloud of dark-brown hair, the widely spaced eyes, the beautiful features.

They were good but not intimate friends, these three. They borrowed from one another, nylons, a handbag, money, if one ran short; they scrupulously repaid. They got along well, recognizing differences in temperament and respecting them. Pat was a romantic, believing in her star. She had wanted to be a nurse, her probationary experience had cured her of that but left her with a bias toward doctors . . . who were, usually, married. But now she had found one who wasn't, although very soon he would be, and to her; which was fortunate, her friends agreed, as otherwise she would have become a hypochondriac.

Evie had had some slight stage experience, in summer stock. But she was interested not in the stage, but in the screen. She was cool and direct and even-tempered. She was extremely ambitious. She said, drinking her coffee:

"This man last night, Dave Gammon — he said he could get me a screen test."

"Golly," cried Pat, "you're as good as in . . . !"

"Are you sure?" Gail asked. "Screen tests cost a lot of money."

"Sure enough," said Evie, "he's the McCoy, I made certain of that . . . a talent scout for Amalgamated." She smiled faintly, "But there could be a catch . . ." she admitted.

"You're so damned cynical, Evie," said Pat.

Evie said calmly, "I have to be . . . a promise is one thing and performance another. This 'I can get you in pictures, darling' isn't just a gag, I've met up with it before. And I'm not in pictures, am I?" She shrugged. "I'm seeing him again tonight and I'll know whether or not we're both wasting our time." She rose and stood against the little archway. She said, "I'll take a flock of photographs along . . . Gammon said, half of the stars haven't good figures . . ." She named several and Pat asked, bewildered, "How do they get away with it, then?"

"Cheaters," said Evie, "falsies. And a good masseuse." She was perfectly aware that her pink and white flesh was badly distributed, too little above the hand-span waist, too much below. She couldn't diet, when she did she lost in the wrong places; and her face showed it. Her face was, literally, her fortune.

"How's Bill?" Gail asked Pat when Evie had left the room.

"Wonderful," said Pat, looking like a child with a Christmas doll, "and we think, late spring. He'll be through interning, and go right in with his father. I'll love a small town, I came from one . . ." She asked politely, "How's Sam?"

34

"As usual," said Gail. Pat didn't like Sam much and Evie frankly disliked him but they were very courteous to him. Early in their association Pat had said candidly, "Isn't it marvelous that we don't like the same type of men?"

They didn't. Gail found Pat's Bill a trifle too self-assured, and clinical, Evie thought him a bore; neither Pat nor Gail was impressed with Evie's considerable string of hard, fast-talking men, minor Hollywood or on the fringe.

Gail got off the stool and smiled at Pat, who was washing up. She said, "Need any help?"

"My turn. Besides, I don't have to work till two."

"I do." She looked at the kitchen clock, said, "Golly," and went to her room to dress. When she was almost ready, the telephone rang and Pat answered it. She called, "For you, Gail," and, as Gail came into the living room, added, "I don't think it's Sam."

It wasn't . . .

"Hello," said Gail . . .

"This is Brad," the quiet voice told her. "I got back a few days earlier than I expected . . . I suppose it's hopeless to ask if you're free tonight?"

"Not at all — as I am free."

"Would you dine with me, then?"

"I'd like to, very much."

"Where?"

"Any place, quiet."

"Good. Shall I call for you about seven?"

She said that he might, and hung up. Funny, she thought, last night, lying awake, she had not thought once of Brad Spencer. She had not thought of him seriously, at any time, until Sam had asked, with that curious forward thrust of his jaw, "Would it be Brad Spencer, by any chance?"

Now she would think of him.

Sam had introduced them, that night in the Cub Room. She had seen him since, quite incidentally . . . once at a charity fashion show which he had reluctantly attended with his extremely formidable grandmother; and once, when walking down Madison Avenue, she had run into him, on a sticky September day, and he had suggested, "Let's go in here and have a long, cool drink." Since then she had had dinner with him twice, meeting him after work. This would be the first time he had called for her, as it happened. Neither Pat nor Evie had met him.

She went back to her room and Evie called, "Was that Sam? I thought maybe he would know something about Dave Gammon . . . he used to be on a newspaper, I believe, before he went with Amalgamated."

"No. It was Brad Spencer."

Evie came in and watched Gail put the last things in the hatbox which was as much a tool of her profession as the carpenter's awl, the painter's brush, the engineer's slide rule of theirs. She said, "You like him, don't you?"

"Very much."

Evie said thoughtfully, "He has practically all the money in the world." She waited, but Gail said nothing. And Evie asked finally, "What does Sam think?"

"There's nothing to think."

"Ask him," said Evie, "Spencer, I mean, if he knows anyone crazy enough to stake a girl to a trip to the coast; car, personal maid, good mink, and a press agent." She smiled. "Maybe he has connections."

"He's a scientist," said Gail.

Evie looked at her oddly. She said, "You're a funny kid. I wonder if you know what you want. Pat knows and I know . . . we're a couple of little steam rollers . . . but you, I don't think you know."

Gail picked up the hatbox. She said, after a moment, "I know, all right."

III

Early that evening Bradford Spencer rattled happily around in his impressive bedroom, prior to keeping his engagement with Gail. He whistled, off key, raking a comb through his thick, mouse-colored hair, regarded himself in an uncompromising mirror and reflected that the plain man had one advantage over the superb specimen of masculinity glorified by the cinema and admired by the ladies. A beautiful girl must eventually reach the conclusion — given intelligence — that it's no fun to share your mirror. The unnotable escort provides a setting, background, contrast, and no competition. A comforting thought.

He looked from the tall windows across to the Park, in the early dusk. He would never tire of this, nor of lights starring the deepening dusk. In spring the haze was violet, in autumn, a dreaming blue; in summer it was shot with gold and in winter shaken into a pictorial snowstorm, swirling about the lights.

A bell rang downstairs, which meant that his grandmother and her companion, Miss

Ellis, were about to indulge in their apéritif of very dry sherry. Brad grinned briefly. His grandmother, Miss Ellis, the servants, the house itself, were all truly out of this world; his world, at any rate. For he was a physicist . . . the man you never noticed in the street, the man to whom no legend had attached itself, the obscure man.

For a time he had broken away, he had been part of danger in the open, the danger anyone could read about in the headlines. He'd managed that by sheer stubbornness, by pulling every possible wire, by shouting down the claim he was essential. But they'd pulled him back, out of the open understandable warfare into the other kind, the secret kind, into the battle of Oak Ridge, from which one derived no wounds . . . if lucky.

He had a wound now, for he had cut himself shaving, which did not enhance his appearance. But, then, he had seldom been in love.

His first experience had taken place at Newport when he was ten and the small object of his tongue-tied affections had attached herself to a more spectacular suitor, aged thirteen, very daring, continually yanked from the watery grave by the lifeguards and alternately slapped and cosseted

39

by a much-married mama. There had been others whom from a distance young Mr. Spencer had adored, particularly, when at twenty-two he had encountered a charming compatriot in Paris. But she was already considering a title. Had she been poor, he realistically reminded himself, she might have relinquished the strawberry leaves, in fact the strawberry leaves would have relinquished her. But she hadn't been poor by a long shot . . . then, at any rate.

Contemplating the evening with Gail, he had found himself smitten with a slight case of the shakes. He wasn't sure that he was in love with her . . . or was he? He tried to rationalize the impulse that had sent him headlong to the telephone this morning in the Pennsylvania Station. He thought, She's a blonde, and she has rather a look of little what's-her-name in Newport, now, it may he added, safely married, and the mother of three sons. The copper-washed hair, the slender body structure, the pointed chin . . .

His grandmother, trotting out for inspection the granddaughters of her old, respectable, well-heeled friends, had advised him upon several occasions that he must marry; and soon . . . There was a sinister implication that if he didn't, before senility overtook him, the Spencer line would perish.

She also advised a charming, intelligent young woman who would share his interests. This seemed unlikely unless he married a female scientist which so far he had not been tempted to do. But a cozy evening at home with his bride discussing nuclear chain reaction did not appeal to him and would certainly not appeal to his bride or anyone else's.

Since encountering Gail at the fashion show his grandmother had done a little gentle probing. He couldn't blame her. She had lost her only child, his father, tragically; and his mother, whom she had also loved, had died a year or so later. She herself had been widowed early. Brad had never known his grandfather. It was natural that she interest herself in his affairs . . . and sometimes regretted quite openly that, as far as her knowledge went, he'd had none. Mrs. Spencer belonged to a generation which believed in a wild oat or two provided they were hothouse grown, or under wraps. What she didn't know was that Brad had sown an oat, in Paris, after he had been refused by his fellow countrywoman. It had been very gay, very expensive and a lot of fun, but would, he decided, pall with repetition.

He heard the creak of the dumbwaiter, and grinned. This was quite a house, sitting narrow and obstinate between two apartment buildings. He yearned to get rid of it but Mrs. Spencer would not hear of it. She had come to the white stone edifice as a bride and intended to remain there until her demise. The house was as obstinate, as unreconciled to change as she was. The marble steps were scrubbed daily, the window boxes bloomed with tulips in spring, geraniums in summer, and dwarfed evergreens in inclement weather. The delicate ironwork was free from rust and the brass shone like the sun. Not hell, high water, or the pleas of realtors could move the Spencer house from its foundations. It was Alexandria Spencer's as long as she chose to occupy it.

Going downstairs, Brad reflected upon the hushed Victorian atmosphere smelling vaguely of port, of conservatory flowers, and, he concluded absurdly, of feather boas. It was a house which reeked genteelly of excellent service and an effulgent past, from the ballroom on the third floor — the servants lived on the fourth — to the basement, and wine cellar. It was a house as well preserved, and as stubborn, as his grandmother, sipping sherry with the desiccated Miss Ellis.

There was a fire in the drawing room and

the Spencer portraits looked down upon Mrs. Spencer, her companion, and the subdued décor. Miss Ellis was as familiar with the room as with the memory of the parlor in a Sussex vicarage which had echoed to her girlish exclamations. She was a tall meager woman, given to beads, bangs, and a perpetual cold in the head.

Brad came in, with his quick light step. He said, "Hi, girls."

Miss Ellis sniffed, but not because she was displeased. She always sniffed. And his grandmother said, "Andrews tells me you are dining out."

"That's right. Early."

Mrs. Spencer set down her glass. She was a small woman who looked as if she had been fashioned from Venetian glass but whose reactions were those of Bethlehem steel. She was over seventy, how much over only Mrs. Spencer and her Maker knew. She wore her delicate, withered face with pride, as if it were a flower, and her still plentiful white hair coiled high upon her head. Her figure was erect and good, her hands and feet extremely small. She wore, mainly, black, gray or mauve. Tonight, it was mauve, in long-skirted velvet, with a fall of lace at the high neck, below the black ribbon caught with a diamond star, her only jewelry, except for a wedding ring. She never wore other rings, for her hands were old so why attract attention to them?

Brad said and laughed:

"You're consumed with curiosity but never admit it, Gran."

She regarded him coldly, she thought. Actually, she could not; she could never feel anything even remotely chilly in connection with her grandson. She had wished him to embark upon a career of diplomacy, and had been bitterly disappointed when he announced that his life would be spent in the obscurity of laboratories. She had prayed that he would be as handsome as his father, and endowed with his mother's almost radiant charm. But Brad's appearance was negligible and his charm extremely quiet.

She said, "I don't pry, Bradford."

He came around, bent over her, and kissed the top of her little head.

"I'm taking Gail Rogers to dinner. Congratulate me," he said.

"Certainly, if the occasion calls for congratulations. But who on earth *is* she," asked Mrs. Spencer, "one of Howard Roger's girls?"

She knew perfectly well that Gail was not of the tribe known to her. In fact, it was down in the diary. She had kept a line a day for some fifty years, she retained all the volumes and sometimes reread them. In these leatherbound books, each surveying five years at a clip, Alexandria recorded her activities but not her emotions. One fairly recent recording read: "Went to fashion show at Waldorf with Bradford. Very dull. Met young woman, a model, named Gail Rogers."

Reading between her own spidery lines she would have remembered that the newer Waldorf had not the atmosphere of the old, that the fashions were perfectly absurd, and she was horrified to find her grandson beaming like a schoolboy at a young woman with obviously no background. She was wholly aware without Bradford's subsequent reminder that many girls in good standing modeled, for amusement or a living. But that was not in their favor. If a girl insisted upon exhibiting herself publicly, then her place was on the stage. Quite a few theatrical persons were accepted and even acceptable. But this newer form of exhibitionism affronted Mrs. Spencer.

Brad said pleasantly, "No, she isn't Howard J. L. Roger's daughter, thank heaven fasting. And you know it perfectly well."

"Are you interested in her?" asked Alexandria blandly.

One of her disconcerting habits was to ask personal questions or make intimate remarks in front of Miss Ellis, or even the domestic staff. She did not consider this lifelong habit ill bred. Rather, she considered the presence of poor Millicent or the servants as nonexistent, when it suited her purpose. And they were so used to it that they no longer were embarrassed by her. She was always kind to them, considerate and pleasant, if sometimes carping a little at what she might consider stupidities. Mrs. Spencer was rude only to her equals, never to her inferiors. As for her superiors, she had none.

She was not, in the usual sense, a snob. She was neither impressed by money — she had far too much, for too long — nor what is known as birth — she was extremely well born, and her position had been attained by the achievements of her ancestors, their benefactions and social consciousness. She did not rustle importantly on committees but she pulled a strong oar in very important boats. She was excited by intellect and accomplishment, without regard for race, creed or color, or condition. She spoke her Victorian mind, sometimes coarsely. She was very shrewd, and aware that a good name can become a bad one, that there are gentlefolk who can barely write their names and that people very poor in material things can be extremely wealthy in matters of the spirit.

Brad said, with her own blandness, "Very much."

"I see." Mrs. Spencer motioned to Millicent to refill her glass, a sign that she was somewhat agitated. She then suggested, "Do bring her to tea."

Brad chuckled. He said warily, "I don't think so. Not that she wouldn't hold her own . . . I'm sure she would. But I'd hate to expose her to you, darling."

"I am not a *germ*," said his grandmother loftily.

Brad flipped a hand at her, said, "Good night Millie," and went on out. When the door had closed Mrs. Spencer took refuge in the sherry. She said dourly, "This might be serious."

Millicent glowed. She was devoted to Brad, whom she had known since his gangling days. She clanked her beads and bangles and pushed thoughtfully at her pepper-and-salt bangs. She asked, "Do you suppose he's in *love?*"

"I don't know."

"He's thirty-two," said Millicent.

"What has that to do with it?" inquired Alexandria testily. "Really, Millicent, you are an idiot. His manner . . . at the fashion show . . ." She reflected, chewing cautiously on a dry biscuit. Her teeth were not all her own and had been very costly. "I've never seen him quite so . . ." Her voice trailed off, she had an irritating habit of not finishing a sentence, no worse than her custom of finishing it, if she wished and dotting every i. She added, "She's a very good-looking girl, taller than Brad, I noticed, and quite striking. Good features, and I believe her hair isn't touched up. Very young and looks healthy. No discernible accent," she added, which didn't mean that she fancied Gail had come to New York via Ellis Island . . .

Millicent asked, still fluttering, "You invited her to tea?"

"Why not," inquired her employer with asperity, "as it is more or less my duty? For if he intends to —"

She trailed off again but Miss Ellis finished that one for her.

"You don't mean," she cried, "you can't think . . . that is —"

"That is what?" asked Alexandria. "Really Millicent, you become more and more incoherent . . . Also, I have always been able to think."

Millicent pink, explained humbly, "I

48

meant . . . you can't think he intends to *marry* her?"

"Certainly not," said Alexandria, "but if he intends to sleep with her I would like to be forewarned."

It was at this auspicious point that Andrews crept in to announce dinner, finding Mrs. Spencer thoughtful and Miss Ellis scarlet. The subject, fascinating as it was, was not pursued. Mrs. Spencer spooned soup, dissected sole, nibbled at a chicken breast, refused vegetables and salad and the sweet without further reference to her grandson.

It was Millicent who thought, Whatever happens, just as long as he is happy.

He was, at the moment. He liked climbing the stairs of the Village flat, stairs which chattered under his feet. He liked the little apartment, and Gail, meeting him at the door, wearing something black, and with an impossible flower tucked back of her ear instead of a hat. Her handbag and fur jacket were tossed over a chair and there were two other girls floating about, whom he hadn't met, and who regarded him with friendly interest.

He said, "I've a taxi waiting . . . I didn't bring the car, because of parking and all that."

Seeing her again was a blow; perhaps he had been kidding himself all the way downtown that this was just one of those things. But merely to look at her was to experience a shock. It wasn't that she was pretty, he knew a great many girls, some far prettier. Her young, enchanting face couldn't, for instance, compare with the remarkable features of her friend Evie. No, it wasn't her face or her figure or her husky voice. It was the effect she had on him, the girl herself, disconcerting and even painful.

He thought, I must seem terribly dull, after Sam.

He asked about Sam, in the cab. He said, "How's Sam? I haven't seen him since that night."

"He's all right," said Gail, with a distinct pang.

"I'll always be grateful to him," Brad said, "running into him, with you . . . I don't suppose I've been in the Stork Club more than three times in my life. Lew Ford dragged me there that time, we'd had dinner at the club and sat around till all hours talking . . ."

Ford was a war correspondent and radio commentator. Sam despised him.

At dinner in the pleasant place he had selected, where the food, wine and service were good and there was no distracting music, he asked about her and she exerted herself to be amusing. Sitting there, looking at him, his pleasant, undistinguished features, she wondered drearily why she had bothered to come. But she knew; because of Sam, and his arrogance; because of Sam and her absurd, unrewarding feeling for him; because of Sam and his challenge.

When she asked Brad about his work, which of course was a routine question, he said, smiling, "You don't really want to know, but you think I expect it of you. I don't. It's as exciting as anything can be to those who do it, but not to anyone else. To anyone else, very dull, I dare say. I'd so much rather talk about you."

She said frankly, "But we've exhausted that, haven't we?"

"Hardly. I know nothing about you."

"You wouldn't like it if you did." She asked after a moment, "How is your grandmother? I thought her — remarkable. But she scared me."

"She scares almost everyone," said Brad. "She used to scare me, but not any longer. She asked, by the way, if I would bring you to tea."

Gail looked startled. She asked, "For goodness' sake, why?"

"She thinks I have designs on you," he

51

said lightly, "or vice versa."

"In your case," asked Gail smiling, "what sort of designs?"

"You mean, what sort of designs my grandmother deduces?" he countered. "Oh, quite dishonorable, she hopes."

Gail thought, I ought to be angry. I ought to be hopping mad. But she wasn't. Spencer, she thought, was a difficult person with whom to be angry. There was something very disarming about him, his amiable smile, his extremely bright brown eyes . . .

She asked thoughtfully, "Should I be insulted? Should I cry, Sir, how dare you? Or maybe I'm confused. Should I be furious with Grandma?"

"Not at all. She's very Victorian," he explained, "and despaired of me long ago. I don't conform. I never made the Grand Tour or whatever it is, and I haven't indulged in the sort of peccadilloes for which she would scold me, while secretly approving."

"What sort of peccadilloes?"

He said, "Oh, affairs, as known in her day . . . Parma violets, hansom cabs, a discreet flat, the usual jewelry, and at the end, a large check."

"How very immoral!"

"Quite. But in her time all well-brought-up young men followed that interesting pattern until they married, and took to security, paternity, and the pursuit of respectability."

"Do you mean to say," cried Gail, "that if she suspected you — or me . . ."

"Say us," he suggested.

"Us, then," agreed Gail, "that she'd ask me to *tea!*"

"Before, but not after the fact," he said gravely. "Yes, indeed, in order to look you over and give, as it were, her oblique blessing."

"Well, I'll be damned," said Gail.

"Me, too. Would you . . . ? I mean, to tea?"

"Why not?" said Gail. "But suppose I have designs on you?"

"So much the better." He added, "By the way, I didn't get seats for the theater tonight. I wanted, rather, to talk. I hope you don't mind."

"I don't," she assured him. "What would your grandmother think if I asked you to return to the apartment with me?"

"The worst," he replied firmly. "In which case she'd withdraw her invitation."

"Let's go then," Gail said, "and not tell her."

"I haven't," admitted Brad, "told her everything." He had a slight, wicked gleam in his eye, and Gail said when the waiter had presented the check and he had signed it, "Then, there was a peccadillo?"

"Of sorts," he answered, but went into no detail, which was, she thought, as they left, very unlike Sam in similar circumstances. Sam had few compunctions. She knew far too much about his life with Betty as well as his less conventional encounters.

It was not successful, the evening at home . . . too quiet, the going a little heavy. After you had talked about books and plays and the weather, what was there? Not even gossip, their one mutual friend was Sam. And the room was still electric with Sam, his anger and his passion, his neglect and his desire, his reluctance and insistence.

It was about eleven when Brad said suddenly:

"I've liked this, but I don't think you have. You need a change." He smiled at her. "You aren't sleepy, so, how about the Stork?"

"But you don't . . ."

He said, "I don't, often . . . but suppose we do now? It might amuse you."

It always amused her, and it was one of the right places in which to be seen. But that wasn't the reason why, presently, she said, "All right," and went to her room to do over her face. It was because Sam would probably be there; he was there, most evenings.

All the more reason for going back to the living room and saying, "I've changed my mind," or, "It's late, and I'm tired," or, "Let's make it another evening."

She looped a heavy gold chain about the high neck of her frock and pinned it with a round seed pearl brooch. Both had belonged to her mother's mother; they were back in fashion again; everything came back in fashion if you waited long enough, even love for love's sake, she thought, even decency and dreams.

She had a crazy little hat, which she loved; she put it on and went back to Brad. And he said promptly, "Take it off."

"What?"

"The hat."

"Why?"

"Anyone who has your hair should never wear hats."

She took it off, tossed it on the couch and said, "All right, let's go."

Mr. Spencer might be an infrequent visitor at 3 East 53rd Street, but he was known. The music thumped, the bar was crowded, but they had a table in the Cub Room and the regulars were there. Brad asked, "What shall it be?" and she answered, smiling, "Milk and something to eat."

She drank very little, one cocktail perhaps before dinner, and rarely anything after; her figure and skin constituted her fortune and she could not afford to imperil them.

They watched the people drift in, they listened to the music, which seemed much farther away than it was. People came from the theaters, from audiences, and from dressing rooms. The writers were there, the motion-picture people, the radio stars. She pointed out several to Brad, who recognized few of the people usually recognized. And after a while Mr. Billingsley stopped at their table for a moment and later champagne appeared, a bottle of perfume and a pair of dice . . . Brad rattled the dice in his palm, and tossed them on the table. He said, "It's awfully hard to make your point."

"Is it?"

"I think so."

She said, looking at him with level eyes, "I don't."

He said gently, "Sometimes all you can buy with money is a pair of elevator shoes."

"That," said Gail, "is a little absurd."

He said, "It's funny how unhappy I once was, because I didn't stretch to six feet."

He was not as tall as she, but, then, she was a tall girl. Yet Sam towered over her, and did so now, coming in straight to their table, letting his friends go on without him; a man she didn't know, two girls she had never seen before, one of them spectacular. And Sam was a little more than drunk.

He said, "Fancy seeing you here, Gail. How are you, Brad?"

Brad said, "Hello, Sam . . . we were talking about you a while ago."

"Nothing pleasant, I assume." He pulled up a chair, and sat down and raised a hand to someone across the way. He asked, "Who's Winchell phoning to, or who's phoning him?"

"He didn't confide in us," said Gail.

Sam grinned. He said, "You made good, didn't you?"

"What'll you have?" Brad asked.

"Nothing," said Sam, "yet." He leaned toward Brad. He said, "Look out for this girl, Brad. I wouldn't be your friend if I didn't warn you."

"He can take care of himself," Gail remarked, and felt cold with anger.

"I doubt it. She doesn't," said Sam, "give up . . . or in . . . not for peanuts, Brad, not even for diamonds; nor, believe it or not, for a two-dollar license unless there's a twenty million dollar chance."

"That," said Brad evenly, "is very wise, if true."

Sam got up suddenly, but not too suddenly. He had no wish to crash over a chair and be gently evicted. He looked down at Gail's face, sweet and cold as cream, and at Brad's steady eyes. He was in two minds about Brad. It would be pleasant, Sam thought, to knock his teeth down his throat, but, on the other hand, Spencer was a good guy, a very good guy. Sam felt so sorry for him that he could have wept, and so sorry for himself that he could have sat down on his haunches and howled. He felt sorry for the world . . . Weltschmerz . . . sorry for everyone save Gail, coolly intent on making a hash of everyone's life . . . her own, Brad's, his . . .

"Nice seeing you, Brad," he said, "and you too, Rusty. Did I forget to say that you are in great beauty tonight?" This was one of his courtly moments. He bowed from the waist, a little unsteadily. "Must join the ladies," he apologized, knitting his dark brows, and departed, a tall man, very noticeable.

Gail said, "I'm sorry."

"Why?"

She smiled faintly. "Sam's unpredictable, I fear."

"He's unhappy," Brad commented thoughtfully. "I don't know him well, of course. But, once, we had a very interesting conversation, to the accompaniment of a

58

great deal of off-stage noise. He was in excellent form. His career as a correspondent was spectacular. He went places he had no business going, you know. All sorts of legends sprang up about him. He had enormous physical courage, a complete recklessness really, coupled with terrific curiosity, and oddly, great compassion and righteous anger. That's why his dispatches were so good. They hit, hard. After I came back I used to read them, with envy. Out of the many, he was one of the few who could tell what he had seen, and get it across to the reader."

Gail said evenly, "There should always be a war where Sam is . . . this one gave him his break. Everything's flat for him now."

"He's doing great work," said Brad.

Gail shrugged. "The time will come when the beating of drums for the returned soldier will die away. It's unfortunate, but true. Just now his column has wide syndication . . . and his book is popular. But people are turning away from the war, more and more."

"He has an adjustment to make," said Brad, "like everyone else."

Gail said, after a moment, "He's writing a novel — that is, he thinks he is. I saw the first few chapters. It's good, but not, I think, good enough."

Brad felt, suddenly, very tired and a hundred years old. He pushed aside his glass. He was aware, in the back of his mind, that people were looking at them, that they had been all along . . . looking and speculating. He was used to that, too. Twenty million dollars, more or less, when attached to an unmarried man provides considerable food for thought and material for gossip columns, despite the fact that he was rarely seen in places where columnists gathered.

He made up his mind, and he asked quietly, "You're in love with Sam Meredith, Gail?"

Gail looked at him. Her heart shook, and her hands were cold. Well, she had come here because she might see Sam . . . a stupid procedure, as she could see him any time . . . she had but to answer the telephone, or to dial a number; she knew all the numbers by heart; the number of the *Planet*, which had "discovered" Sam Meredith; the number of his untidy apartment, the numbers of the places where he might reasonably be found at some time during the course of an evening.

She said, weighing her words, "Yes. That is, I was . . . I'm not perfectly sure, now."

"Yet you'll marry him? Forgive me, this is an impertinence."

"Why?" Her gray eyes were the color of storm. "No, Brad, I won't marry him."

"But, if you love him —" he began.

"Maybe that's why. Also, Sam's not the domestic type. If he marries again —"

"He's been married?" asked Brad, astonished.

"Of course. She's a very nice girl," said Gail soberly. "I met her before I knew him. She's remarried, happily." She picked up the black lipstick with the white stork symbol and turned it over in her hand. She added, "If he marries again it will be against his will and his better judgment. A girl would be a fool to start with two strikes against her, Brad."

"But if they loved each other — Sam and his hypothetical girl — who isn't in the least hypothetical —" He broke off and grinned at her wryly. "What am I saying?" he murmured.

"Oh, love!" said Gail.

This was not a noisy room, even though it was not very large and many people came and went. But sometimes in a lull you could hear a single voice, clear and urgent. Such a voice reached them both, from a far table, a girl's, alive with excitement . . . "Sam *darling!*" it cried, in italics.

"Yes, love," repeated Brad stubbornly.

"What's the matter with it?"

She said, "I wouldn't know. I'm just an unbeliever."

"You can be in love and not believe in it."

"Sometimes," said Gail, "when you're dreaming, you know it. You tell yourself, deep in the dream, I'm just dreaming, and soon I'll wake. There are more durable things," she said drearily.

"For instance?"

"Respect, companionship, security," she said.

Brad shook his head. He asked, "I wonder what has brought you to that conclusion, at your age. How old are you, anyway?"

"Twenty-two."

"I'm ten years older," he told her.

Gail asked, after a moment, "Could we go now? I have to be up early, tomorrow . . . or is it today?"

"Just as you say," he answered, and presently they left and heads turned and voices spoke . . . "Rusty Rogers," someone said fretfully, "I don't see *what* they see in her, of course she's good looking, in a standardized way but models are a dime a dozen . . ." and someone else commented, "Twenty bucks an hour, isn't it?" and a man asked, "Was that Brad Spencer? I've never seen him before."

But the dark girl at Sam's table put her hand over his and whispered, "You're clouding up. What's the matter, did I say anything?"

In the cab Brad spoke, carefully. "You'll come to tea, with my grandmother?"

"Should I?"

"Why not? You'll like her when you know her. She's quite a person."

"Does she often ask your chance female acquaintances to tea?"

"If she thinks I'm interested in them."

"Has it happened frequently?"

"A couple of times . . . in error. It was a waste of effort, as Gran was mistaken . . ."

Gail laughed. She said, "My next move is a little too obvious, I think."

"No," said Brad. He leaned away from her, in the corner. "The book of rules assures us that one nail drives out another. I hadn't known about Sam. At least, I wasn't certain. Tell me, honestly, is it a clear field now?"

"It always was, really."

"Despite Sam?"

"Yes." She thought, This isn't happening and if it is . . . She drew a long troubled breath. "I wonder," she said carefully, "exactly what you mean by a clear field."

"My intentions, to coin a phrase, are excessively honorable. But I'd give you

63

plenty of time, Gail."

"You'd better give yourself plenty of time, too."

"Sam," he began, "won't like it."

"Sam asked me to marry him," said Gail, "or rather, he assumed that I would, and with gratitude. He was big about it," she remarked acidly, "because it's entirely against his principles."

"And?" asked Brad. He held his breath a moment. He thought, She's been badly hurt. He experienced an enormous tenderness and pity, sharper and more compelling than desire.

"I refused."

The cab stopped at the brownstone house but Brad made no move to get out. The driver asked, "This the place, bud?" and he said, "Yes. Wait a moment, will you?"

He leaned forward and the street light illuminated his grave face, the bright brown eyes. "May I call you?" he asked.

"Of course."

"My grandmother will, also." He added, "She's meticulous about some things, Gail; but not about others. She's extremely forthright. It's probably a form of arrogance. She speaks her mind when it suits her to do so . . . on the theory that attack is better than defense."

"You're warning me?"

"Perhaps."

"All right," said Gail. "Does she know anything about me?"

"No."

"Do you?"

"All that seems necessary."

She was silent and he added, "Could we be engaged to be engaged?"

IV

He put his arm around her, gently, demanding nothing. He asked, "Well? You've nothing to lose, you know."

And everything to gain, she thought. Her head ached with a sudden violence. She said, with an effort at lightness, "That's unwise of you, Brad. I might take you up on it."

"I hope so. In the interest of research, do you dislike my arm around you?"

"No," she said truthfully. It was even pleasant, the arm to lean upon, a shelter, the promise of safety.

"Or — this?"

He bent and kissed her, not too casually, and that was pleasant too . . . not exciting, not painfully pleasurable, but pleasant.

She said, "No, Brad, I don't dislike it."

"Good," he said. "Well, think it over. I'll call you within the next few hours . . . I may have to go off to Washington again but not before the end of the week."

She could see him smile, seemingly undisturbed. She thought, He's a strange person, and was troubled because she could not read him clearly or fit him into any familiar pattern.

He got out of the cab and spoke to the driver. "Wait for me, will you?" he asked, helped Gail out, and took her to the door. He did not offer to shake hands. He simply looked at her, still smiling and said, "Thanks for a very hopeful evening."

"Brad —"

"What?"

"Never mind, just thanks, for everything."

"Sometime you will finish what you wanted to say and then thought better of. This isn't, perhaps, the right moment or the right place. Let me have your key."

He took it from her, and opened the door. "Good night," he said and went back to his cab and she heard, as she climbed the stairs, the door slam and the car start.

In the cab, he thought, Who has hurt her so much? Sam, of course, but it isn't altogether Sam, there are other wounds.

He was a stubborn man and a patient one. His work called for stubbornness, patience, endurance. It also called for hope.

He thought, We have plenty of time, and was instantly aware that he was not so certain.

Gail fumbled for her other key, at the door of the flat. A light burned in the little living room, and it was silent there. The girls were in and asleep. On the telephone table she saw the propped note, with Evie's scrawl across its face. Evie had written: "Gail, that madman, Sam, called twice — he woke me up, the louse . . ."

When? she thought, standing there, in her fur jacket and shivering a little from nerves and fatigue, before or after we saw him?

The telephone rang again with a crazy shrillness, telephones sound so much louder and insistent after midnight, and she lifted it from the cradle and spoke softly into it. "Yes?" she asked.

Evie's head poked itself around the door of her bedroom. She said crossly, "For Pete's sake . . . oh, you're in, Gail . . ."

"Gail?"

"Yes."

"This is Sam. Remember me, poor but dishonest?"

She said, "Sam, you waked Evie up, twice, you're impossible . . ."

"Tell her she requires no beauty sleep." His voice was somewhat loud, and his words blurred. "I gave you time to get home . . . if you did go home."

"I am home. . . obviously."

"Put Spencer on, baby."

She said evenly, "He isn't here."

"Strictly from etiquette," he said approvingly.

"Sam, it's very late."

"Oh, sure . . . Should she ask him in?" he said. "No, of course not . . . not if he's a nice young man with twenty million dollars and innocent of evil."

She said, "You're drunk . . . and this is a stupid conversation."

"We'll decide about that tomorrow," he answered, and hung up abruptly. Her eardrums hurt, first with the clatter, then with the silence. She put the phone back on the cradle gently and turned. Evie was still standing there, a robe tossed over her shoulders, her small feet bare; disheveled, and pink from sleep, she looked enchanting.

She came into the room and sat down in a big chair and curled her legs under her. "What cooks?" she asked. "I couldn't sleep, anyway . . . thanks to your young man."

Gail sat down and took off her jacket. She said, "Brad took me to the Stork. Sam came in, with a couple of girls and another man. I never saw any of them before. He stopped at the table . . . he was pretty well plastered. He was still there when we left. I suppose he thought we'd had time to get back, when he phoned."

"Where were you?" asked Evie. "Not that it's any of my business."

"Outside, talking, in the cab." She leaned

her head back against the chair, "I'm awfully tired," she said.

"Look," said Evie, "I don't want to stick my neck out and I suppose the reason the three of us get on so well is because we don't . . . but why don't you give Sam the brush-off? There's no percentage in things as they are."

"I did, last night."

"Oh?" Evie lifted an eyebrow. "And he won't stay brushed?"

"I don't know."

"You'll find out. I liked Brad Spencer," said Evie thoughtfully. "No glamour boy, except for the gilding, but a solid citizen. Do you like him, Gail?"

"Yes."

"Is it possible," Evie asked, "to divorce him from the money? I mean, subtract the money from him and look at what's left?"

Gail said, after a moment, "No."

"That's too bad," Evie told her, "because maybe he rates it. But me, I couldn't either. I suppose he's used to it by now."

Gail got to her feet. She said, "I'm half dead . . . night, Evie."

But Evie went to the bedroom door with her and stood there, watching Gail take off her frock. "In your shoes," she said, "I'd latch on to Spencer . . . no matter *how*. But then I'm ambitious, I'm not plagued by scruples. Which doesn't and won't make me a tramp because I'm too smart for that. But you . . ." She shook her head. "Sam Meredith's bad for you," she said somberly, "in marriage or out of it. He was bad for Betty, but he'd be worse for you. Betty's all body and no brains. Watch your step," she warned, and went back to her own room.

When you're so tired you don't sleep. Gail lay awake and went back over the evening, step by step. It made very little sense. She got nothing out of it in retrospect except that Sam wasn't giving up, probably because she had not given in, and that, although he had not said so in so many words, Bradford Spencer was in love with her.

She liked him, she liked him very much. Liking was more durable than love, and if you made a promise you kept it.

But she was afraid to sleep, because if she slept she would dream.

Brad called, at noon. She had no engagement until two, and had slept late. She was alone in the flat, drinking her coffee by the sunniest window in the living room when he telephoned. He asked, "Are you all right?"

"I'm fine."

"Could you bring yourself to dine with

me again? We have unfinished business to discuss."

She did not want him to come back here, no matter what the other girls might leave unsaid and said. After a moment, "All right . . . suppose I meet you, around seven, at the same place?"

The work went badly, the photographer for the fashion magazine was testy and fault finding. The lights were blazing hot. When she had finished she ached, and there was barely time to get home and dress. She would be late, she thought, looking at her watch. Pat, bless her domestic heart, had ironed some blouses for her. Gail selected one, white, with a little frill and put on a black suit, and her fur jacket and went, hatless, to the door. Evie was out but Pat was in, cooking dinner for Bill. It smelled good.

"Have fun," said Pat. "Evie's off with the new man again. She says it looks hopeful."

Gail waited awhile for an empty cab to pass. She was shaking with nervous impatience when one cruised around the corner and she put up her hand to attract the driver's attention. But the cab wasn't empty. She had been mistaken. It stopped and Sam got out.

He said, "Just in time to take you to dinner, Rusty."

"Sorry," she said, "I have an engagement."

"My error. Let me be the first to drive you there," he said, and stood aside. "I hope it isn't in Westchester."

There was nothing she could do, short of making a stupid scene. She got in and Sam after her. "Where to?" he asked politely.

She told him, setting her little jaw, and Sam repeated the address to the driver. "Nice, select place," he approved, "extremely expensive and refined, like, I assume, your host."

She asked, "Sam, what's the use of this? You're being absurd . . . and last night you were —"

"Truthful," he interrupted. He put his arm around her but she sat rigid by an effort of her will power.

"Deep-freeze?" asked Sam. "Well, that's awfully interesting, dear."

"It's no use," she said again, "none at all, not ever."

"Gail, don't be a fool," he said roughly, sincerely, all the mockery gone. "I won't promise you anything . . . except that I'll love you. I'll get away from you when and if I can, I'll drink too much, I'll raise hell with you generally, but if ever two people belonged together —"

"You thought that once before."

"No, I didn't. I fell in love with Betty, yes, but —"

"I don't want to hear about it."

"Okay," he said. "With you, it's different . . . which is a cliché if I ever heard one."

She said, "I won't marry you, Sam, not if you beg me to, every day for a hundred years."

"This is the last time," he told her. "And I'm not begging. I'm asking."

"No."

"It's too bad you picked out Spencer," he said, "though wholly comprehensible. I hate being sorry for the guy, but I am."

She said, leaning forward, "Stop at the next corner, driver, please."

The cab slid obediently to a stop but Sam put his arm across her, and held her back. "I'll be a gentleman," he said, "if it kills me."

He got out and addressed the driver. He said, "Take the lady to her destination, Eros, she has a rendezvous with the national debt."

The door slammed, the car moved on. Gail looked back, and saw Sam standing there, tall, a little stooped, under the street lights.

The driver asked, "Is he nuts?"

The tears rose in her throat, and she said drearily, "In a way, I suppose he is."

She wanted to cry, Turn around, somehow, anyhow . . . catch up with him . . . Let me open the door and say, Darling, get in . . .

Promises are stupid. You make them as a frightened compassionate child, a child afraid of shadows and ogres, a child who has learned too early to love, to pity and to resent that she must. For love and pity are burdens, and a child is not very strong.

Forget the quiet hands, brushing your heavy hair, forget the sacrifices and the weariness, forget the slow step on the dark stairway and the voice imploring, Give me your word. Forget the warning and the shaken breath, and the breath which was silent and the strange man saying, "It's over."

But she could not.

When the cab stopped again Brad was there, waiting. He put out his hand to her, to help her, paid the driver and took her inside the restaurant. He said, "You look as if you had seen a ghost."

"I have," she admitted, and added, "two."

"I've ordered dinner," he said, "and Martinis. I hope that's all right."

They had an uncrowded corner table. The cocktails came and Brad lifted his glass to her, smiling. He said, "To no more ghosts . . ."

During dinner he talked and she listened. He spoke of his work, "one of those plodding things," he explained. "You wouldn't think it could be exciting, you'd think all the excitement had gone from it . . . as of August 6, 1945 . . . I am not discounting the implications and the shadow of what may well be a permanent terror . . . I am talking about the people who worked obscurely, each on his own job, each on a piece of the explosive puzzle . . . knowing very little until it was put together . . . Now, it's day by day, and step by step."

She asked, "Do you think I could possibly learn something about it?"

"I am sure you could. How good were you in math?" he asked, smiling.

"Not very, I'm afraid."

"Never mind." He told her about some of the men with whom he worked; and the one woman in his particular department . . . "very attractive," he said, "very brilliant . . . She's an Austrian . . . our side got her out, and over here, a long time ago. There's quite a story attached to it."

"What does she look like?"

"Not like the accepted idea of a hen scientist," he said, "with a string of degrees. Small, fair, quiet . . . and about thirty-five."

"She sounds perfect, for you," said Gail casually.

"But isn't. That's the unfortunate part. You don't fall in love where it's sensible. Besides, she is married."

"And her husband?"

"He's here too. That is, what's left of him."

Gail's mind shuddered away from the opening chasm, filled with darkness. She said, "Poor thing —"

"Yes. Both of them. Let's talk about pleasanter matters."

"For instance?"

"Us," he said promptly. "Let's stay here until late and talk about us. Mainly you. I wish this was a small town and you had a large devoted family and I could march up the front steps every evening and be looked over by your father. Maybe he'd like me after a while. I shoot a fair game of golf, and play good contract. Your little brothers and sisters would hang around but I would sit them out in the living room. And perhaps your mother would indulge me after a while, coffee and doughnuts on winter evenings . . . lemonade in summer . . ." He broke off. "Have I said anything to hurt you?" he asked.

"No, of course not." But she was conscious that her hands were unsteady, and her mouth.

He said contritely, "I'm sorry, Gail. I was just thinking . . . how hard it is to do satisfactory courting, these days. It's always over bars and tabletops, in cabs, at theaters . . ."

She said, "Not always. You must know a great many girls with — living rooms and devoted families, even in New York."

"I do indeed," he said, "and want none of them. But we must talk, you and I . . . if we are as I hope, engaged to be engaged. After we've talked come the preliminaries we have skipped . . . the bus rides and the drives into the country, in the spring; the movies, and the plays, the weekends in Connecticut with my grandmother . . . she has a hideous old house there, or didn't I tell you?"

She said soberly, "Do you mean all this, Brad?"

"I mean it. First, let us talk about Sam."

"Must we? I thought, last night —"

"Not enough, last night. Last night I learned only this; you were in love with him . . . and are still . . . or at least you aren't sure whether you are or not. But you will not marry him."

"No," she said steadily.

"Why?"

"I've told you."

"I don't think so."

She said, after a moment, "In order to know why, I would have to talk about myself, a good deal."

"That's what I want you to talk about."

She said, "My mother was a remarkable person, and never very strong . . . she drove herself, until it killed her. She was married quite young. My father left us when I was about four. I don't remember him, I have just a dim impression of a big man who laughed a great deal. She bored him, after a while, and so did I."

"Is he alive?"

"I don't know. I don't think so. Once, a friend of his came to see us. He said my father was very ill, and in a charity ward in a Chicago hospital. My mother gave him — this man — some money. She said she did not want to know *which* hospital . . . She had loved my father, very much for a long time. But afterwards, I think, she came to hate him."

"Tell me about her."

"We went back to her parents when my father deserted us," Gail said. "They were Kansas people . . . my grandfather was an overworked doctor, in a rural section, my grandmother, an invalid. My mother was their only child. They took us in and loved

79

us but we were a burden on them. My mother went to work. She was utterly untrained . . ."

"And your father's people?"

"He had none that I know of . . . my mother had met him when she was visiting in New York. He was working in a bank then."

"And?"

She said, "My grandmother died, and then, when I was seven, my grandfather. We had the house, and little else. My mother did all the things she could do, sewed for the neighbors, baked for them, went to stay with their children, took a clerking job in a shop. When I was about ten we had to sell the house. And we left town. There was a man there, one she had always known, who wanted to marry her."

"And she wouldn't?"

"She couldn't. She didn't know if her husband was dead or alive, otherwise she might have," Gail said evenly, "because he had money. Not a great deal, but he would have made us comfortable."

Brad said, "I see. She never made any inquiries about your father?"

"Later, some time after the man who knew him came to see us. That was here in New York, not long before her death. She wrote to all the hospitals in Chicago, but they replied there had been no one of that name . . ."

"Perhaps I could find out." He took a little card from his pocket, and a pencil. "When was this?"

"During the winter, four years ago. I was through high school, and in business school. We were living in furnished rooms. My mother had been working for some time as agent for a special type of corset . . . She died just before the new year, shortly after I had taken a job in an advertising agency."

"You loved her a great deal?"

"Yes. I was so sorry for her," said Gail, "so *sorry*."

"She wouldn't wish you to carry such a burden," he said oddly.

Gail was silent. She said, "All our life together . . . we had no home, not even my grandfather's. I mean, she was the sort of woman who needed a home, her own, her own things around her. We came to New York by degrees; the Kansas town first, then other towns where she had friends who tried to help but couldn't much. Furnished rooms, rackety little hotels . . ."

He said, "You didn't tell me your father's name."

"Morrison Rogers."

He wrote it down and put the card away. He asked, "You have no picture of him?"

"She had . . . I destroyed it. He was very big, wide shouldered. His hair was dark red, his eyes were blue . . . She told me that."

"Why did you destroy it, Gail?"

"I had always hated him for what he did to my mother."

"And she? You said she hated him, too."

"Yes, but she was still in love with him. She tried . . . not to be. She didn't want to be."

"So you don't want to be," he said quietly, "with anyone, not even Sam?"

"Especially not with Sam." She looked down at the dark fluid in her coffee cup. She said, "My mother asked me to promise her . . . that I would never marry for love. That I would marry for money. Not, of course, quite so brutally. All she wanted, she said, was that I be safe. She said, *You're never safe if you love someone.*"

"I see." He was quiet a moment, thinking. Then he said, "We may be able to trace your father, Gail. Although we haven't much to go on, just a secondhand description and a name which, very likely, he didn't use."

She said, her face strained and white, "It doesn't matter. Now you know what I'm like, Brad."

"Not yet, not altogether. But I know that you are lovely, that you have been hurt, that you are honest. It's enough to go on."

She said, "Brad, you can't be in love with me."

"Why not? I find it extremely easy," he told her, smiling.

He said, "I will be honest with you, also. I have few illusions about myself. I'm a very average man . . . amiable enough, intelligent, fortunate in a job I like and can do well, and which I earned . . . in the sense that it couldn't be bought. I am not a businessman. My inheritance is managed for me. When I say I would be equally happy without the inheritance I mean it. I have a few close friends. I have been in love once only — unless you count an unrewarding romance when I was about ten . . . There have been, now and then, the peccadilloes we discussed last night; they were of no moment, but it is comfortable to look back on generosity. There might have been women who'd fall in love with me — as I have with you — heart over head — but I didn't happen to meet them. Shall I give you time, Gail? Till, let us say, the spring? Time to be with me, to talk, to argue, to know each other, a little? You see, when you have a great deal of money and no, as the posters say, added attraction, you expect, if you marry, that the money will be a factor. Therefore, should you fall in love with someone who seems to be all you ever wanted and is honest in addition, you've been rewarded beyond your most absurd hopes."

"What would you expect of — such a girl?" she asked.

"Of such a wife? Companionship, affection, fidelity. Is that the catch? Sometimes a man, or woman, isn't faithful, even to someone he, or she, loves."

"You ask very little, Brad."

"That's a delusion. I ask nearly everything."

"Why of me?" she said helplessly, and a little frightened.

"I don't know. If you're in love, you don't know why."

She said, "I don't — I didn't know why with Sam. He is all I've ever wanted . . . I mean, with my reason."

"Love's not reasonable," said Brad, "nor fair. I'm not. I offer inducements, and am aware of it. More so, after learning about your childhood, about your mother. She was on my side."

"I know." She was white again, and he asked, "Shall I take you home now?"

She nodded, he spoke to the waiter, signed the check, and they left the restaurant. But as a cab drew up and the doorman stepped forward, Gail asked, "Let's walk, shall we? It's a wonderful night."

"If you wish," he said, "but you wear such foolish shoes!"

It was good to walk; the autumn air was cool, it held the electric quality that is Manhattan's own. They walked down Park, and then Madison, and finally down Fifth Avenue. They window-shopped and talked of trivial things, and people turned to look after them because the tall girl with the glowing hair merited a second glance.

When they reached Thirtieth Street Brad hailed a cab, and put her in it despite expostulations. He said merely, "Your feet hurt."

She admitted it, smiling. "But if you say, I told you so . . ." she warned him.

"I shan't." The cab moved on, and she sat quiet, waiting, and finally he said:

"There's one more question. I believed when I kissed you last night that I am not unattractive to you. I didn't expect a world-shaking response; on the other hand, I certainly didn't want pretense, even the slightest, even the pretense born of — shall we say, sympathy?"

"I wasn't pretending."

"It's the one thing," he said, "that we can't afford, you and I . . . I, because I love you, so

85

much, and you, because you do not love me."

"I know," she said.

He leaned to kiss her and she kissed him in return, sweetly and without reserve. You can feel attracted to a man you don't love. She knew that. She had experienced such attraction before she knew Sam. It could be dangerous, that knowledge. In this case, it was not, it was a cause for sober rejoicing.

The cab stopped at the brownstone house and Brad said, as they went to the door together, "Is it a bargain?"

"If you wish . . . and for you," she said, "a bad one."

"When I go home," he told her, "my grandmother's door will be open. It isn't very late. Millicent will have brought her hot milk, laced with a little brandy, and Gran will be sitting up in bed reading. She'll wear a pink satin bed jacket, or a blue one perhaps. She'll hear me come in and pull off her glasses and call to me. And I'll remind her that she spoke of asking you to tea. She'll do just that. Millicent will write the dictated note in her pretty hand. And if you come, my grandmother will crack a delicate whip . . . but it may sting. Will you come?"

This was another challenge and, as such, she met it. She said, "I'll come," and watched him, as she had last night, take the key from her and open the door. She said, "Good night, Brad," and he went back to the waiting cab. She thought, going up the stairs, Spring isn't so far away and in six months almost anything can happen.

$\mathcal{V}$

"Write the girl," said Alexandria imperiously, "and ask her to tea for — let me see . . . a week from Sunday. Usual time."

On the previous night, when Brad came home, his grandmother had been, as he prophesied, awake and reading. The only deviation from the picture he had drawn for Gail was the bed jacket, which was ivory, sprigged with roses. She had called him as he came up the stairs and their conversation had been brief.

"You're home early," she had remarked.

"Too early. But my girl pursues a career."

The sound Alexandria made was not so blatant as a snort, but it served.

"Your girl? Meaning, I assume, Miss Rogers?"

"Yes, indeed." He looked, she noted, extremely cheerful and she detected, replacing her glasses, the faintest smudge of lipstick, punctuating his smile. Her old heart plunged. But gentlemen do kiss, and do not tell their grandparents.

Brad had grinned at her cheerfully, picked up her book, commented, "Trash," without censure, and put it down again. He had then inquired, "I thought you had threatened to ask her here for tea?"

"Threatened," she repeated austerely, "is that the word, exactly?"

"Leave us not go into semantics at this hour," he had advised pleasantly, kissed her good night, and departed.

Remembering this, Mrs. Spencer issued her edict, sitting in the small, charming morning room, which she was pleased to call her office, while Millicent, hunched over the fragile desk, jerked around, startled. Millicent had been plodding through the mail, drawing checks in reply to charity appeals, and doing accounts. It was mid-October and Mrs. Spencer paid her bills on the 15th.

"What girl?" bleated Millicent anxiously.

"The Rogers girl. Her given name is Gail. Bradford neglected to give me her address. I dare say she is in the public telephone book," said Alexandria, who wasn't.

Miss Ellis leafed the pages of an engagement calendar. She said, "But Bradford is going away again . . . a week from Thursday . . . and you are giving a small supper party that evening. He said he wouldn't be here."

"Quite," agreed Alexandria, with fragile menace.

Poor girl, thought Millicent, prepared to love, adore, and protect Miss Rogers if she proved to be a gentlewoman, and kind if she seemed right for Bradford.

Alexandria said in her sinister little way, "I'd like to talk to her alone."

Millicent was not offended. "Alone" did not mean "without you." It meant, without Bradford. Millicent was part of the décor, and knew it.

She wrote the letter. She had never learned to type and indeed her functions did not include clattering on the keys. Mrs. Spencer herself rarely wrote a letter. She signed them, as she signed her checks, with a flourish, but she wrote no one save Bradford, when he was away from home for a long time, and of course, to herself, as it were, in her diary. But she would no more have sent a typewritten letter to a friend, an acquaintance, or even a stranger than she would have danced the samba. Her business mail was attended to by efficient secretaries in the office that managed the Spencer Estate.

"Send it by hand," said Alexandria.

All her important invitations were sent by hand, a well-known peculiarity. But this was the first time that Pompston, the elderly chauffeur, had been known to drive the ancient, but extremely good town car to the Village, where, parking it with misgivings, he climbed the stairs, after pressing a buzzer, and knocked upon a door.

Pat was the only one at home. She admitted him, astonished, but no more astonished than he. In faded blue slacks and a sloppy shirt, with her red hair in pigtails, Pat was housecleaning.

"Is Miss Rogers at home?" inquired Pompston.

"No, But —"

He said kindly, "When she comes, will you give her this note, little girl? It's from Mrs. Roderick Spencer." He looked pained as she took it from him. "Try not to get it dirty," he warned.

"I'll try," said Pat, dead pan.

When, toward evening, Gail returned, Pat, dressed to the teeth to dine with Bill's parents, in town from the country, gave her the note and narrated the manner of its arrival. She said mournfully, "No lollipop. I should have held out for a lollipop. I bet he's never heard of bubble gum."

Gail opened the thick, ivory-colored envelope, addressed to her with "By Hand" in the corner. It was in the third person, and stately.

She handed it to Pat and said, "Well, what do you know?"

"Not a damned thing," Pat admitted. "What does this betide? Rice and old shoes?"

"Arsenic and old lace," said Gail. She had spent the day wondering if she was crazy, or if Brad was. She asked, "Did anyone telephone?"

"Sam. He said to tell you he was booked for the first rocket trip to the moon and wanted to know if you'd come along for the ride. Some flowers came. I fixed 'em . . ."

Roses, quantities of them, in a big blue jar, the card beside them. Gail rose, carrying Mrs. Spencer's invitation, and opened the card envelope.

"Spencer," deduced Pat. She sighed. "I wish Bill was rich," she said dreamily, "it would be wonderful. But he couldn't be rich and still be Bill. Also, when he's rich — and he's going to be — I want to have a hand in it. What are you going to do about Sam?"

"Nothing. Should I?"

"I don't know. You worry me. You aren't excited . . . I mean, about anything . . . Bradford Spencer or Sam. I couldn't live if I wasn't excited. I'm in a dither all the time . . . it hasn't always been fun but now it is, all the time. I recommend it," said Pat.

Evie came in, looking soulful. She had been looking soulful, for hours, eyes washed with dreams, hair caught with stars, beautiful lips parted, as if shaping to a kiss. It had been boring but necessary. Evie's picture, in plentiful color, would launch a new lipstick, which would be named Dream Kisses and sell for one dollar, plus tax, up to two hundred and sixty plus, encased in solid gold and encrusted with jewels.

"What cooks?" asked Evie, unable to undo her expression.

"Mrs. Spencer, with gas," said Pat, "she's asked Gail to tea."

"And is Gail going?"

"I'm going," said Gail. "Anyone have any very genteel stationery or must I rush out and buy a costly box?"

Evie had some unencumbered by hearts and flowers, the envelopes not lined in stripes or checks. "To be sure," she apologized, "it ain't engraved but maybe that's not expected of the working girl."

Gail sat down at the mutually shared desk, a contribution of Pat's, and wrote her reply. She wrote a good, not at all mannered, and quite readable hand. She accepted, also in the third person. And remarked, setting her fist upon the blotter, "I wonder if I should learn to curtsy . . . and has anyone three feathers?"

"We're out of rye," Pat said.

"For the hair, darling, for the hair." She felt as if she should wear feathers in her hair, glass slippers on her feet; also that a padded cell had its advantages.

Tonight Gail was going out with Evie, Evie's Mr. Gammon and a friend of Mr. G's. Evie had implored her to do so. "It won't be bad," she pledged, "dinner, theater, and the Stork. Of course, I run the risk that Gammon may take one look at you and throw me on the cutting-room floor . . . a little previously. But he wants gay companionship for his pal . . . it seems that they were buddies in public relations foxholes . . . and you're it."

"I'll efface myself," said Gail kindly.

The telephone rang as she was dressing and Brad said, "I hope it was understood that we had an engagement tonight, and every night."

She said they hadn't had . . . "I'm sorry," she told him, "but I promised Evie I'd go out with her."

"Tomorrow then? I'd bring you back early and get a late train to Washington . . . Did you hear from my grandmother?"

"I did. She's asked me to tea, a week from Sunday."

"The old son of a gun," said Brad, and chuckled.

"You didn't expect her to?"

"Certainly, but it so happens I'll be away over that weekend."

"Should I decline?"

"That, my darling," Brad said, "is up to you."

"I'll go," she said firmly. "She knew you were going away?"

"I dare say. Is it all right for tomorrow night?"

It was all right. She hung up, and presently the doorbell rang and Mr. Gammon arrived, extremely articulate, a sleek young man who knew everything and everyone, towing a tall, dour individual whom he introduced as Hank, fresh from the salt mines, and the best goddamned script writer in Siberia, California.

On the appointed Sunday, at four-thirty, Miss Rogers was entertained — but not very — by Mrs. Spencer.

She saw Brad several times before then, and they discussed the situation. "You mustn't mind," he said apologetically, "but I hope you do. I'm a civilian, yes, but what I'm doing comes under the head of government business. So I go when I'm sent for and sometimes when I'm not. I wish I could be with you Sunday. Don't let her throw you. She'll try, of course."

"Which seems somewhat old hat," she told him.

"It is, but she wears it with dignity, audacity, and sometimes it becomes her. Be patient with her," he urged unexpectedly, "she's old, she lives in another world, and is fond of me. Not that that gives her the right to be rude to you, and she may be, you know . . . or, again, she may not," he said thoughtfully. He grinned. "If she's rude, it's a good sign."

"You confuse me," murmured Gail.

They had settled down to a curious relationship. It was not that he took her for granted or, if he did, he was careful not to show it . . . but as if he took an eventual understanding for granted. They talked a great deal and laughed considerably. Before that Sunday came, they had seen a couple of movies, rather good, and one play, very bad. They had dined in various places, wherever their fancy took them, once the St. Regis, once the Automat, and another time at an Armenian restaurant. They had ridden a bus uptown and back and they had gone to a shooting gallery where with some astonishment Gail had watched Mr. Spencer demolish duck after ill-fated duck.

He was fun to be with; she liked being with him. He made no demands. He did not speak of the future; tacitly he permitted the future to take care of itself. He kissed her, but not too often or too insistently. He frequently told her that he loved her. He sent her books and, often, flowers.

Evie, restless because Mr. Gammon had returned to Hollywood, full of promises but without performance, said, "You could command mink and diamonds at this stage."

"I don't want them," Gail said.

"Don't be silly."

"All right, so I'd like them, who wouldn't? Mink, sables, diamonds and sapphires, rubies and emeralds. Handfuls."

"All in good time," said Pat, "and legal!"

On Sunday, Gail blew herself to a cab and drove uptown, arriving a polite five minutes late. She wore her black suit, her fur jacket, a pale-blue blouse, her best nylons and treasured shoes . . . they had toes and heels; she felt that Mrs. Spencer would prefer toes and heels — as a matter of fact, she did, too. She wore, because doubtless her hostess was not accustomed to free-wheeling hair, a sketchy bonnet, the merest halo of black, spiked with pale-blue feathers, and, in addition, the violets Brad had sent. On the card he had written, "Keep your chin up but don't lead with it. And thank you, darling. I realize you are merely being kind to me and at the same time indulging an obstinate old lady whom, despite myself, I also love."

She put the card in her handbag as a talisman and standing on the marble steps in the dreary darkness of a day which had swept on and off since early morning, thought, But this is absurd, why have I come, what am I doing here? It's a sort of *acknowledgment* . . .

She'd made a bargain. Maybe this was part of it. She lifted her chin, the line clean and firm from her ear lobes, and relaxed her mouth consciously, as she did before the camera, and Andrews opened the door.

The aura, the personality of the house came instantly to meet her, to weigh her in the balance. She was sensitive to atmosphere. She could feel the house looking her over . . . she could smell the house, its age, its respectability, its warning. She thought, It's like the iron curtain. I must tell Sam.

But she hadn't heard from Sam again. She might never hear. Even if she did, she didn't want to hear.

She was taken to the drawing room and Mrs. Spencer turned from the contemplation of a bowl of hothouse flowers and smiled at her.

There was another woman in the room, to

whom Gail was presented, but she might as well not have been there. This was Millicent, of course, Gail thought, the self-erasing companion of whom Brad had told her, all beads and bangles, with anxious kindness in her faded eyes and hands which were never quite under control. But Millicent could bound about, arranging chairs, unnecessarily, and be reprimanded for it, too, fussing with cushions, and chattering interminably and you still wouldn't notice her, not with Alexandria in the room.

Tea was served on a heavy tray. Andrews staggered in with it, the poor old man, thought Gail angrily . . . kettle and pot, creamer, sugar bowl, the fine, almost translucent cups, the trays of tiny sandwiches. "Or," asked Alexandria, suspending her hospitable hand, "would you prefer a cocktail, Miss Rogers?"

"No, thank you," said Gail sedately.

"Tea," said her hostess, "is a reprehensible custom . . . one grows too dependent on it. You don't drink?" she asked guilelessly.

"Oh yes," said Gail, as guileless, "occasionally and not much. I can't afford to, I'm afraid."

Alexandria agitated an eyebrow. "I am afraid I don't understand. Lemon, or milk?

Or if you wish, cream. Sugar?" she asked, and then, "Bradford likes his with rum," she commented.

"Milk," said Gail, "no sugar, and yes, quite strong, if I may."

Millicent looked approving. After such a fashion did she like her tea, several times a day.

Gail took the cup from the steady old hand. She explained gently, "I'm a model, you know . . . for artists, for photographers, and at fashion shows. It's only sensible not to drink . . . the figure," she added carelessly, "and the skin, they show it eventually."

She settled back in the corner of the couch. She was certain that Mrs. Spencer was waiting for her to cross her noteworthy legs. She did not. As a matter of fact she had been taught not to, or, at the most, at the ankle. She sat easy, and erect, her straight young back firm against the couch.

"Do you like your work?" asked Alexandria. "I thought you looked charming at the fashion show . . . you wore the bridal gown, as I remember."

"It was very pretty," said Gail, expressionless. "No, I don't care for it particularly, Mrs. Spencer. It is exacting, and very often tiring. But I do not know how to do anything else."

"I see. It's too bad that Bradford couldn't be with us today," said his grandmother. She wore a single string of pearls, and the velvet throat band. Her dress was gray, and with the usual touch of lace. Her hair was done high, and held with gold and tortoise-shell combs, and Gail thought, She's wonderful . . . she should be in a glass case. I'd feel safer if she were!

"I'm sorry, too," said Gail, drinking the good strong tea, and setting her cup beside her to bite into a sandwich so fragile that it might have been composed of manna and, she thought, probably was.

They talked of books, presently — and Mrs. Spencer almost concealed her astonishment that Gail had read a book — and of plays. Mrs. Spencer had seen a play and had not liked it. They spoke of music. No, Gail did not attend the Philharmonic and was quietly baffled when her hostess said, sadly, that she missed dear Mr. Bagby, very much. Mrs. Spencer then explained Mr. Bagby and his well-patronized concerts, "which were, my dear, long before your time."

The second cup of tea was poured and Alexandria, stimulated, sharpened her mother-of-pearl weapons. She said, "I am an impertinent old woman . . . I was taught not to indulge in curiosity or personalities, I assure you, but I am old and willful, and forget my lessons. Please tell me about yourself."

"There isn't much to tell, Mrs. Spencer."

Alexandria discarded the foil, picked up a hammer and began extracting nails, she hoped.

"You are a New Yorker?" she inquired.

"No, my mother's people were Kansans. My mother and father met and were married in New York. I was born, however, in Chicago."

Alexandria looked slightly alarmed as if Mrs. O'Leary's cow had suddenly walked into the room.

"You were brought up there?"

"No place, particularly." Gail began to enjoy herself. She thought, I wish Sam was here, he would like this. "My father," she went on, "left Mother and me when I was quite small. For a time we lived with her parents. My grandfather was a physician."

This was a blow. Doctors were eminently respectable; that is, most of them.

"Your mother is living with you?"

"She is dead," said Gail shortly, and folded her lips, and Millicent, watching, quivered for her. "I live with two friends, also models, in a small apartment."

Alexandria put down her cup. It was time

to get down to cases. She said, ignoring Millicent, who had been waiting for this, dreading it, but not daring to depart even if she wished, which she didn't, "You are a very handsome young woman, Miss Rogers." She smiled. "I am not astonished that my grandson has fallen in love with you."

Gail felt a small, warning shock. She had expected anything; but not exactly this. She felt very sorry for the bangled Miss Ellis, who was stirring about in a big chair not far away and clashing spoons and cups, in a frenzy.

"Has he?" she inquired politely.

"You know, I am sure," said Alexandria, "and, again, will you forgive my impertinence?" She pulled out a stop or two and permitted her voice to waver. She said, "He is all I have . . . and holds, I may add, my entire interest. His happiness is of paramount importance to me. I asked you to come here — knowing that he would be out of town — because I hoped you would speak honestly with me."

Gail thought, All I ever do is speak honestly and I'm getting sick and tired of it!

"Yes?" she asked cautiously.

"I have known Bradford all his useful life," said Alexandria, realizing that this was uphill work, and wanting to shake the girl, so unrevealing, so unfortunately quiet, "he is a remarkable person. I do not want him to be hurt. For many years he has had no serious interest in — women. I believe that he is serious about you. If so, I am quite powerless to — advise him. In short, he is in a position to do as he pleases. But one thing I must know. Do you love him, Miss Rogers?"

"No," said Gail, quite pleasantly.

Millicent gabbled, incoherent, and Alexandria's black eyes were brilliant with amazement, and with sudden anger, which she deplored but could not control.

How dare this girl *not* be in love with Bradford?

Alexandria drew a steadying breath deep from the diaphragm, and was plagued with grudging admiration. She had expected protestations of undying devotion, even a little maidenly confusion, true or false. She would have preferred not to believe the protestations; would have maintained she could not believe them. It boiled down to a simple formula: a suitable girl would be, naturally, madly in love with the Spencer scion; an unsuitable girl would merely hope to feather her nest with solid gold plumage. Yet Mrs. Spencer could not stomach the lack of pretense; it blunted her weapons and illogically wounded and infuriated her. Also, her common sense warned her that a candid woman is unusual — and dangerous.

She glanced at Millicent, saw that she was plum colored with indignation.

Alexandria reassembled her arsenal.

"I'm a fatuous old woman," she told Gail, smiling, "and therefore a little shocked."

"But not sorry?" inquired Gail sweetly.

"Yes, and no," said Alexandria, whose New England ancestry often asserted itself. "As I have said, I don't want Bradford to be hurt. On the other hand . . ." she paused delicately.

Gail communicated with herself in a forthright, vulgar fashion. Nuts to this, she thought, irritated. She put her cards on the table, aware that she held all the aces.

"On the other hand," she suggested, "you are relieved?"

The bright black eyes looked straight into hers. And Alexandria replied gently:

"As you have been frank with me, you will not be offended if I, too, am plain spoken. You are a very attractive girl, my dear, you have youth and beauty and you are also courageous and intelligent." She paused, and now her smile was singularly winning, and then went on, as Gail thought, This sounds like a recommendation for a ladies' maid, "But I would have been distressed to see you and Bradford marry. For your sake, as well as his," she added.

"Why?"

"For a variety of reasons," Alexandria answered promptly. "A — a mutual attraction is desirable if not sufficient to guarantee a good marriage. An enduring relationship is usually premised upon a similarity of background, and of tastes."

Gail said indifferently, "Brad and I like the same things."

"I wonder," asked Alexandria, "why we are arguing? Of course you like the same things now, although Bradford, a serious scientist, would not long enjoy, I fancy, the sort of life that must interest you."

Gail laughed outright. She said, "Come, Mrs. Spencer, you've been reading books and gossip columns." She could have sworn that she saw the old woman's backbone stiffen visibly. "Like most young people I enjoy dancing, good restaurants, the theater . . . and, now and then, a night club. As a matter of fact, in my job, I have to be seen in the so-called right places, every so often. It's part of the picture. But that doesn't mean that I couldn't settle down to an orderly home life."

Millicent choked slightly and Mrs. Spencer said sharply:

"You have admitted that you do not love my grandson. Are you trying to tell me that, if he asked you to marry him, you would not?"

"He has asked me, Mrs. Spencer."

Alexandria was white under the film of powder, the very sparing dusting of rouge. She said, "And . . . ?"

"I haven't accepted," said Gail, "and I haven't refused. We have an agreement . . . Brad suggested that we be engaged to be engaged . . . until spring."

"You know, of course, that I shall repeat this fantastic conversation to Bradford?"

"Oh, yes," Gail said, "but it isn't necessary. He knows that I'm not in love with him."

Alexandria received the blow, and rallied. She said, "Then he's more of a fool than I've ever believed. Or do you expect to fall in love with him — by spring?"

"No," said Gail evenly, "but I like him very much. I have never liked or respected any man as much. We have a good time, we like being together. He interests me, very much. I admire his standards, his way of life, and his work. I don't understand his work, of course, and sometimes I don't wholly understand him. But given intelligence —" she paused and added — "you were kind enough to say you thought me intelligent, perhaps I could grow into understanding."

Millicent said suddenly, "I beg your pardon," rose, and fled from the room. It was a brave thing to do as she had never departed from Alexandria's presence without direct, or implied, permission. But she told herself, I simply cannot endure it; our *poor* boy, she thought, running up the beautiful stairs. She suppressed another thought, which was that, for once, Alexandria had met a worthy, however mistaken, adversary. Millicent reached her room and in its virgin shelter, sat down upon her bed. She said aloud, "I shall warn him, it is my duty!"

Alexandria cast a slightly astonished glance after the small form of her deserting companion. She waved her hand toward a silver box on a table near the couch and asked, austerely, "Do you smoke?"

"Occasionally, thank you." This was one of the occasions. Gail took a cigarette and set the match flame to its tip. She needed a cigarette at this juncture and it was one of the rare moments when she felt that she could do with a drink as well.

Alexandria expressed no disapproval for, if she had, it might have been mentioned to

Brad, and Brad, no doubt, would inform the girl that his grandmother had indulged in a postprandial cigarette long before it was de rigueur for gentlewomen; only, of course, in the privacy of her home or the homes of close friends; never in public and mainly because, at the time she acquired the habit, her husband had been immensely amused. But she hadn't smoked for several years, upon the advice of her doctors.

Gail smoked quietly, and waited. And Alexandria asked:

"*Do* you intend to marry my grandson?"

"I don't know," Gail said. She looked through the veil of smoke at the older woman. "I would be foolish not to, wouldn't I?" she inquired. "As, surely, I shall never again meet anyone as eligible!"

"Very well," said Alexandria shortly, "so you'll marry for money. Have you considered how unfair it would be to Bradford?"

"Yes. That is why," Gail murmured, "it seems best not to take any hurdles until spring. But I would make him a good wife," she added firmly, "undemanding, affectionate and . . . faithful."

"An old-fashioned term, these days," said Alexandria, unmoved. "But does he not deserve more?"

"Who has more?" asked Gail. "Most men

have less. They may start out with a violent —" she hesitated, used the quieter term, "attraction, on both sides. But the marriages that last — didn't you say they are based on more than that?"

"Certainly not," said Alexandria, vigorously and mendaciously. This dreadful girl had an accurate memory. "A man who gives his entire heart deserves one in return. The original attraction does not pass with the years, it merely becomes, as you phrase it, less violent and finds compensations."

Gail asked, "Why not *start* with the compensations . . . respect for each other as individuals, shared tastes, and family interests?"

Alexandria flushed deeply, her sensitive, lined skin suffused with color. She repeated faintly, "Family?"

"Naturally," said Gail, "all things being equal. Did you expect that I would not fulfill my share of marriage, if possible?"

The flush subsided and Gail's heart misgave her. This was her enemy but she was old and frail. She added gently, "I am tiring you, Mrs. Spencer."

"Not at all. One more thing. Have you considered that you would not be fair to yourself? You might fall in love with someone else, when it was too late. Or do you subscribe to the theory that it is never too late, that you can indulge yourself within marriage, or, as young people do, terminate your marriage whenever the mood seizes you?"

"Anyone," said Gail, "who marries, thinking, if it doesn't work, I can get out of it, never *meant* it to work in the first place. I would mean it to, Mrs. Spencer. And I am not liable to fall in love." She folded her lips together in the manner that Alexandria had observed, earlier in the afternoon.

"Why," asked Alexandria, "should you be immune?"

"For a number of reasons."

Mrs. Spencer rose, and Gail came to her feet, in one flowing easy motion. And Alexandria said, "I must warn you that I shall repeat our conversation to my grandson."

"Of course," said Gail. She did not offer her hand nor did Alexandria. They stood facing each other for a moment, the girl so much taller, so alive with youth, and Alexandria felt as if her hoarded vitality had been sapped from her. She made a curious little gesture with one hand, one of dismissal and of bereavement as well.

And presently the door, with its beautiful iron grille, closed quietly behind Gail by Andrews hands, and she stood a moment on the steps. The rain had ceased, but still threatened. The Park was ghostly in the dusk, the street lights came piercing through, the ground mist rose in lazy swirls of fog, vague and obscuring.

She felt chilled, and shivered. She wished Sam was here beside her, that they might go together somewhere gay and warm, loud with crazy music and the sound of voices. She wished she might tell him all that had been said this afternoon. She thought, it's not for me . . . I'll turn and ring the doorbell and ask that grim old man to let me in. I'll go back into that room and say I didn't mean it, don't worry, I won't see Brad again.

No. She had made a bargain and she would stick to it, and when she reached the flat, which was empty and dreary, when she unpinned the fading violets with their too-sweet odor from her jacket, there was a Western Union messenger at the door, and a wire from Brad.

CALLING YOU TONIGHT ABOUT ELEVEN, it read, HOW DID THINGS GO WHAT YOU NEED IS A GOOD STIFF DRINK ALL MY LOVE BRAD.

She laughed aloud, standing there with the yellow paper in her hand and looking toward the clock on the desk. It was always fast, that being the safer way in this house-hold, but Brad had timed his telegram very neatly.

Pat came in. Bill had an emergency, their date was off, she announced, dismayed. "And we were going out to dinner. You look bushed. What happened?"

"Nothing," said Gail, and shed her halo hat and her jacket. "Pleasant tea, much pumping, the works."

"Did you like her?"

"I don't know that anyone could, except her own generation or her own flesh and blood," answered Gail, from the bedroom. "She's a pint-sized Tartar, arrogant as only umpty-ump years of family and money could make her. But she's quite a person."

"What did you eat?" asked Pat, who was always hungry.

"I drank mostly, tea that you could walk on and gnawed at a sandwich or two . . . so thin I couldn't taste 'em."

"The rich always starve," said Pat gloomily. "Are you going out tonight?"

"No."

"I'll fix us something here," Pat suggested. She was becoming a notable cook, which she sometimes regretted as Bill had warned her he would rarely be home on time, or home, period.

"Fine," said Gail, "we'll listen to Charlie, and Allen, Winchell and Louella and have an evening home, just for a change."

She was reading, Pat had gone to bed, and Evie wasn't in as yet when the telephone rang and Brad said, "I'm still in Washington. Believe it or not, I've worked all day. I'll be home tomorrow . . . how about dinner?"

"All we do is eat," she said.

"It becomes a habit. Was this afternoon very bad?"

"You'll hear all about it, if you see your grandmother before you see me."

"I meant, was it bad from your viewpoint? I've already heard from her. She rang me at the hotel, around six this evening. I wasn't there. I called her back, an hour ago. I waited to call you, thinking you might be out."

Gail said, "Well, now you know the worst."

"She wasn't very explicit," said Brad comfortingly, "as she hates the telephone. But I got the impression she meant to convey."

Gail said carefully, "Perhaps you would rather not have dinner tomorrow night."

"On the contrary, it seems too long to wait. Gran didn't tell me anything I didn't already know, darling."

"Brad, I sometimes think you are out of your mind."

"Hope springs eternal," he reminded her, "or didn't you know? No, I'm perfectly sane. And I'd rather love an honest woman who didn't love me than a dishonest one who claimed that she did. For how could I be sure? Good night, Gail, I'll see you to-morrow, about seven, at your place."

VI

Brad came back to town, called for Gail at seven, and they went out to dinner. He asked, over cocktails, "How was yesterday? And don't spare the horses," and she answered, "In a way, I enjoyed it," and smiled. "Suppose we talk about something else until we have a little more privacy?" she suggested.

"Very well . . . and after dinner, what?"

"Shall we return to the apartment? The girls are, as usual, out," she said.

So, after dinner they sat comfortably in the flat and Brad leaned back against a corner of the couch, smoked and looked at Gail. He was tired, and at ease and, he dared believe, happy.

"Now," he said firmly, "give."

"Your grandmother," said Gail obediently, "doesn't approve of me. I am afraid we took off our gloves. I am certain she hoped I'd lose my temper, throw things, behave, in general, like a fishwife, whatever that is. I can't imagine being married to a fish," she added thoughtfully.

He said, "I've seen her, Gail. I went home from the train, to change, and there was an hour to spare. We spent it together."

"Good. Then, you have the picture? Her version. Old master, no doubt."

He asked, "How can it possibly matter? She finds you quite beautiful and extremely honest."

"Also," added Gail, "too damned well brought up to suit her." She watched the flicker of astonishment in his eyes, laughed, and said, "My mother couldn't give me much. She couldn't give me, most of the time, a proper environment and, at no time, the frills . . . no dancing or piano lessons, no parties on birthdays and holidays. She couldn't even give me the sort of education she wanted. But she made me mind my manners and she made me educate myself. She said that when a girl had money, family, and all the protecting things perhaps she could afford to be badly behaved and ill mannered. But not otherwise. Also, perhaps, she could afford to be ignorant."

He said quietly, "She gave you a great deal, Gail."

"Your grandmother," said Gail, "asked me if I was in love with you and I said, No. She was delighted. She believed that such an admission would automatically rule out marriage. I told her it didn't, necessarily, and that you knew it."

"I know. Much of your conversation was repeated to me."

"She warned me it would, but I had assumed it." Gail pushed her hands through her heavy hair, and shook her head as if to clear it. She said, "It's up to you, Brad. You have never quite believed me, I think. Now that someone else tells you . . ." She paused and asked, "Wouldn't it be better if you went through that door, now, tonight, and never came back? You love your grandmother and you are all her life. I realize that. If we go on seeing each other . . . whether or not it comes to anything — it will make her terribly unhappy. And there isn't a thing I can do about it."

He said, "I'm sorry if she's unhappy, believe me. But it can make no difference. I love you. I'll never love anyone else. Perhaps I'm one of the people who would rather love than be loved. I don't know. Anyway, that's the way it is . . . I'll walk through the door, yes, but I'll come back and keep on coming back. You'll have to marry me to get rid of me."

"How?"

"Oh, trips and such," he said vaguely. He leaned forward and put his hands on her cheeks, cradling her small face between his hands, looking at it closely, and with love.

He said, "Yet it wouldn't be fair to you, I know. Maybe I'm more unscrupulous than I thought."

"Mrs. Spencer speaking," said Gail, not moving. "She pointed that out to me too. It wouldn't be fair to her grandson, she said, as he deserved the suitable girl who would suitably love him. It wouldn't be fair to me, she added kindly, for I might fall in love elsewhere — too late . . . that is, she asked, if I considered love, though married, too late. She suggested that I didn't . . . that I would be of the modern school, demand a divorce a week from Tuesday and a big fat settlement. She didn't mention the settlement."

Brad dropped his hands. He asked, "And are you of that school? I don't believe it, but I'm asking."

"No. If I make a bargain, I keep it."

"Then," he said smiling, "we both take risks. Who doesn't, in any marriage, however entered into, Gail?"

"That's right." Her mind fled back reluctantly to the dark bedroom and the bed with the sagging springs; so many rooms, so many beds, and always the same weight of compassion and distaste . . . the child lying straight and taut in the darkness, the woman weeping beside her. Gail could taste the tears, she could feel them. And no matter

119

how wide the windows or how cool and fresh the wind, somehow always the odors . . . it was as if you could smell sorrow, as well as the faint scent of talcum, of pitiful cosmetics. "I have to keep up," her mother said . . . and, too, the odors of the house, of people and kitchen, of dust and decay.

If I had married Sam, Gail thought drearily, there would have been many tears and great loneliness.

Brad said, "You look so white. You're tired, dear?"

"A little . . . but not as tired as you must be."

He rose, pulled her to her feet, and kissed her. "We'll call it a day," he said. "I can't afford to let you be bored with me . . . that would be fatal . . . and there are many days ahead of us. Our entire lives, I hope."

"Wait a minute. Did Mrs. Spencer . . . say anything . . . Of course she did," she answered herself, irritated, "and I don't want to pry."

"She said nothing that you can't know. It is natural that she regards me as a dashing Prince Charming storming around on a white charger. She resents the fact that you aren't lying down under said charger's hoofs. I suppose that's natural, too. On the other hand, she has always wanted me to have exactly what I want . . . even when it came to my work. It isn't the work she'd like me to do but, as it was my desire, she'd put no stone in my way, even if a stone were handy. I believe she's always felt disturbed over the fact that she couldn't dispense, or occasionally withhold, largess. But my grandfather made a curious will. He adored his wife but he was besotted about his name. Hence, the grandsons, if any, were not to be dependent on the women in the family. I was the only grandson, Gail. My grandmother has an extremely large trust fund from which her income is derived, and also life tenancy of the houses. But that's all. She couldn't cut me off with a shilling, even if she wished. I have a trust fund too . . . certain sums of the principal arrive at stated periods . . . when I was twenty-one, twenty-five, thirty . . . the next when I'm forty and then the rest is tied up for my son, or sons. I am an appallingly rich man, even allowing for taxes and the dollar devaluation."

He put his arms around her and held her close. He added, "That's the way it is and I'm glad. I want you to have everything you've ever wanted or ever will want. I want you to be safe, all your life long. And if this is a form of bribery . . . try to forgive me."

"There's nothing to forgive," she said.

After he had gone she did not do the several things she had planned: the washing of her stockings, the ironing of lingerie, and straightening up of the small untidinesses that were normal to the household. She let the routine go and sat there thinking, very much alone.

Brad would make it easy for her to keep her promise; he would make everything easy. She was, she told herself stubbornly, already very fond of him. If you want to put it another way, she was beginning to love him. She was not in love with him; in that, the difference lay, an enormous divergence, a disparity she could recognize, if not yet evaluate. She did not turn cold and hot when he came into a room; nor feel her bones melt when he touched her; yet neither did she feel the reluctance or even revulsion you were supposed to feel in the circumstances. The books were wrong . . . in the books you loved or did not; responded or could not.

But when she was with Sam the books, however torrid or banal, however manufactured, were right; she *did* turn hot and cold; her bones *did* melt . . . because she had been in love with Sam, and must still be, she thought unhappily, if thinking about him disturbed her so profoundly.

I'll get over it, she told herself, I must.

How?

Can you get over it by saying, I must, I shall, I will, I have done so? She knew you could not. It was like believing. You didn't believe in anything by telling yourself so; the conviction must spring from within, without explanation, without, even, proof. Simply, you believed.

She rose, walked across the room, picked up the telephone and dialed Sam's number, listening to the whine of the sharp, complaining ringing. She thought, absurdly: I'm not hearing his phone ring; they just do that in the telephone office somehow; you hear something buzz and you think it's Sam's phone and you can see it, sitting there, ringing away for its dear little black life . . . there are newspapers on the floor; there are papers and magazines and books on the desk . . . there's an empty glass . . . there's a bottle of Scotch . . . the silly black cat is crawling around, playing with bits of manuscript, the clock ticks and the phone goes on ringing . . . the pin-up girls are on the walls, unframed, curling at the corners . . . they always curl at the corners.

The operator spoke and remarked that the party didn't appear to be rushing to the telephone, or a facsimile thereof.

Gail hung up.

She went into the bathroom, made a face at the laundry basket . . . a pox on suds, on ironing boards. I'll go to bed, she thought, and get some sleep.

When Sam came, an hour later, she was drifting off, willing herself into the black engulfing tide, soft as velvet, drowning as water; willing herself not to dream, only to sleep. She heard the hammering at the door, sat up and thought, drowsily, Drat her, anyway. It would of course be Pat, who always forgot her key.

She switched on the lights and looked at her clock. It was a little past eleven . . .

She was halfway to the door when she heard Sam's voice. He said, "I know you're there, Rusty. No back talk."

Now she was wide awake, and went barefooted to the door and spoke through it. She said, "I've gone to bed."

"Well, get up," he said testily. "You are up, by the way."

"Yes and no. Go 'way, Sam," said Gail, her heart in her mouth. All right, so swallow your heart, its bitterness and its uncertainty. Eat it, if necessary. Isn't that an old Chinese custom or something? She found herself laughing, helplessly, almost hysterically.

"Is that a joke, son?" inquired Sam solicitously.

"Please go away."

He said, "I'll stay here until hell freezes over . . . such an original phrase. Until the milkman comes, until the postman knocks, until the landlord collects the rent. I'll stay until the next world war and the atomic end of mankind. This is a filibuster, darling. I'll talk, sing, recite, declaim, orate, and otherwise give cause for the neighbors to call the cops. Therefore, O beautiful and idiotic, come out, come out, wherever you are or take the consequences. I feel I am confusing my games," he concluded querulously, "but surely you perceive my reasoning?"

She did. He was quite capable of making more than a public nuisance of himself. "You'll have to wait until I'm dressed," she said.

"Why?"

She did not answer but went back to her room and inserted herself into underthings, a bright skirt, a sweater . . . a pair of stockings . . . she hunted for garters and loafers. She ran a comb through her hair, spent a brief moment before the mirror. Then she marched into the living room and heard Sam whistling softly under his breath. He was whistling "Always."

She opened the door and he said brightly, "Corny, wasn't it?"

If he had been drunk, even half drunk, she could have borne it somehow, but he was entirely sober. His crazy hair was brushed, he wore what she recognized as his best suit, his shoes were shining.

She said, "I don't want you coming here."

"People don't like bills, they don't like taxes, they don't like dying. But bills and taxes happen to most of us . . . and dying's a trick which everyone learns." He slammed the door and took her in his arms. "How about it, Rusty," he said softly, "how are you going to die? Decently, all passion spent, in a dreary bed, with costly specialists attending your last hours and the grandchildren waiting for the reading of the will, or are you going to smash up with me, tomorrow, next month, in a dozen or fifty years . . . fall off a mountain, out of a plane, into the sea . . . but together?"

"Sam, Sam . . ."

"Stop crying, damn it," he said. "Stop. This is the last time. Have I said that before? The very last time."

"Let me go!"

"Never."

But he did and she staggered a little, as his compliance was abrupt, groped for, and found, a chair. Sam walked to the coffee table and picked up a pack of cigarettes. He took one out, his back to her, flipped his lighter, and then turned.

"My agents tell me that l'affaire Spencer progresses apace," he said.

"We're not going to discuss that," she told him, regaining something of her composure.

"I begin to lose patience with you. Sometimes I ask myself, why I bother. There are hundreds of girls, as pretty, prettier, with just as good or better minds, as well as legs. There are hundreds a damned sight more generous," Sam told her, "and as much fun. Then I remember you, or I see you again, and I stop asking. I don't know if your effect upon me is due to a chemical reaction or what. I don't care. I am not interested in academic biology either. I've stayed away . . . and now I'm back. You wish I was dead or unborn or a thousand miles away, don't you? Well, I intend to live a while longer, I can't undo my parents' regrettable, consequential impulses, so the best I can offer is distance . . . if you want it that way."

"What do you mean?"

"Look." He came over, sat on the arm of her big chair and pulled her roughly against him. "Rusty, I'm going off on a swing round the country . . . stopping at villages, small towns, farms, cities. I'll talk to GIs in schools and colleges, banks and gas stations, in hospitals, in poolrooms, in theater lobbies, in hotels and flophouses. I'll talk to them in bars and restaurants, in their own homes, in their parents' homes; in shacks and dumps and joints; in huts and attics, in good solid frame dwellings with trees in the back yard. I'll talk to them on trains, and planes, in trucks and taxicabs . . . What's cooking, Joe? What's your gripe, if any? Was it as you hoped and dreamed, as you believed, the home-coming? Was it easier or harder, the adjustment? Do you still go for the corner drugstore and the hamburger . . . the girl next door, the girl who waited . . . as we said you would, when you were fighting and we were reading about it? How is the girl next door, by the way? Did she wait for you or did she marry someone else . . . the 4F guy, the black market stinker, the hero with more medals than you and more points so he came home faster? Or did you forget her. . . . did you marry the girl from England, Wales, Belgium, Australia, Ireland? . . . There are a lot of angles, Rusty, and I'll cover 'em. I'll write my column wherever I hang my hat. I'll do some of the traveling by car and, some, if I want to, on foot. And I'll be gone a long time, as long as it suits me.

Columns?" he said. "I've a million of 'em —
with due credit to Mr. Durante — and a
book too, and a couple of novels . . ."

She was sitting up, holding him away from
her, her eyes brilliant. She cried, "It sounds
wonderful, Sam."

"Okay, so it's wonderful. And you'll be
along, Rusty. This will be our show. You can
talk to the girls," he said, "and kiss the babies for me. Is it a deal?"

For one completely insane moment her
heart cried, Yes . . . yes, so loudly and surely
that he must have heard. Indeed, he did
hear, for her heart's voice spoke in her eyes
and her shaken mouth, and the rising color
in her face, and he kissed her and said, "I
knew it!"

Gail pulled herself away. She said, "Sam,
please go over there, sit down . . . anywhere
. . . away from me."

The cigarette he had dropped in the ash
tray still burned; the smoke ascended, lazy,
expiring. Smoke does get in your eyes.

"Scared?" asked Sam, and moved away
from her and across the room with his tall,
tired slouch.

Listen, said someone, not in the room,
someone not anywhere, listen to me. Do you
know what it will be like, after a while? Oh,
maybe not on this trip, but the next or still

another . . . being left alone in dirty little hotels, waiting for a phone to ring . . . for hours . . . maybe days . . . surely, after a while, nights . . . or being left alone in a neat little flat somewhere, still waiting for the ringing or a letter . . . and one day the bell won't ring or the postman come. You know that. Is it worth it, the voice inquired, for the little you'll have at first?

"It won't be a little," Gail said aloud and Sam asked, "What did you say? Gail, stop looking like that."

The voice said, Much or little, it will end . . . and you'll live a long time afterwards.

Gail rose. She said, "I can't go with you, Sam. Not this time or ever."

He could protest, argue, hammer at her, urge. He was good at all these. But he did nothing. He looked at her and then he said flatly, "I believe you mean that."

"Yes."

"Okay. I'm not very bright, am I? Give my love to Mr. Spencer, poor devil."

He crossed the room without looking at her, opened the door, and closed it quite softly.

On Christmas Eve, Brad came to the apartment. Pat was with Bill and his parents, and Evie, the day after Thanksgiving,

130

had departed for Hollywood. Mr. Gammon had proved, to everyone's astonishment, the McCoy. On the first of the year, a pleasant girl, a friend of Pat's, would take Evie's place.

Brad had suggested that they spend Christmas Eve together. He had added, "If we can be alone, and if you can cook."

Gail had retorted that, naturally, she could cook . . . after a fashion.

So on Christmas Eve they ate broiled chops, baked potatoes, a green salad, and a bakery tart, and opened a bottle of champagne which Brad had sent in a few days before.

The little range served, and the chops were neither under- nor overdone. Gail set the card table, in the far corner of the living room, with the best equipment the flat offered, and wore an enveloping apron over her green frock, with a sprig of holly pinned to the shoulder. She removed the apron before dinner and said, over the wineglass, "I'm glad you were here to open it . . . it defeats me somehow. Merry Christmas, Brad."

The packages he had brought were on the couch, a dozen of them. She looked over at them and smiled. "Convention dictates . . . books, flowers, candy," she reminded him.

"How long since?"

"Years."

"There's a small package there," he said warily; "it's for Easter really, unless you change your mind between now and midnight. You cook an elegant chop, you bake a wonderful potato, you toss a superfine salad . . ."

"And patronize a good bakery?"

He laughed, looking relaxed and contented. He said, "A toast . . . to Christmas . . . to all the Christmases . . ."

"What are you doing tomorrow?" she inquired.

"Family dinner, very stuffy. We have no close relatives, only a few extremely remote cousins who crawl out of club windows and out of brownstone dungeons to regard the tree and stuff themselves with entirely too much food . . ."

Gail looked down at the table. "No appetizer, no soup, no fish, no vegetables . . . we'll have scurvy," she said.

"Let's, it might be fun."

She said, "As a matter of fact, I hate to cook. I don't like anything about a kitchen, and I hate dishwashing."

"What a wonderful wife for a rich man!" he said admiringly.

"Do you think so?"

"I have thought so, for some time. And what are you doing tomorrow, Miss Rogers?"

"Pat is going to Jersey to be with her people. She asked me, too; it's a big family, very haphazard, very jolly. Her young doctor will be on duty . . ."

"You might unaccept, Gail and come to dinner with us."

"The family dinner?"

"It could be. Have you noticed," he inquired, "how mild, how like spring, December is?"

The snow was deep, and the ice rutted the gutters, and the wind cried around the buildings. Gail laughed. She said, "Drink your coffee and smoke, while I clear away."

"I'll do the dishes," he offered, "much as I dislike the thought."

"Let them stay in the sink. Pat's so starry-eyed I can persuade her to do anything."

When they came back from the kitchen, after he had carried trays and they had scraped and stacked, he said, "It isn't midnight . . . but . . ."

"Turn on the radio," Gail ordered, "it's not fair to open presents until then."

There were programs of carols and they listened sitting close together; carols and Christmas plays and people managing somehow to infuse a written script with the brief, beautiful annual wonder. And in a pause between programs, when the battered little box was silent, he asked:

"How's Sam?"

"I don't know. Have you been reading his column?"

"Yes. It's good . . . it's very damned good."

She said, "I wonder how many people will like it . . . we forget so soon." She had said that before, she thought.

"Have you forgotten?"

But he did not mean the war, nor the returning men, nor those who were to return and those who never would. And she waited before she answered.

It had not been very long since Sam closed the door softly and went away. Or was it forever, an eternity? There were no letters, no foolish telegrams. Other times when he went away the Western Union boy came three times a day or perhaps not for a week. And there were no telephone calls.

You forget, the hard way; with desperation and in tears, with determination, with promises which you break and make again. But somehow you manage. She looked at Brad, waiting, and thought how fond she was of him, how good he was, how kind, what fun they had together. She thought, He is patient, he asks so very little . . .

So she said, "Yes, Brad, I've forgotten."

He took her hand and held it close. He said, "Let's hunt for some carols again and listen, without talking."

At midnight she opened the packages . . . books, candy — "no flowers," he admitted sadly, "unless you count the holly a little earlier."

"Or the table tree," she reminded him. It shone from a corner, a living tree in a round white porcelain pot, hung with miniature lights and tiny decorations frosted with silver.

Nylons, and handkerchiefs, a ridiculous lapel pin, frankly costume jewelry, a mammoth poodle to remind her of the poodle they had once talked to at the Plaza, one Sunday after luncheon.

In a little box, a smiling Chinese god in ancient ivory, his infinitesimal carved hands invoking a blessing . . .

After a while she opened the smallest box, the square one, and presently the ring lay in her hand, an emerald, very large, but not too large, and very beautiful.

He said, "You like emeralds, they become you, and they are like the spring, translucent, green, young . . ."

She weighed the ring in her hand; it was heavy, she thought, very heavy . . . not with the weight of stone and carats, nor of setting . . .

He said, "Well, foolish of me, I suppose . . . rushing the season, if there is to be a season."

Gail put the ring back in the box. It was not yet spring, she would be more certain when the Easter parade flowed down the New York streets and all other streets.

She picked up a little package from the table by the couch, and said, "I have this for you, Brad."

It was a silver lighter, and he opened it and exclaimed and leaned to kiss her. He had dozens of lighters, she knew, but he would like this one the best.

She said, "And something else."

"Gail?"

"I'll come tomorrow," she told him unsteadily. "You really want me . . . come, I mean, to the family dinner . . ." He took her in his arms, and she said presently, half crying, because she was frightened, and half laughing, because why need she be frightened, ever again, "Now it's I who rush the season."

She wore the emerald, it was a little too large and slid around on her finger. It was green fire, green sea water, it was the green of an impossible star, the green of new leaves and fine springing grass . . .

"You have made me happy," he said, "for the rest of my life. If only I can make you a fraction as happy."

The radio was still on, they had forgotten it, a clear voice singing an old song, and bells ringing . . .

She made her pledge aloud. Not many do, nowadays, yet all, or most, must make it, in their hearts. But Gail spoke the words, so gentle and outmoded, so hopeful and believing:

"I'll be a good wife, Brad," she said.

VII

Shortly before one o'clock, Brad kissed his
fiancée a belated good night and an early
good morning and departed. He was be-
mused with the pleasant idea that Gail would
accompany him, as a Christmas gift for Alexandria . . . "she goes to bed but not to sleep,"
he insisted. But the project did not appeal to
Gail. It seemed bad enough that Alexandria
be informed by her grandson that Santa
Claus had brought her the realization of her
worst fears without presenting that realization, in person, at such an hour, and she said
so, flatly.

"But you don't expect me to keep this to
myself?" he asked, like a small boy.

Mutely, Gail prayed that Alexandria
would be asleep and not listening for rein-
deer on the roof. She tucked Brad's scarf
around his neck, kissed him again, saw the
door close, and went to the window to look
out. Presently she watched him emerge
upon the street and wait there until a cab
cruised by; he hailed it, climbed in, the cab
drove off. Gail sat down, and lighted a cigarette. She put it out, almost instantly, went

into the kitchen and tied an apron around her. A fine time and season to be washing dishes. But she was wide awake. She felt very odd, alternately hot and cold, as if she were coming down with something. She watched the suds, too lavish for the soap shortage, spin up in the sink, took off the emerald ring and put it on the shelf, from which it winked at her. She felt . . . how did she feel? Soberly happy, frightened, and, somehow, trapped. The last idea appealed to her as ridiculous. She told herself straightforwardly, *I'm* not the one who's trapped.

It wasn't too late; she could wait a while and then telephone the Spencer house, heedless of the time; she could say, I can't, Brad, it's too serious a step for us both and too unfair to you.

Don't be a dope, said the emerald, using the vernacular. This is what you wanted, isn't it? And aren't you lucky? You can keep your promise and without difficulty. He might have been fat and greedy, demanding and selfish. He might have been old and withered. He might have been much married and disgusting. You're so lucky you should be on your knees. You like this man, remember? You're fond of him, you respect him, and when he takes you in his arms you don't instinctively pull away. Brace up . . . and Merry Christmas.

She washed the dishes and wept into the soapy water. Silly to be crying on Christmas morning with her life, her fabulous life before her. She thought, with passion, I'll be right for him, I'll do anything. I can take the old lady and her antagonism, I can take anything.

What did she want? The wild wonder, the absorption and loss of self, the rosy clouds on which to walk, upheld? The wonder diminished, the absorption was no more, the self was recovered, the clouds dispersed . . . this happened to the most ardent lovers . . . it would happen to Pat, it would have happened to Gail had she married Sam. Marrying Sam would have been as much against her better judgment as his. What had been between them was too fragile to take the weight of daily living. I would have never had a peaceful moment with Sam, she told herself unhappily.

Who wanted peace?

She answered that one. I do, she thought, I want it more than anything in the world.

Can money buy it?

She dried the dishes. Money couldn't buy it . . . she was adult enough to know that; but money helped. Not money itself, the cash in the hand, the figures in the bank book, but the knowledge that you were protected against the sharp cold winds that blow alike on rich and poor. You could build quite a structure with money; you could not build a structure strong enough to shut out death or illness but you could build one which would be a fort, equipped to fight.

She heard Pat running up the stairs, slipped the ring back on her finger, and returned to the living room, the table tree shining bravely, the holly at the windows, the wrappings of Brad's packages strewn on the couch . . . the presents standing on tables and chair . . . books and perfume, the foolish poodle . . . all the evidences of his thought for her.

Brad got out of the cab before the house and glanced up. The lights were on in his grandmother's room. He gave the yawning driver, a man chilled to the bone in a sweater under his coat, a considerable bill. "Well, thanks, chum," said the driver, astonished, for this guy was obviously sober, "and Merry Christmas."

"The same to you," said Brad, went up the steps and let himself into the hall. On the landing, he switched off the downstairs light and a moment later rapped at his grandmother's door. It was not unusual for her to read very late. And today was Christmas. He thought, with tenderness, When she was a little girl perhaps she did not sleep, thinking of her stocking and the tree. But he was uneasily aware that tonight her wakefulness would have little to do with Christmas . . . but a great deal to do with his absence from home tonight.

She said, "Come in," and Brad opened the door and looked at her, smiling. He said, "Merry Christmas, Gran . . . but you can't have your presents until your breakfast tray arrives."

She said, "I believe you have already received your major gift."

For happiness shone from him. Loving him as she did, it was impossible not to rejoice. But she feared and distrusted the source of the happiness.

Brad sat down on the edge of the bed, a gesture she deplored yet endured, and put his arms around the frail, thin shoulders. He said, "I'm a very happy man, Gran . . . and Gail sends her love."

"That, I do not believe. She is an honest young person and has no more love for me than I have for her."

Brad sighed. A man had trouble with his women. He said, "I believe each of you respects and admires the other."

"In my case, and in a manner of speaking, you are quite correct," said Alexandria. She looked very old and tired. She kissed his cheek and her lips were cool and dry, like withered flowers. She smelled faintly of talcum and of a very light, expensive perfume. "I have always wished the best for you," she said, "and I have always prayed for your happiness. You are taking a very serious step . . . she *has* accepted you?"

"Yes, and we know it's serious. I am sure Gail does, and I do when I am sensible enough to reflect upon it, which, at this juncture, isn't often."

"Naturally," agreed his grandmother. She thought back fleetly to her own engagement. All very correct, with Mr. Spencer calling on her parents. She remembered the dress she had worn, the room in which, a little later, they had sat together and alone. Over fifty years ago.

She said gently, "I hope that Gail will be with us tomorrow."

The given name came hard, and she thought it absurd. A girl should be called by a name with generations of use back of it; Mary, Sarah, Elizabeth. In her own generation, Alexandria had been quite usual, Victoria, Ann . . .

She had taken the blow, rallied, and now she marshaled her forces. They were still considerable, despite her age, her disappointment, and her enormous, emotional fatigue.

"I think so, if you ask her," Brad stipulated. He added, "Poor kid, what an ordeal," and then perceived the slight spark in his grandmother's black eyes, a wicked little ember. "Don't gloat, Gran," he advised.

"I'm not gloating. What an unattractive word and accusation."

He said, "It would be an ordeal in the best of circumstances. Let's not kid ourselves that this is one of the best. But the Christmas cousins are amiable if vacuous . . ."

"Really, Bradford!"

He said, "And I quote. That's what you said about 'em last Yuletide. And it's as good a time as any for a family announcement."

Alexandria's heart, slow in its latter days, accelerated uncomfortably. She asked, "You plan to marry soon?"

"Why not?"

There was no reasonable reply, nor valid arguments. There could be no proper calling of the involved parents one upon the other nor could Gran officiate *in loco*

144

parentis. For Gail had no parents; she had no one.

"I suppose you are right," she agreed.

"Try to get some sleep," he said, "for today is considerably advanced and will be moderately exciting."

After he had gone, after the lights were out and the wind blew chill, and smelling of snow, Alexandria looked into the darkness. She would make the best of it. Usually the noblesse oblige attitude made sense, spared embarrassment, but was sometimes hard to maintain.

If that girl hurts him, she thought, if she *dares* . . . Her black eyes were a hawk's, her heart had hawk's eyes, too.

Not many hours later the telephone woke Gail and Brad said, "Merry Christmas again, darling. How does it look to you this morning?"

"Wonderful," Gail answered sleepily. The weather beyond her windows was not at its best, but, for Brad, the sun shone and it was June.

He said, "Gran wants to speak with you. She wants you to come to us today. I'll call for you, if you will. It will be hideously dull and stuffy, but the cousins, I promise, will depart at a reasonable hour."

145

She could say, No. She could say, Soon, Brad, as soon as tomorrow, but not today. But he wanted her to come and she owed him a great deal; not the value of the emerald and all for which it stood, but for trust and patience and good faith, so she said, "I'll come, of course. What time?"

"It's regrettable, but we'll dine at four, a most unchristian hour," he told her. "Gran's ancestors progressed from two-o'clock dinner to four and then to six. I believe my grandfather was served at seven; and in my youth, it has stretched to eight. But nowadays Gran dines early and all holiday repasts are fixed at four. I advise a slight case of starvation, prior to plum pudding. Is three too early for me to come? It seems a couple of years away. I haven't slept," he added simply, "I couldn't spare the time. I alternated between marveling at my luck and the black fear that you had changed your mind. . . . Thank you, darling. Hang on a moment, while I plug in a phone in Gran's room."

After a moment Alexandria spoke. "Gail?" she inquired, and then, "Merry Christmas." Her tone was frosted as a Christmas tree, glittering as tinsel, and a delicate chill was communicated over the wire. But her words were cordial, if restrained. "Brad has told me his good news," she said, "and I greatly hope that you will dine with us en famille today."

Gail said that she would be happy to dine.

A little later Pat came into the living room. She had spent ten minutes upon her return last night, looking at Gail's ring, and exclaiming, "Holy cow!" But Gail was too tired to indulge in girlish confidences at that hour and had postponed them.

Now, Pat eyed the emerald as if it were an adder and said, "I could have sworn that I dreamed it." She embraced Gail, with abandon. "I can't believe it's legal, leave me touch the hem of your nightie. Aren't you going to wire Evie? Look, are you still coming home with me today?"

"No," said Gail, "I'm awfully sorry. Would you make my apologies? Brad's grandmother just asked me to have dinner with them, Pat."

"Well, sure," said Pat, and collapsed upon the couch. "What a headlight, ducky, and green for Go. I'm so happy for you, I could yell." She did so, at the top of her healthy lungs and added, "Lucky the people across the hall are away. How I envy them, going south. I suppose you'll be too, or aren't you being married soon?"

"We haven't discussed it."

"For Pete's sake!"

147

"There hasn't been time," Gail said, laughing.

"Gail, if you get married before I do, I'll kill you. No, I won't, I'll stand up with you instead. And you'll have to be my matron of honor instead of bridesmaid. That should give my wedding quite an air. How about pushing some practice Bill's way?" inquired Pat. "You know, Park Avenue stuff?"

"I'll go around with a sandwich board," Gail promised, "reading, from left to right, 'Patronize Dr. William Gaines, his wife is my best friend.' "

"A bonzer idea," said Pat, who had once met an Australian. "Gail, are you happy?"

She said gravely, "I'm very happy, Pat."

"Look," Pat's upturned face was very serious, "be sure, be awfully sure . . ."

"I am sure. Brad's a wonderful person," said Gail gently, "and I don't deserve him."

"Sometimes I feel that way about Bill," said Pat, "but at others I know damned well he doesn't deserve me! What about Sam?" she asked hurriedly.

"What about him?"

"Nothing. I won't stick my neck out. Only, if it's out of . . . of spite or anything . . ."

"It isn't." Well, thought Gail, angry with herself, you have some pride, haven't you?

148

You can't let people go around thinking Sam has just taken off without so much as by your leave so you've taken Brad as solace. A lot of people would hoot at that; some solace, they'd say. She said aloud, "Sam asked me to marry him, Pat."

"You turned Sam down?"

"That's right."

Pat got up. She shook her head, and then patted Gail's cheek. She said, "I like Brad fine, the little I know him."

She thinks, Gail told herself, that I still love Sam and that I'm marrying Brad for money.

Well, wasn't she? she asked herself coldly. Money, security, and a sober happiness.

Dinner at Mrs. Spencer's was one of those things that went on and on. There were three cousins, two female and one male, but almost indistinguishable one from the other, save in a matter of dress. They were all drab and desiccated. They ate an enormous amount for people so painfully thin. Millicent also was at dinner, in her best plum-colored crepe, with the Jensen brooch and bracelet Brad had given her elaborately displayed. She did not display Mrs. Spencer's practical gifts, the warm underwear, stout stockings, wholesome sweater coat, and very substantial check. She drew Gail aside before dinner, to shake her hand and to say, quavering, "I am very happy for you." But Millicent had been crying. Her eyelids were faintly pink, and her rabbity little nose.

Mrs. Spencer made the announcement during the dessert course . . . plum pudding and a mammoth snowball of ice cream, laced with fruit and brandy. She rose, small and erect, in a black velvet frock, Brad's orchids, little, rosy stars, pinned to her shoulder, and lifted her wine glass. She said, "We must drink to Gail and Bradford's mutual happiness."

The cousins were astonished. Eva, the widowed one, wept; Florence, the spinster sister, was seized with a fit of choking; Junius, the male, marched stiffly to Gail's place and imprinted a chaste salute upon her cheek. None was disturbed, albeit curious and, in their mummified way, excited; for none stood to lose nor gain, whomever their remote relative married.

It was painful, but bearable.

The cousins departed, in Alexandria's car, somewhat before nine o'clock. Now it was time that the domestic staff be officially apprised of the change in the family situation. Each had been with Alexandria for a long time; Andrews, and Cora, his wife, who cooked; Sarah, Alexandria's personal maid; Gertrude the parlor maid and her sister Harriet who officiated upstairs. These were on duty, Christmas as on other holidays, as was Pompston the chauffeur. He, together with the laundress and the kitchenmaid . . . who was new, for kitchenmaids are always new — would be informed later. It was a stately occasion.

Then they sat in the drawing room and Alexandria sent Millicent upstairs to the safe to fetch a small jewel case. When Millicent, sniffling, brought it, Alexandria opened it. She said, "These are not intrinsically very valuable, but they have sentimental association . . . some of these pieces were my mother's, some were her mother's, and some were my great-great grandmother's."

They were lovely things, garnets and jet, onyx and pearls, rose diamonds, emeralds, sapphires, and most of them were in sets. Mrs. Spencer looked at them for a moment. No. They would be wasted on this girl. She kept the fabulous pearls in the safe deposit, the diamond necklace and other heavily insured jewelry, which she rarely wore. She looked in a little compartment and said annoyed, "But this is not the right box, after all, Millicent."

Millicent fluttered and Brad compressed his lips. He could read his grandmother's mind, crystal clear. Not for Gail the lockets and twin bracelets, the necklaces and rings which were dear to Alexandria's heart, although she did not wear them.

Millicent, convinced that she had been unjustly reprimanded, toiled upstairs and returned with another jewel case. Halfway down, the reason dawned upon her too, and she was suddenly quite pleased about the whole thing though the subtlety was, of course, wasted upon Miss Rogers.

This case contained pins, rings, a number of bracelets, and the everyday pearls. Carefully Mrs. Spencer selected a bracelet of alternating diamonds and emeralds which her husband had given her, one Christmas, and clasped it on Gail's wrist. She said, "It matches your pretty ring, my dear."

She did not add, because doubtless Bradford would break the news to Gail, if she became his wife, that the pearls now in the bank would be hers. Those were entailed. They were Alexandria's only until her grandson married. They were extremely well known, and every so often a healthy young woman was escorted to the bank as to the Minotaur, to sit, well guarded, with the pearls around her bare throat so that they would not lose their glowing life and color.

It was quite an evening.

They were married before the end of January, despite Alexandria's remark that she considered a long engagement sensible. "But," said Brad, "we are getting no younger; that is, I'm not — Gail of course will always be about six. And what are we waiting for anyway?"

The announcement went to the press, suitably worded, and the plans for the wedding were made. Gail made them. It was her wedding. She wished, she said, to be married in the small neighborhood church which she sometimes attended, and where she had found the clergyman very friendly. She discussed this with Alexandria and Brad shortly after the New Year.

"I'm not quite a heathen," she said, smiling, "although I admit I sometimes oversleep on Sundays."

Alexandria said briskly, "But I hoped you would permit me to give you your wedding, Gail."

"A wedding," said Gail, "is the concern of the bride's parents or, if she has none, of her relatives . . . and, failing relatives, of herself."

Alexandria was in two minds, a unique situation and confusing. She had accepted

the unfortunate situation, she hoped grace-
fully. She had told the tearful and twittering
Millicent that there was nothing she could
do about it. Her curious friends, dancing on
the doorstep, were received with cordiality
and China tea, but little information. Her
intimates, venturing to inquire, did dear Alexandria approve? were informed that, naturally, she approved, why should she not?

The columnists had something of a nine-
hour wonder and those who dallied with the
social news, in a cozy fashion, dipped their
pens in their hearts' blood and wrote feel-
ingly of thc bcautiful young model and her
happy millionaire. It was usual, and Gail,
who had been living in a world built up by
publicity, sought and unsought, for some
time, accepted it as a matter of course. Evie
wired from the coast, "for heaven's sake ex-
clamation point" and then telephoned upon
the promise of her first contract. She asked,
"Who's standing up with you as the phrase
goes . . . silly, isn't it? You don't expect
prone attendants or is it supine?"

"Pat," said Gail, "and, if you'll come,
you."

"Darling, I can't, I am having the works
. . . getting myself a figure, speech lessons,
all the rest. But why don't you and Brad
come on out after you're married?"

Gail said sincerely that she would like nothing better. But she was leaving the wedding trip to Brad and somehow she could not quite see him as the happy bridegroom in Hollywood.

Alexandria argued for some time about the wedding. A small one, as obscure as possible — except that Brad could never be obscure — would be to her liking; but, on the other hand, her pride panted after the processional pageantry of a wedding at St. Thomas's.

Brad ended all discussion. He said, "Gail shall be married just as she wishes; in a balloon, on the radio, or in an airplane. By a justice of the peace if she prefers. I am only incidental. Besides, I like her plans."

And so they were married in the church of Gail's choice; and the bride wore a new suit, the color of wet sand, and sables, the gift of the bridegroom's grandmother. She did not wear the pearls, which were hers as soon as the words were said, because, while modest pearls are worn with a sweater, modest or otherwise, those the approximate size of mothballs are not. As for the sweater, it was handmade, and delicate as the most lacy blouse and the palest shade of green. Her little hat was pale green and sand colored, and she was one of the prettiest brides anyone had ever seen.

Brad's best man was his friend, Angus McKenzie. They had grown up, gone to school and the university together. Angus flew on from Chicago, but his wife, expecting her second baby, could not come. He was a big man given to infrequent speech and no gestures. He was kind to Gail, she liked him but was aware that he withheld his judgment.

There were no other attendants except Pat, and a few guests. Bill came, getting the afternoon off and with eyes for none save the bridesmaid, which was proper. The cousins came, and a few intimate dowager friends of Mrs. Spencer's. Gail had asked Pat's people and three of the girls she knew best and was amazed, making out her meager list, how few of all those she knew she wished to be present. But a number of Brad's friends came, and all who worked with him at the laboratory, including Helena Sturm, the Austrian scientist of whom Brad had spoken to Gail. She was a pretty woman in an entirely natural way, her fair hair was simply dressed, her skin fine and clear, her blue eyes direct. Gail had met her prior to the wedding, and admired her very much. She did not quite dare like her; Helena was pleasant but not easy to know.

She regretted, she said, that her husband was not well enough to come. Gail knew that Dr. Sturm was confined to a wheel chair, because of injuries in a concentration camp, but Helena always maintained the fiction that, just today, he was not well enough.

The reporters gathered, there was no way to avoid them. This was a quiet wedding but no hole-in-a-corner affair. Mrs. Spencer was inwardly outraged, but outwardly agreeable.

There was no reception. Alexandria had offered the house and mild merriment, but Gail refused. If Brad didn't mind, she said, she'd rather not.

So that was that and after the wedding Gail aimed her white and green orchids at Pat and they went out to the car, in the darkness of a threatening winter day, and drove along the icy roads to a small inn in Connecticut, where they spent a few days. It was a good interlude, with log fires in the big bedroom and country roads to tramp over: with a frozen river beneath their windows and unobtrusive service.

When they returned to New York, Pompston met them, before the Century pulled out, bringing the extra luggage which had been left at Brad's and taking the car back to the garage. Alexandria and Millicent were with him, to wish them a good journey. They stood in the echoing station, under the painted sky, said the usual things, and all longed for the train to depart.

They went to Arizona, for Brad was giving himself a month or better. He was his own employer, the laboratory was his, and he had had no holiday since well before 1941 unless you excepted his war experience, the training and the brief time overseas, which hardly seemed in the nature of a vacation.

He had advised Gail diffidently, "Don't get a lot of clothes, darling, you can pick them up in Arizona."

This touched her and she had kissed him, saying, "I won't, I promise, and the exchequer wouldn't run to it anyway, even with discounts. But, on the other hand, you deserve a wife with two frocks to her back."

She bought carefully, cotton dresses, a print or two, the necessary accessories, for she would not arrive with an empty trunk. Her savings account was flat as last night's wine before she had finished, but not until she was married did she feel free to draw upon the money Brad had settled on her.

He explained it carefully, as if embarrassed. He had made a will, he said, "and arrangements."

"If I die, darling, you become my heir; also Gran's, by the way. The only strings to

the money are attached to our mutual heirs."
He had smiled then. "The hypothetical sons
and daughters of whom my grandfather took
note. But I'll live a long time. And also I've
made a settlement on you, which you'll have,
come hell and high water, whether I walk out
on you — a fantastic prospect — or you on
me, in what is known as high dudgeon . . .
what is it by the way, and should we try on
for size? Understand?"

He was making it easy for her, she understood, and nodded, her eyes filling. He was
very good to her.

At the Arizona ranch they lived in a comfortable cabin and took their meals with the
other guests. And sometimes they drove
into Phoenix and it was fun to buy clothes
there, sun suits and bathing suits, Levi's and
giddy shirts, Mexican blouses and full, gay
skirts.

In every way, Gail's husband was good to
her, gentle, not asking more than she could
give. Yet she could give a good deal, she
learned, because she was so fond of him,
and grateful . . . and to be grateful without
resentment is a marvelous thing. Her reactions were natural and happy, and were not
burdensome to her. For her response to
Brad was not weighted with the crushing
load of an absorbing, urgent love, one which

cannot rejoice in the pleasure of the moment but must devour the beloved. Gail knew nothing of such love; she had once experienced its shadow but, as it were, only in prelude. So now she was happy in an uncomplicated fashion, under the bending skies and the violet shadows of mountains.

Their cabin looked over a cacti garden, and across to a swimming pool. It was a very de luxe ranch, complete with wranglers, square dances, and scenery.

Gail swam, very well. She had learned in a YWCA pool as a child. And she danced, even better. It amused her that she had been here before, at nearby resorts, snatched there by plane and away again, before you could say Desert Fashions.

She had learned to ride, after a fashion, in a New York academy, mainly because Evie took lessons — "It's essential if I'm to go to Hollywood," Evie said — and because it had not proved too expensive. In Arizona she took both tennis and golf lessons, one on a resort hotel court, the other at the club . . . for Brad enjoyed both games, and she wished to be able to play with him. And all this, the friendly cocktail parties, the desert picnics, and the excursions by rented car, filled up the sparkling days, made them pass so quickly you had scarcely time to think.

Walking, riding, sitting by the fire in the cabin, for the nights were cold, they talked, about themselves for the most part. Each added to his picture of the other, filling in the outlines. Brad was the only person to whom she had talked long and openly about her mother, and from the beginning.

"I no longer dream about her," she said, one afternoon as they lay in long chairs outside the cabin and watched the sun decline in glory. "Isn't that strange?"

"No, darling."

He was brown from the sun, and Gail had acquired an even, dark gold, her gray eyes brilliant against it, her hair spectacular. Now and then an unregenerate tourist found his way to the ranch, and seeing Gail at the pool, in a white bathing suit, whistled loud and long or, crossing the border in his uninhibited thoughts, exclaimed admiringly, "Ole, ole!"

"Why?"

He said, "When you're happy — and you are, aren't you? — perhaps you do not dream."

But he knew, as she did, and as any psychiatrist could have told them, why. It was not because she was happy that the dreams had gone, but because she had kept a promise.

Now there was regret to take the place of

dreams, a regret familiar to so many . . . if only she had lived, if only I could have shared this with her . . .

She said abruptly, "I never told you how she died. I came home and found her. It was cold and wet and she had been out working; calling on people, being turned away . . . carrying the cosmetics, I think," she said drearily, "in a little case. Her face was flushed . . . her breathing —"

"Don't, darling."

She went on, "I ran out and got a doctor. The landlady had called one, but he didn't come. I knew of a good man, someone had told me. We took her to the hospital, and put her in a ward — we couldn't afford anything else. They did all they could . . . even to sulfa drugs, not what they are now . . . And she came home. She was cured, they said. And then one day . . ." She looked away from the mountains and at him. " 'Her heart,' the doctor said, when he came, 'It's all over,' he said. And it was."

He said gently, "Try not to grieve. It's much to have known her, Gail . . . I scarcely remember my mother."

"But this — peace," said Gail slowly, "and the desert . . . the air and the mountains and all the sun. It pours down. It would have been wonderful, Brad . . . we

162

could have done so much."

He said, a little oddly, "You have done much," and she looked at him quickly and asked, "What do you mean?" and after a while he reached out for her hand and held it, and answered, "I think you have laid a little ghost."

That night, changing for dinner — one didn't dress, here, it seemed more amusing to charge long-dress and dinner-coat prices and then frown upon them — Gail turned from the mirror. She said, "Our time runs out, and I'm scared."

"Don't be." He came to stand behind her and look at her reflection.

"It's your house," she said, "and yet it isn't."

She had wanted their own place, no matter where. But there were obstacles. There were places out of town, big, unwieldy, demanding more service than it was now possible to purchase, which were available at a price. But Brad had said, available or not, he could not be so far from the laboratory . . . and, sometimes, he warned her, he stayed there very late at night. Apartments in town were difficult for anyone to come by and, besides, there was his grandmother.

He had said, "It will be a sacrifice. But she

163

is old, she will be very lonely. I understand what I ask of you and I don't, for a moment, urge it. But — if you could see your way . . . ?"

It was reasonable that he would ask his wife to live in his house . . . reasonable that he would consider Alexandria, whose life tenancy had, in all probability, no great amount of time. He gave her so much; Gail could give a little. But it would not be her house nor would she have the ordering of it. Alexandria had offered that, instantly. She asked merely that Gail would, if possible, retain the servants. "I have proposed pensioning them," she said, "but they're afraid of independence . . . they have been too long in service."

And Gail had said, "If I come here to live, everything must be unchanged."

She was aware at the time that Alexandria was studying her, and wondering. She told Brad that, early in their marriage. She said, "Your grandmother isn't certain whether I am being docile in this matter, or just lazy."

Now she reached back and touched his hand as it lay on her shoulder. She said, "I'm being foolish. It is your home, of course, and mine."

They walked to the lodge under brilliant stars and went into the lounge, which was filled with people. And a man looked up, detached himself from a group, and came toward them. He slouched when he walked, his hair was uncombed, his clothes disreputable. He towered over them both, and said, smiling, "Hi, you two."

Brad put out his hand. He said, "For God's sake . . . did you know we were here? Why didn't you phone? You'll have dinner with us, won't you?" and Gail asked, her voice sounding loud in her own ears and as if shaken by the terror in her heart, "But what in the world are you doing here, Sam?"

VIII

Sam's brown and weather-beaten face expressed apparent astonishment and delight. He'd be damned, he said, several times. He added that you could have knocked him over with a palomino when he saw them coming in. He shook Brad's hand hard, and said, "With your permission?" as he bent to kiss Gail's golden cheek. She found herself shrinking from the brief touch of his lips, and babbling, she told herself angrily, inanely, "Well, Sam!" over and over again.

Sam said, "I wish I could eat with you two but I'm pledged to that flea-bitten gang over there, as they drove me out from town. We're celebrating something. What, I wouldn't know. Nice guys, two reporters, one banker, a cattleman, and a couple of others. Gail, you look, as the girls say, but wonderful."

She said she felt wonderful.

Brad asked, "How about a drink . . . would your friends join us?"

Sam was sure they'd be delighted and so when the introductions had been effected, they went to the cocktail room, off the lounge. Brad canceled his small table, asked for and procured a large one. The place, which looked like a tack room, was half filled, and the other half was rapidly arriving. It was curious, as Brad had once remarked to Gail, how doggedly resorters combated the effects of fresh air, exercise, sunlight, and relaxation with alcohol.

Gail sat next to Sam and made the required effort. She said, "All I know is what I read in the papers, so I take it you've been around. What are you doing in Arizona?"

He said, "Just what I've done elsewhere. I'm driving, in this instance, stopping off at dude and regular ranches, crashing people's modest or palatial homes, spending time in hash houses, gas stations, machine shops, and corrals. I'm not interested in the viewpoint of visitors to the resort places, but the guys dragged me out here, for which I'm grateful, now." He smiled at Brad across the table and addressed him directly. "Very belated congratulations," he said. "I saw the announcement, and meant to wire but I was in the Kentucky backwoods at the time and, as Gail will testify, I was born a procrastinator . . . two weeks after I was expected. As for the wedding item, that caught up with me somewhat late." He turned back to Gail. "Will you take a rain check on the wedding gift?" he inquired. "How about a couple of off-color turquoises?" He then assembled the eyes and ears of his friends and lifted his glass. "To the bride and groom," he toasted, and managed to make the harmless, usual, rather touching words slightly sinister. "As a matter of fact, Spencer owes his good luck to me. Old Sam, the involuntary Eros. Never a bridegroom but always a dope. This is what comes of introducing a friend to your best girl."

There was laughter and one of the native sons remarked that if he had a girl like that he'd keep her under wraps.

It was very gay, and as they all knew who Brad Spencer was they were welcome to draw their own conclusions.

Sam asked about Pat and Evie. When he reached California he'd look up Evie, he promised. "If she brushes me off I'll mangle her," he said. "I knew her when. But perhaps she hasn't been dipped in platinum yet — which would be plating stainless steel, by the way — and so will have an hour for a chum."

The conversation became general and under the cover of the give-and-take, Sam lowered his voice and said, "So you brought it off, Rusty."

"That's obvious, isn't it?" asked Gail. She

added, "Or would you like to see my marriage lines?"

"Don't be feline, darling. I've never seen you look better; sleek, sunny, smug. That's a pretty little piece of glass you're wearing. But you'll get fed up with it, not that Brad isn't one of the best, but between the millstones of Science and Upper Fifth you're going to be ground to an unlovely pulp. It's not for you, pie-face . . . the ritual dinners, the box at the opera — not quite as top drawer as that used to be, alas. And emerald manacles can chafe like the lowly handcuff. What nightmares you'll have, instead of gilded dreams. But then you made your bed and you'll lie in it, for a while. I concede the monogrammed sheets."

"You're displaying very bad taste," said Gail. Anger rose in her, a good sensation, hot, heady, making her feel alive.

"So, I'm to rejoice? That's strictly from bilgewater," Sam said. "And I wish to God I hadn't seen you again, if it's the last time it will be fine with me!"

People were drifting from cocktails to the dining room. The spectacle of mink coats or sable capes slung across linen-covered shoulders and flannel shirts amused Sam, openly. It was material for him, he said, in contrast to all he had been seeing. How to rough it, in ten easy lessons.

The group broke up, shortly after, and parted at the door of the dining room, Sam and his friends going to a table reserved for them on the transient side of the room, and Brad and Gail to their own table by a window that looked across to the mountains.

"Sam looks blooming," remarked Brad when their order had been given. He pushed aside the vase of bright fresh flowers but did not look at her too closely. And then asked, evenly, "Did you mind, very much?"

"I minded," Gail answered candidly, "but why, exactly, I don't know. Something about his general attitude. There are times when Sam becomes too jovial and disagreeable for endurance."

"I overheard what he said to you," Brad told her, "that is, some of it. I couldn't help it."

"I'm sorry," she said. "Please don't be upset. He was just being nasty." She looked at him and tried to smile. "I mind more, if you do," she said.

He said, "Oddly enough, I didn't, except for you."

They saw no more of Sam that evening, except when passing his table the lifted hand and the crooked, characteristic grin.

Mentally, Brad walked cautiously. He had observed more than he was willing to admit. It would have given him great pleasure to invite Sam Meredith to step outside under the big burning stars and there to knock him senseless, among the uncomfortable cacti. But Brad was a reasonable man. He was considerably shorter and lighter than Sam, and neither battler nor boxer. But if he had been seven feet high and suitably proportioned he would not have enhanced himself, he felt, in Gail's opinion, by such a gesture. Do you knock a man down — provided you can — because your wife was once in love with him? He repeated the "was," firmly, to himself; or even because he is, comprehensibly, still in love with her and due to this condition makes certain observations neither courteous nor kind?

That night, while, as she assumed, Brad slept less than an arm's length away, Gail lay wakeful and listened to the coyotes holding their maniacal conversation, sounding forlorn and hysterical. She was angry with herself. It was idiotic to experience excitement, terror even, and both curiously pleasurable, because Sam Meredith had made his appearance. Her anger spilled over into a form of illogical exasperation with her husband. He was inhumanly even-tempered, irritatingly understanding. There are disadvantages, she thought, in being married to a gentleman, who lived by some high code of his own and observed all the rules.

She had worked herself into quite a tizzy when she recalled her refrigerated remark to Sam. "You're displaying very bad taste," she said. Now it struck her forcibly that she must have sounded rather like Alexandria. Perhaps you got that way by osmosis?

She was thirsty, her mouth dry, and she got up and went quietly into the bathroom. But Brad spoke. "Are you all right, Gail?"

"Of course." She had just reached for a glass and it eluded her fingertips. It was conceivably the last straw, metaphorically speaking. She seized the glass and deliberately flung it . . .

It broke and her tension with it and she began to laugh, leaning against the washbasin, catching a glimpse of herself in the mirror, the flushed face, the overbright eyes. And Brad padded in, saying, "What the devil — did you cut yourself, dear?"

"No . . . do be careful . . . you'll walk on the pieces." She added, "I broke the darned thing, it slipped from my fingers." She ran the water, took another glass, and drank.

Brad put his arm around her. "Dope," he said, "there's a thermos by your bed."

They went back to bed, pausing a moment to watch the moonlight flow through the windows. Gail pulled up her blankets, feeling drowsy and relaxed. What a fool she was. What had she expected . . . or wanted? A scene, the sort of routine unpleasantness that might spring from such a situation? Naturally, she didn't want scenes, nor unnecessary emotion, nor, she thought, with defiance, Sam Meredith.

Upon their return to New York, they went directly to the Spencer house and slid smoothly into that plush-lined, polished pigeonhole. It was hard to do much redecoration these days but Alexandria had managed new curtains and upholstery in the time that had elapsed since the engagement. Brad's own suite was now comfortably adapted for two people, his large bedroom and bath and the study, now turned into a living room, while Alexandria had taken a small adjoining guest room and bath, and made the bedroom into a dressing room for Gail, with a daybed in it "in case of illness," she had explained, very deadpan, and the bath had been gaily renovated. All very attractive, and glamorous, as Pat remarked, paying her first call and afterwards going downstairs to drink tea with Alexandria, who had taken a remarkable fancy to her at the wedding.

Breakfast was almost, if not quite, like having their own place, for Alexandria had not breakfasted publicly for a great many years, and the breakfast room was preferable to the dining room, being smaller and uncommonly sunny. Gail could pour the coffee and pass the toast, after Andrews had departed, and look at Brad, screened behind his newspaper, and feel quite married. But after he had gone to the laboratory, time limped. There was only so much she could do; she couldn't spend all her hours shopping or reading, walking or resting.

Tacitly, Alexandria kept out of her way. They usually lunched together if at home and Gail was free to join her at tea or not, as she pleased. There had to be one large, elaborate tea in order to present Brad's wife to his grandmother's friends, and a succession of small, stately dinner parties. Helena Sturm came upon several occasions but not because Alexandria liked her. She didn't, she couldn't, she said, "share the enthusiasm now current for foreigners, except some of the English," but because Brad was sorry for her and liked having her there. "She leads a very confined life," he explained to Gail, "works her clever head off at the lab, and then goes home to sit with

Erich. He's looked after, daytimes, by an aunt who has lived here for many years and keeps house for them."

At one such dinner, black tie and a hope that the gentlemen would not linger too long with the old port and regrettably new cheese, Helena and Gail found themselves talking quietly together after the ladies had withdrawn. Helena wore a muted-blue dress, long, giving her deceptive height. Her fair hair was parted in the middle, and drawn to the nape of her neck. She used little make-up, except a light lipstick. Gail, trying to draw her out, found it difficult. Helena had little interest beyond the laboratory except chamber music. She played the cello, she said, and added that her husband had been a fine amateur musician, both piano and violin. "Especially violin," she said. She added, smoking, "Often we have had a few friends in and Brad comes, and plays violin. Rather well." She asked, "Do you play, at all?"

"No," said Gail, "I wish I did." She concealed her astonishment upon learning that Brad played, and her ignorance. She said, "I have not been musically educated, Mrs. Sturm, either as a performer or as a listener. But I like music."

Helena's small pale face became more animated. She asked, "Then, you could come to us some evening, it would not too much bore you?" Her accent became a little more marked. "Erich has missed seeing Brad in our house, we both have."

"Of course," said Gail, and a moment later the men came in from the dining room.

When they were upstairs that night she asked Brad, "Why didn't you tell me that one of your accomplishments was playing the violin?"

"The fiddle," he said promptly, following her into her dressing room. "I don't know. Didn't occur to me. Maybe I thought you'd better find out things gradually. I took lessons as a kid with great reluctance, when I was in school I fooled around some, because I liked it. But I never had much time. Did Helena tell you? She knows dozens of better violinists and it must half kill her to hear any of them because, I understand, Erich could have been a professional, he was that good. He was a medical man, you know, a surgeon."

"I didn't know. She wants us to come there one evening," she said. "They have missed you." Gail sat down at the dressing table and began brushing her hair and he watched, fascinated always by the living texture, the sweep, the amazing color. It was a

176

very cold night and the electricity crackled in the brush, the hair clung to it.

He said, "If you can take it, dear, we'll go. Erich's not easy to take. You could, after the first moment, accustom yourself to his disfigurement I'm sure. But he's a violent man, moody, difficult, bitter."

"I can take it," she said confidently.

She wasn't so certain, meeting Erich in the small apartment. Helena had made the most of every inch of space, the living room itself was large, quite uncluttered, and comfortable. There were flowers around, and the coloring in the room was subdued and restful. There were several people besides Gail and Brad, a pretty Frenchwoman, who sang, a young man from the laboratory whom Gail had met and whom she suspected of being futilely in love with Helena, and another Austrian couple. Seeing Erich Sturm for the first time was a shock although she had been prepared. He had once been a very big man. He still looked big, in his wheel chair, his shoulders very broad, and his head massive. His hair was white and his face was scarred. He had eyes as black as Alexandria's, and they were bright and seemed young, at first. His hands, which he kept hidden as much as possible, were badly crippled; how, she dared not ask herself.

They talked, there was music, and she watched Brad play. He looked at her, in protest and appeal, half laughing, half serious before he raised his bow. He played, she thought, very well. She sat beside Erich and listened and watched his face soften and the black eyes, which were sometimes like obsidian, soften a little, too.

She said, "I know so little about music, Dr. Sturm, but surely that was very good?"

He said with his heavy accent:

"It was charming. Your husband, Mrs. Spencer, is a naturally good musician. My wife is quite wonderful; the others, more than adequate."

The French girl sang, to Helena's accompaniment, and after a while there was a simple supper, and much good wine, and when they left Erich Sturm, looking at Gail, asked abruptly, "You will come again?"

"I'd like to, very much."

"You are beautiful to see," he said, in his uncompromising way. He must have once had a deep, sonorous voice. Now it was high and querulous. It did not suit him. He added, "I like your husband. He is a fine young man. Money has not spoiled him. He has been very kind to me and my wife."

He shifted his glance to Helena, talking with Brad, and it was dark with a rooted misery. Gail's heart shook. She thought, She is all he has, he loves her almost beyond reason.

Going home, Brad said, "You were depressed, I think."

"A little, at first; and now and again while we were there. It's pretty awful. I don't mean Dr. Sturm's appearance, Brad."

"I know. He was a great surgeon, and he was not of nor in sympathy with the party. They couldn't make him do the things they wanted him to do. As for her, she could have been very important to them . . . only she wouldn't conform. She got out just in time. Scientists all over the world knew of Helena Sturm, were, in some instances indebted to her. She didn't want to leave Erich, but he compelled her, for he was afraid for her. So she was got out — it's a long story — first to Sweden, afterwards to America. Erich might have made his escape before it was too late, but he wouldn't. He had patients who looked to him for life. He'd perfected a very delicate, dangerous heart operation, there were about three men in the entire world who could perform it, at the time. When the Nazis caught up with him he was operating. By God, they waited until he had finished. I don't know how he made them but he did. He was eventually shunted from one concentration camp to another. His last stop was to have been just that; at the most infamous of them all. But he was liberated shortly after his arrival. One of the army doctors recognized him, he had known him in Vienna. Eventually, Helena was able to get him over here. He is greatly improved in general health; and he has been able to lecture to small groups, from his chair. He can't demonstrate his operation but he can explain it, and the slight deviation that makes it his own, as a signature is personal."

She said, "He is terribly in love with his wife."

"It would be easier," said Brad, "if he weren't."

Just before they reached home he said, "Another letter came from the detective agency today."

He meant, the agency he had employed to find out the whereabouts of her father, if he still lived; failing that, the authentication of his death. Gail had seen the first reports, which had come in just prior to their marriage.

"Did they find anything?"

"Nothing. But there are a great many cities in the United States, towns, villages . . ."

She put her hand on his, and leaned

against him. The young veteran who was now their chauffeur, as Pompston was exclusively Alexandria's, looked in the mirror, grinned and looked away. Swell couple, he thought, halting at a light.

She said, "It seems hopeless . . . we don't know where, or when, or by what name . . ."

"Nothing is hopeless."

Gail said after a moment, "I have no affection for him, Brad. You understand that. I have only a sort of inherited hatred. No, that's not the word. The word is resentment. I don't want to see him, if he's alive. I don't think I even want to know . . . This was your idea, remember?"

He said, "You don't mean that. You'd rather know."

She knew, early that spring when, coming in from lunch with Pat, Andrews opened the door and said, expressionless, "A gentleman is waiting, madam."

She asked, "For me? Who is it, Andrews?"

She thought, Sam? But Sam wouldn't come like that, early in the afternoon. Sam would telephone. Sam would ask, What would it cost me to get past the guards?

"A Mr. Rogers," said Andrews evenly.

"Rogers? You're sure?" She lowered her voice, felt that she was white, knew that she felt almost ill with nervousness. "Did he ask for me . . . or for Mrs. Spencer?"

"For Mr. Spencer first," said Andrews, "and then for you."

"Where is Mrs. Spencer?"

"She has gone out, madam," said Andrews; "she will be home for tea."

He stood aside and Gail went into the drawing room. Her knees buckled and she was conscious only that she wished Brad was with her.

A tall, painfully thin man rose from the couch by the fireplace and put his cigarette in an ashtray. She saw all the little unimportant details as one sees them, at such a moment. She saw that his clothes were very worn, but that his shoes were polished. She saw that his hair had once been red and was now a streaked gray. She saw that he had smoked a good deal, that the ashtray was full and the silver box stood open. She saw that he looked a little like the picture her mother had kept, and which Gail had destroyed. She thought she remembered his eyes; they were still very blue.

He said, "Gail? It is Gail, isn't it?" He smiled and made no move toward her. He added, "Absurd as it sounds, I'm your father." He waited a moment and added, "You can't accept that, can you? In the cir-

182

cumstances, I don't blame you. You look very white. Please sit down."

It might have been his own drawing room.

She sat down, folding her hands, one within the other. She said, "If you *are* my father — you don't expect that I —"

"Will fall on my neck with filial raptures? No, not at all. It isn't blood," he said, "but association that makes the bond."

She said, "It's hard to believe that you are my father. The last I knew of you was when a — friend of yours came to my mother and said you were very ill in a Chicago hospital. She gave him money for you. We did not hear again. She wrote, finally, to the hospital. No one of your name had been there at that time."

He said pleasantly, "I wasn't there, under that name. I have found it convenient to use a number of names. Do you recall my alleged friend's name?"

"No."

"I didn't get the money," he said regretfully, "but then I was never fortunate in my choice of friends! I was ill in Chicago. I recovered. Gail, is your mother living?"

She said harshly, "No."

"I see. I thought not. I inquired for her, after I asked for you. Will you tell me — ?"

"No. How do I know who you are?" she

cried. "What proof have you?"

"Look in your mirror," he said softly, "the same shaped face, the same modeling of the head." He took out a battered wallet and gave her a picture and she looked at it, blindly. It was small and badly executed and showed her, as a baby, in her mother's arms. She had its duplicate upstairs on her desk in the living room.

"You could have obtained this, somehow," she said.

"That's so. From someone dying next me in a ward, or under the wheels of a car, a drunken man thrown in jail overnight . . . which has been occasionally my lot," he said mildly, "or for vagrancy . . . but I did not so obtain it. What do you know of me?" he asked.

"Very little." She set her jaws to keep her mouth from shaking. Her hands were cold, and she felt the sweat spring out on her upper lip and along her hairline.

He said, "I met your mother in New York — how old are you now — twenty-two, twenty-three? She was the daughter of a Kansas physician. The town in which she lived was called Forden. Her father's name was Ralph Manning; her mother's Jane. I forget her maiden name. Your mother was the only child. She came to New York to visit a friend who had moved there. Her name was Dorothy Sampson. She lived in an apartment on the Upper West Side. The exact street escapes me. I had met her brother casually and came with him and others to the apartment. Your mother and I were married in New York . . . I was at that time working in a bank. I may add I have been a number of things before and since — an actor in a road company, the manager of a small theater in the West, a hotel clerk — and I have held other positions less respectable."

She said, shaking, "You could have learned all this, too."

"I could indeed," he said easily, "but that, too, would be hard to prove."

She said, "My husband has tried to trace you."

"He isn't the first," said the tall man, amused. "But, at least, I owe him nothing." He looked around the room. "You are very beautiful, and, I may add, as fortunate as you are lovely."

She was silent, because there was nothing to say, and she was wretchedly unhappy. She had thought of it, very differently . . . if they found him . . . she had thought of an old man and an ill one. The first premise was absurd to begin with, for he was not old, he was, she thought, not more than fifty. She had believed that she would see that he was cared for, dutifully, if without forgiveness, because perhaps her mother would have wished it so, having loved him for so long, no matter what he had done to her. But now the picture changed. He was not old, he was not ill, and he was not, as perhaps she had also pictured, repentant.

He said, "I may add that I have been in San Francisco. I saw, long after its occurrence, the news of your marriage." He added, "Has anyone ever called you Gay?"

None but himself, when she was a baby. She could not recall it; but her mother had told her, a great many times. "I believe that he loved us," she would say, "I believe that he thought the world of you. 'Such a gay baby,' he said. He called you Gay."

He watched her face change and went on, "Still someone, sentimental, and half delirious, might have told me that, too. Shortly before your mother and I — shall we say — parted company, I had a slight accident. Do you remember it?"

"When I was four, my father deserted us. No, I don't remember."

"Of course not, at four." He laughed, his face relaxed and charming, despite the deep lines, the unhealthy skin. "But perhaps she told you? She was always a backward, rather than a forward looker, and very talkative. I came home one night, somewhat the worse for drink, as they say, and I stumbled on the roller skates of the child who lived across the hall. I fell and cut my shin and perhaps it was that which made me determined to forsake domesticity. There is always some deciding factor, often quite small. Did your mother ever tell you of that incident?"

She said unwillingly, "Yes."

"I am a little sorry for you," he said musingly. "Not now, oh, never now. But in retrospect, while your mother lived. You must have had a blow-by-blow description of those five years with me . . . not quite five, you were born in the eleventh month of our marriage."

He pulled up his trouser leg, casually, his frayed sock fell about a thin ankle and there was a faint scar, a thin white line.

He asked, "Are you convinced? Or should I resort to the Ouija board? Your mother would remember me. She had a tenacious memory."

She thought, I mustn't shout or scream or ring for Andrews . . . I mustn't do anything. Her anger was black and bitter, it rose in her throat and choked her. She asked, her voice drained of color, "What do you want?"

"You're very abrupt," he murmured. "Your mother was not able to afford — the graces, was she? No, I can see that. But you walk like a model. One account I read said you had been one. Could not you be less — brusque? I could of course make the implausible but pleasant answers. I could say, I have come to die on your doorstep. Very uncomfortable that would be; and with proper care I am good for thirty years. When I was in college . . . did your mother ever tell you I had once graduated from a university?"

"Yes, she told me," said Gail.

"I was voted the man most likely to succeed. We shall see." He went on after a moment, "I could say I had come to you for the love of which I had by my own depravity and cruelty deprived myself. But that isn't so, my dear. I do not find you any more lovable than you find me. I am of course delighted at your success and impersonally charmed by your appearance, standardized but attractive."

She said desperately, "Will you get to the point?"

He looked at her, without speaking. Her twenty-third birthday had been last week. Brad had given her a party; he had also given her a small, lovely string of pearls. The Spencer mothballs still reposed in the safe deposit. He had given her the sable cape flung over the chair. She was aware of these and of the handmade shoes, the black suit, the plain, finely tucked silk blouse . . . she was aware of the emerald, of the pin that caught the blouse at the high neckline, a birthday gift from Brad's grandmother. She was aware, for the first time, of the money she represented, every cent of it; from the cost of the hairdresser to that of the hides of little animals, from the price of jewels to that of the suit — a few yards of material cut by a famous hand . . .

He said amiably, "If you insist upon knowing, I want money, my dear, and a lot of it."

"That's blackmail, you know," Gail said.

Her father raised an eyebrow. "How? You jump at conclusions, and coarse phrases. I have threatened you with nothing. With what could I threaten you? It is not unusual to have a father, although very unusual never to have had one. Surely the Spencer family is so old, so established, as well as so financially secure, that the shock of an unregenerate in-law would not rock it to the foundations? There is of course the little matter of a kindly law which frowns upon the nonsupport of destitute parents. And, I assure you, I am destitute." He turned his

189

pockets inside out, with a gesture; they were empty. "How I begged, borrowed and stole my way here from the coast is something I abstain from telling you. But it would all make an excellent newspaper story," he said thoughtfully, "and I can give it the necessary color and detail."

She said, with contempt, "No decent newspaper would print it."

"Why not? Anything that happens to a Spencer is news."

"I owe you nothing," Gail said.

"Because I left you, and my wife?" He smiled, a little. "My dear child, and I do mean child — think twice. You have heard one side of the story only. I was, to begin with, very fond of your mother, I was even in love with her. She was pretty, she was passionately in love with me. I was earning enough money to support a wife, modestly. But I did not like the way I was making it. Had your mother had means . . ." He sighed. "But she hadn't. I knew that, she did not deceive me, and in the first roseate weeks it seemed unimportant. But when I — shall we say — resigned from my job things were somewhat different. I found myself with a pregnant and demanding woman. She was a good woman, Gail, believe that I respected her. But she was — dull. She loved me too

190

much and she was too good. It is difficult to be married to a saint. Nothing I would do or say could shake or anger her. I could make her weep but never rage. I could do anything to her but leave her. She would have followed me, she would have worked for me, she would have crawled on her hands and knees. Don't look like that, my dear. There are all sorts of men. I am not the type that thrives in a hothouse. So I left her."

She was sick, sick to her bones, sick in her flesh, sick in her mind. "I — I can't sit here and . . . Please go," she said pitifully. "Tell me where I can reach you . . . I will get in touch with you . . . I must talk to Brad, I must see Brad."

He said, "I'm afraid I'll have to stay here. A park bench has no telephone, and a Salvation Army shelter —"

The doorbell rang and Gail rose. She said, "That is Mrs. Spencer."

She heard Andrews open the door, heard Alexandria's voice and Millicent's. She went, staggering a little, to the hall, and Alexandria, about to go upstairs, turned to look at her. She said sharply, "What has happened?"

"Mrs. Spencer, could you call Brad?"

Why, the girl's in bits and pieces, Alexandria thought. Funny how everyone was vulnerable at some point or other. She had thought her grandson's wife composed to the point of hardness. She spoke to Millicent. "Go on upstairs . . ." she said, and Millicent, looking aghast, went. Alexandria took Gail by the shoulders and shook her slightly. She said, "Control yourself. No, you are not going to faint. You are going to tell me what has happened."

Andrews had said, as Alexandria came in, that Mrs. Spencer had a caller, and she had heard, as she passed, a man's voice; she had even glanced in and seen him, a middle-aged man, sitting there.

He had risen and was now standing at the entrance to the living room. He was smiling. He looked, in a battered, very unpleasant way, distinguished. And Gail said dully:

"This is my father, Mrs. Spencer."

IX

Alexandria regarded Morrison Rogers and assumed her most impenetrable mask. In the eighteenth century gentlewomen protected their delicate complexions with trifles of velvet, linen or silk. Alexandria cared for her physical skin with pure soap and water, with unguents in winter and a tilted parasol under the sun. In any season she was mindful of her dignity, and shielded herself from a display of emotion, her own or anyone else's, behind a smooth façade integral to her by temperament and upbringing. No stranger, and few friends, had seen her evince anger, disappointment, or even pleasurable astonishment. In her immediate family she rarely laid the mask aside; now and then it slipped a little, as Millicent could testify.

Gail held her breath, her heart pounding. To a certain extent she felt that she knew Brad's grandmother; at least she had learned to read with some accuracy the thermometer and barometer, gauging temperature and forewarning of storm. She was therefore prepared to see Alexandria's apparently spontaneous smile, practiced and meaningless, sun glittering on ice, and to hear her exclaim, "What a pleasant surprise!" and correctly to evaluate the adjective.

Alexandria offered her small hand, and Rogers bent over it thoughtfully. His own smile was a reflection of hers. When he straightened up, his dark eyes met eyes as dark. They took each other's measure, aware of caution, like fencers or chess players. He thought uneasily, A hard old nut to crack. In his circuitous, uncomfortable journey across the continent he had pondered upon Mrs. Spencer, the only close relative of his unknown son-in-law, and rejoiced in the reflection that there would be no difficult male relatives. He had visualized Alexandria as arrogant, pampered, but easily disarmed by flattery, the dowager stuffed shirtwaist, verging upon the senile. As for Brad, he had dismissed him with the contempt of the man who has nothing, because he's been unfortunate, for the man who has everything, through no talent of his own. Rogers did not consider his circumstances of his own making nor Brad Spencer's of his; Brad had simply inherited a horseshoe. Given opportunity, Rogers would have been, he believed, on the top; without the unearned Spencer money, Brad would have been just another average young man. The newspapers had spoken of Bradford Spencer as a scientist but Rogers had dismissed that, shrugging. Money makes possible all pastimes. If one rich boy bought baseball clubs, another could afford race horses; still others collected blondes, pictures, outraged husbands and lawsuits, or delirium tremens in costly surroundings: If Spencer wanted to fool around with test tubes or whatever, it was as unimportant. But Spencer's grandmother was something else again and Rogers, often astute, revised his campaign.

Alexandria turned to Gail. "Why don't you telephone Bradford," she suggested, "and see if he can come home? This is quite an occasion." She made a gesture of command which Gail read clearly. Pull yourself together, it ordered, and follow my lead.

Andrews still hovered in the hall, and Alexandria indicated that he was to take her outdoor things, and to serve tea at the usual time. She motioned Rogers into the drawing room, still smiling.

Gail went upstairs, a long climb when there was neither youth nor eagerness in her step, and encountered Millicent in the upper corridor. Millicent inquired, Was there anything she could do? and Gail replied, No. She added, aware that Millicent had no love for her yet believing her kind and trustworthy, "My father has turned up, unexpectedly, Miss Ellis. He's with Mrs. Spencer now and I'm going to call Brad."

"Your *father!*" Millicent, sentimental as a valentine, was overcome. "How wonderful," she breathed, "how happy you must be."

Gail said nothing; there was nothing to say. She went down the hall to her suite, entered her sitting room, and shut the door. Millicent, in a mild snit, retreated to her own quarters to comb her somewhat frowzy hair, powder her nose, and reflect upon the situation. The girl was hard as nails and quite unnatural. She was sketchily acquainted with the outlines of Gail's history and the fact that her father had long since shaken the dust of domesticity from his graceless heels. But Millicent, herself forgiving and romantic, was steeped in the rainbow-after-storm school of fiction, and she could see it all clearly . . . the remorseful parent, seeking his child's compassion, his last days illuminated by a daughter's love.

A pretty picture, in the usual tradition.

But no one could long live with Alexandria and not be exposed to realism. Millicent put down her comb and thought, horrified, but he never tried to find her until now!

Gail, at her desk, dialed Brad's private number at the laboratory. His secretary, an efficient, discreet man, not young, answered, and she asked, "Is Mr. Spencer free to come to the telephone, Mr. Jonas? This is Mrs. Spencer."

"I'm sorry," said Jonas, "but he went out over an hour ago and has not returned, Mrs. Spencer."

"It's terribly important," she said. "Is there any way I can reach him?"

"I hope no one is ill," he began, the urgency in her voice having disturbed him, but she said quickly, "No . . . it's not that."

He speculated briefly, wondering, as he answered, "Mr. Spencer went to the Sturm apartment, Dr. Sturm isn't in the laboratory today. Her husband is ill. She telephoned after lunch and Mr. Spencer went as soon as he could, to see if he could be of assistance. Have you the Sturm number? If not, I'll give it to you."

"Never mind," Gail said, "but if he telephones or returns, will you ask him to call me? . . . Thank you, Mr. Jonas."

She hung up and sat there, shivering despite the warmth of the room, drawing idle circles on the fresh blotter with her pen. You weren't supposed to feel as she did. *Honor thy father* . . . but how could you honor a man whose life was built upon dishonor, who had darkened her formative years with the shadow of her mother's grief and disillusion? Blood was not thicker than water, she thought, the water under the bridge.

If he had come to her ill, beaten, exhibiting the slightest penitence, she would, she assured herself, be certain to experience the warmer impulse of pity, beyond what would have seemed mere obligation. But her father appeared in good health, was not defeated, and she was certain, regretted nothing. He was, in short, a cool and dangerous man.

She went into the dressing room, to rearrange her hair, to employ a little rouge, which she seldom used, and to redden her lips. She was making excuses not to go downstairs, and knew her own cowardice. What were they saying to each other? What was Alexandria thinking?

Alexandria, erect in a straight chair, was thinking that every step counted, the last as well as the first. And the initial conventional fencing was almost over, a brittle, tentative clashing, very courteous.

Rogers brought it to a conclusion, no blood drawn. He disliked wasting time, in certain circumstances; and judged that he need not waste it with this integrated old woman. He said, "You must wonder why I have reappeared, Mrs. Spencer?"

"Not at all," she denied sweetly. "I quite understand your anxiety to see Gail again."

"I'm afraid you do," he agreed, with a consciously rueful smile, and she thought, He has charm; he has been educated in many schools, some conventional. He has — an air. There is good blood here, she decided further, all the more dangerous, in a bad man.

She said briskly, "The amenities can be dropped. The facts are clear. I'll state them briefly. You left Gail and your wife when Gail was a child. Since then you have evinced no interest in their welfare, or circumstances, until recently, when, I assume, you learned that your daughter had married my grandson."

"That is substantially correct," he agreed, with insolent admiration, "and, if I may use a vulgar phrase, Gail has done very well for herself, I am happy to say."

"Extremely well," conceded Alexandria mildly, "as my grandson is an exceptionally fine person; intelligent, sound, and I may add, realistic."

"Indeed? How gratifying," he murmured, and went on, "I was astonished to learn from Gail that her husband had tried to trace me. Had I been in her position, I would have concealed the existence of so unsatisfactory a parent."

"Gail is very honest," said Mrs. Spencer; "moreover she was not certain that you did exist."

" ' 'Tis true, 'tis pity; and pity 'tis 'tis true,' " quoted Mr. Rogers. "How I managed to survive, I don't know; nor why. Perhaps for this agreeable moment? Has Gail told you anything about me, Mrs. Spencer?"

"Nothing," answered Alexandria pleasantly, "that would lead me to believe your survival desirable."

"I admire your frankness. I meant, however, did she tell you anything of my antecedents? Come to think of it, she probably knows very little. My grandfather was an Englishman, one of a large family, land poor, with a good name and little else. An unfortunate younger son, he came to the States while his brothers entered the usual professions, army, navy, and the church. He settled in Boston, married a distant connection, with some means, and prospered. My father, an only child, attended Harvard University. Upon his graduation, he did not see eye to eye with my grandfather. He had no interest in the family business, which was merchandising. This was clairvoyant of him, as the business was badly hit by the panic of 'ninety-three, never recovered, and vanished in the year I was born. Meantime, my father had gone west where he married a beautiful, unsuitable young woman, his landlady's niece. I am sure you can understand his parents' dismay," he said smoothly, "and the fact that he was cut off with the customary shilling. There wasn't much more, anyway. But my parents were hard working and thrifty. They sent me east, with enough to take me through the university and bring me to New York. They died in the influenza epidemic of 'eighteen. I am not, by the way, a hero of the First World War. I am happy to say that a football knee kept me out of it. The rest of the case history you know, or surmise. I have had good times and bad. I assure you that all graduates of my university, however desperate, do not go about crying 'Rinehart!' as I have seen depicted in the motion pictures. A college education is seldom legal tender for a tolerable meal."

"All very interesting," remarked Alexandria, "but beside the point. How much do you want, Mr. Rogers?"

"I do like a woman who arrives quickly at the right conclusion," he told her. "How much? Let me see . . . Not, I assure you, the small sum sufficient to keep me from the gutter. Incidentally, it isn't a bad place, once you get the hang of it. No, Mrs. Spencer. An assured income, upon which I would be able — shall we say — to travel. I have seen a good deal of the world, but not all, and at my age one doesn't join the navy."

"Ridiculous," she said shortly, "and out of the question."

"Are you sure?" he inquired. "Have you considered the publicity angle? I mentioned it to Gail, the human interest story, replete with sobs. She is an idealist, I'm afraid, as she believes no paper would print it. What do you think?"

"Much as you do," said Alexandria dryly.

"I suppose you could have me arrested," he said dreamily, "although upon what charges? Disturbing the Spencer peace? But that wouldn't read well either, would it?"

Andrews interrupted, bearing tea, and Rogers relaxed. "It's been a long time," he said, observing the silver, "this is very pleasant."

Alexandria asked how he preferred his tea. He told her and took the cup. He was thirsty, if not for tea. He found the lacing of rum tantalizing. Also, he was hungry. He debated this. Should he wolf the sandwiches, which might arouse her sense of duty, or nobly refrain, merely nibbling the unsatisfactory edges? Perhaps the effect would be the same. This was a very smart old girl. He would nibble, with open restraint.

She said, "Mr. Rogers, Gail will join us presently, together with my companion, Miss Ellis. We will therefore postpone our discussion."

"Quite," he agreed, heard Gail coming downstairs, and rose as she entered. She sat down, without looking at him, close to Alexandria, accepted a cup, and addressed Alexandria. "Brad's not at the laboratory," she said, "but if he returns there, before coming home, or if he telephones, Mr. Jonas will have him call me."

Her voice was steady enough. Alexandria looked at her with moderate approbation. She asked, "Is Millicent coming?"

Millicent arrived, twittering, and Rogers came to his feet again. Introductions were effected, and Millicent thought, Oh, dear, what a very distinguished-looking man. She sat down and Alexandria gave her tea. The conversation was general, and absurd, Said Millicent, "Did you have a good trip, Mr. Rogers?"

"Uncomfortable," he replied, smiling,

"but traveling conditions are not at their best." He directed an amused look at Gail and Alexandria, and Millicent was aware of Alexandria's frown. But, she argued, agitatedly, to herself, He had to come from somewhere!

The weather. The weather was always safe. "So unseasonable for March, so warm," said Millicent, fluttering, "of course at home — in England that is — spring comes much earlier."

No one could dispute it. Mr. Rogers drank his tea and consumed his sandwiches as if he didn't care whether he ate or not and conversed mainly with Millicent. Gail said nothing whatever.

Andrews came in to say that Mr. Spencer was on the wire and would Mrs. Spencer care to have a telephone brought in? He addressed Gail and she said, a little wildly, "No, thank you," fled into the library, shut herself up in that great, book-lined room and took up the instrument.

Her father commented, "Nervous, isn't she? But then, most people are today . . . old and young, mildly neurotic."

Gail said, "Brad . . . ? Brad, can you come home?"

"What's wrong?" he asked instantly.

"It's my father . . ." To her horror she

began to cry, crying helplessly into the telephone.

He had never seen her cry. He couldn't see her now but he could hear her. He said, "I'll be right there, darling."

When he arrived, Millicent had vanished, as had the tea service. Rogers waited implacably, Gail was there, very quiet, and his grandmother. He thought at once that he had never seen his grandmother look even a shade helpless before; she did now.

"We will omit the usual courtesies," said Alexandria. "And make this very brief. In short, this is Gail's father. He has come here for the express purpose of procuring funds."

Rogers was observing his son-in-law. Not much to look at, neither height nor breadth. But he had learned, the hard way, to estimate men. This man had steady eyes and a firm mouth; also, considerable chin. Not at all the type he had expected. If his daughter had married Bradford Spencer for money, she might, at that, get a bonus. Nice for her, he thought impersonally; for himself, he was not pleased.

Brad said cheerfully, "Well, that's to be expected." He had not sat down, and now he put his hand out to Gail, and she rose and he put his arm lightly about her shoulders, for a moment. Then he said, "Suppose you run on upstairs and you, too, Gran?"

Alexandria was stunned. She said, "Really, Bradford . . ."

"I'll handle this," said Brad.

Gail turned her back and left. She did not, and could not, speak. She stood aside to let Alexandria precede her and when she reached the top of the stairs she found her waiting. And Alexandria said, "Come into my room a moment."

Her suite was at the other end of the hall. It was big, and cluttered. All the things she most treasured, senseless bric-a-brac, some valuable, some worthless, all the old photographs, sewing baskets, bits of bronze, glass, ivory and enamel jostled elbows in her sitting room. She said firmly:

"Sit down, Gail."

Gail sat down, in a fat small chair. Alexandria disappeared into her bedroom and Gail heard her talking to her maid. When she emerged she had taken off her frock and folded herself into a hand-woven, shapeless robe. She lay down on the chaise longue, pulled a cashmere shawl over her slippered feet and relaxed her muscles deliberately. She said, "Go ahead, cry if you want to . . . it will do you good."

"I've cried, and it didn't," said Gail. She had made herself presentable before returning to the lunatic tea party, but her eyelids were still somewhat swollen. She added, "If only you knew how I feel . . ."

"I'm not you, I can't know; but I can imagine, I think."

Gail said, "To have this happen —"

Alexandria interrupted. "My dear child," she said, her patience thin, "it was bound to, if the man was alive. Surely you could foresee that?"

"I didn't," said Gail humbly. "But Brad tried to trace him. Did he tell you?"

"Your father did; Bradford did not. Had he done so, I would have counselled him to let well enough alone. But, as it turns out, it doesn't matter."

Gail said, with some spirit, "Tracing my father wasn't my idea, it was Brad's, Mrs. Spencer."

"Men are more sentimental than women," said Alexandria, "although, now that your father has traced you, I don't think Bradford will regard him with sentimentality. And I wish you would find something to call me other than Mrs. Spencer. It would please Brad, and I would prefer it. If you have a child, he will grow up thinking our relationship on a very odd basis. You aren't, by the way, pregnant, are you?"

"No," said Gail, startled.

"You looked extremely well when you returned from Arizona," said Alexandria, "but I have noticed a certain moodiness —" She broke off, and added, "I wish you wouldn't look so forlorn. Fretting over that — that mountebank downstairs won't remedy matters."

"I never dreamed he'd come," said Gail. "I thought he was dead . . . I hoped it. Does that seem terrible to you?"

"Not at all. Practically everyone has someone whom they wish dead, admit it or not. Mine was the aunt who brought me up. I escaped her when I married. As for your father, his kind lives forever, barring happy accidents, and it was simpler for him to find you than vice versa . . . owing to the extremely unpleasant lack of privacy that exists in this day and age."

Gail said, "I don't want Brad to give him money; if anyone must, I should. Yet that is Brad's money, too . . ."

"Very commendable," commented Alexandria, "but, on the other hand, if he is arrested for vagrancy — and I have no doubt it would be simple and delightful for him — how, exactly, would that look?"

She regarded Gail thoughtfully. Up until now she had had a very meager picture of her background; the hardworking, sacrifi-

208

cial mother, of respectable, average stock, the formless, faceless father who might be anybody or nobody. Granted his recital was true — and there was no particular reason to doubt it — Gail's paternal inheritance was decidedly mixed . . . and one which would pass to her children. County English, thought Alexandria, mercantile Boston . . . and essence of very black sheep. If ever she'd seen a Jack-of-all-trades, and master of none, he was downstairs in her drawing room now; clever, amusing, attractive, too indolent or indifferent to be interested in earning a living; a man who, doubtless, drank, gambled, wenched, spent royally when he had it, cadged when he didn't, booked a hotel suite with his last fifty dollars or spent a week in the local jail, with equal equanimity. And who now, without more than the effort of crossing a three thousand mile stretch of space, had struck it rich — or so hoped.

And probably had.

"What's Brad saying to him?" Gail demanded. "He — he frightens me Mrs. . . . I mean — Gran —"

It stuck in her throat and Alexandria misliked it also, but there it was. And Alexandria said, "He won't frighten Bradford. Sometimes I think you have a good deal to learn about your husband."

Whatever he had to say, it didn't take long. Brad came upstairs two at a time and his grandmother called to him. "We're in here," she said.

He came in, pushed her feet away and sat down on the end of the couch. He said, "Don't look so grim, Gran." He smiled at Gail. "And you, don't look so scared."

Gail asked, "What — happened?"

"Your father," Brad said, "will go to a swell hotel tonight . . . that was the hardest part — finding a room. But I managed. He will eat, and, I hope, sleep and he will meet me tomorrow at the office. I'll have Renton there."

The office was the estate office, Renton was the older member of the law firm that had the Spencer business.

Alexandria asked, "What do you propose to do?"

"I propose," said Brad, "to offer him an income or, if you like, an allowance, one upon which he cannot starve, which will provide him with a decent roof, three meals a day, proper clothing, and the usual comforts. No more, no less, no drawing ahead upon it, no lump sums; just so much, paid monthly as long as he refrains from annoying or otherwise embarrassing Gail. And as long as he keeps out of New York."

"He won't agree," said Gail hopelessly.

"All right," said Brad; "he can take it or leave it."

Alexandria prophesied, "He won't take it . . . in which case he will go to the newspapers . . . he'll find some reporter willing to listen . . ."

"Okay," Bradford said.

"No!" Gail got to her feet. "No, Brad, I won't have it."

"Why?"

"For your sake," she said, "your grandmother's, and your work."

He said, with a faint touch of astonishment, "How can it possibly affect any of us, Gail? What your father has become is not your doing. Any story that would be printed would have to say that he left your mother. There's no way to gloss over that. Suppose he says she threw him out? It would be hard to swallow. A young woman with a small child and no other means of support? Be sensible. And any newspaper reader, knowing that he had left, would deduce why he came back."

"Naturally," Alexandria agreed, "and I hope your optimism is justified." She thought, I couldn't have handled it better myself; possibly, not as well. She was proud of Brad, irritated with herself, and impatient of the whole situation. She had grown somewhat accustomed, if not resigned, to Brad's marriage. She respected his wife, although she was not fond of her. And Brad was happy, poor wretch, which was the main issue. This, however, was what came of marrying into the blue, as it were, knowing nothing of the complications that might arise. Marriage for two was difficult enough with the future complications never dreamed of in the first fine careless rapture, but a marriage which included wayward relatives was another matter. If Brad had married someone of Alexandria's own selection . . . ? Yet she was honest enough to admit that the family ramifications of her friends were not entirely desirable; what family was? The beautiful, suitable Marlow girl, for instance . . . her father drank like a fish, and not water; the Elton child suffered from a mother whose early affairs had been a scandal, if never made public; the Richards child's older brother had been kept out of jail merely because his father was able to cover his depredations; and the charming Kirkley girl had an aunt in an expensive institution for the mentally disturbed.

Alexandria sighed. She said, "Let's dismiss this for the time being. And as you are dining out, Gail, hadn't you better get some rest?"

Gail and Brad were dining with old friends of Brad's, and ordinarily Gail would have looked forward to it, as she liked the Wades, who were pleasant and in whose attractive apartment she felt the comfortable atmosphere peculiar to places inhabited by happy people. But now a shadow crossed her face, it would be hard to maintain, evening long, the attitude of the carefree bride. Brad, watching her, said quickly, "We can call it off, dear, if you'd rather."

She opened her mouth to say, Yes, please, Brad, but seeing Alexandria's vigilant regard, answered, "No, Brad, I'd like to go." She was aware that Alexandria would retain her poise and be mindful of her social obligations in the face of family disaster. She would not, of course, dine out if a member of her family was seriously ill or had suffered a fatality. But family problems or disturbances would not constitute obstacles in the path of her duty; she merely left them at home, properly pigeonholed.

When Gail and Brad reached their suite, Gail took off her frock and started her bath. She pinned her heavy hair on top of her head and undressed while Brad prowled about his room. They were not dressing, and Andrews had put out a dark suit and the proper accessories. Brad asked, through the open door, "Mind if I invade your privacy?"

He sat on a slipper chair and Gail, immersed in bubbles, soaped herself vigorously. "You look," remarked her husband, "about fourteen. I like your hair like that."

She smiled automatically. After a moment, she said, "Let's talk about it, Brad. There is no use ignoring it cheerfully."

"Why not?"

"I'm afraid of my father. He's dangerous . . . I feel sure your grandmother agrees with me."

He said, "I don't think so. He's an enormous bluffer, really, so I feel that he'll come to the conclusion that the bird in hand would be more rewarding than the flock in the bushes. You needn't see him again, dear. I'll make that a condition."

She said somberly, "We'll always have it hanging over us . . . like a time bomb."

"They don't hang over."

"I would have given anything to spare you this."

He rose, patted her topknot, and said, "I like it, rather. It makes me feel closer to you, Gail."

For the first time she realized that Brad was conscious of a deficiency in their marriage . . . a lack not supplied by his love for her, nor her affection for him, nor by mutual esteem and to a certain extent, tastes; nor, even, by what seemed a satisfactory physical relationship. Yet she had not pledged perfection nor had he expected it, she told herself stubbornly, nor had she foreseen the sense of guilt that now oppressed her, and had, if in a lesser degree, since the beginning. It could become intolerable. Brad was so reasonable, and so kind; and, in her own way, Alexandria. They were both maddeningly self-contained. Gail thought that if once — just once — Alexandria would lose her control, descend to a common level, or Brad would blow his top — if he had, for instance, that night in Arizona, with Sam — she would feel better because less inferior.

She remembered that she had not asked about the Sturms, and did so while they were dressing.

"He gets this way now and then, by spells. Helena can't do much with him, the aunt of course, nothing. Today it was worse than usual," Brad said.

"How?"

"Black, despondent, railing at everyone and everything. I can understand it," Brad said, "as he has lost a profession which was dearer to him than his life. He also believes that he has lost something equally dear . . . Helena. He is, in his own estimation, no longer a man. He believes that she deceives him."

"Deceives him?" Gail said, incredulous.

"In her attitude; he thinks it's just pity, or duty . . . whatever you want to call it. She can't persuade him otherwise, when he reaches this physical and mental nadir. So he turns on her, threatens her and himself. The poor little old aunt goes to pieces, naturally. It's happened before."

"What do you do?" Gail asked.

"What I can. It isn't much. I talk with him, try to reason. Before this happened to him he was, Helena assures me, as reasonable as most men, perhaps more so. Anyway, I stand by until he snaps out of it. That's pretty bad, he's always so miserably remorseful and humiliated."

"But the doctors."

"Can do little beyond sedatives, and, when he is more himself, talking with him. Their doctor was there this morning and again while I was with him. He's tried for a long time to persuade Helena to have Sturm properly cared for."

"You don't mean committed?" she asked.

"I doubt if he is medically insane," said Brad. "He has a marked emotional instability, and physical pain as well. A private institution dedicated to rehabilitation might do a great deal for him. Helena doesn't think so . . . her logical scientific mind doesn't function in this instance. She believes it would mean his ultimate destruction, the confinement and constant watching, even under the best conditions. She pointed out that, though his injuries physically confine him, he is, within the restrictions they impose, free to be with friends, with her, and to do as he wishes. He has a home, she said today, and love. She's convinced that any other situation would throw him back into the hopelessness he suffered, after his injuries, during his imprisonment. I can see this, but for her own sake I wish things were otherwise. She's a valuable human being."

"I expect she depends on you a good deal," Gail said.

"Probably. Most of her friends, refugees like herself and Erich, aren't of much help, much as they'd like to be. They have their own problems . . . those of mere existence, and worry over the people close to them who aren't here." He looked at his watch. "Better get going," he suggested.

He had made her rest after her bath and now it was close to the time when they would be expected by the Wades. Gail finished dressing and they went downstairs to look in on Alexandria and Millicent before leaving.

It was unfortunate that, after a pleasant dinner, the Wades' neighbors, from the next-door apartment, dropped in.

"I asked them," Mrs. Wade told Gail, "as you and Betty know each other and she's anxious to see you again. They moved here last fall, we became corridor and elevator acquaintances. They seem exceptionally nice and have a charming little boy."

"Betty?" asked Gail, and no warning bell rang in her mind, occupied with other matters.

"Her name is Rolland," said Mrs. Wade, "but we're already on an informal basis. Surely you remember her . . . small, fair, looking younger than she probably is? She was married before, she told me, to a newspaperman. He's been very successful lately . . . I don't remember his name."

"Sam Meredith," said Gail. "Of course. I'd forgotten Betty's married name." She was aware of Brad's quick glance at her as he sat across the room smoking with, and talking to, his host.

"Rolland is likable," said Wade. "He's in the insurance business. He hooked me, almost before I knew it, not long after they moved here. As a matter of fact, he did me a real service."

Gail said, "I'd like to see Betty again."

She saw her, shortly afterwards, looking blooming, as blonde, almost as childish in appearance, but a little rounder in figure. She and her husband greeted Gail with cordiality, and Betty said, "It's wonderful seeing you. I assure you I meant to write at the time of your marriage but young Pete was busy having measles —"

They had no time alone until Gail was ready to leave, when Betty followed her into the Wade guest room. She asked, "Do you mind my saying how glad I am for you? I was afraid it would be Sam."

"It wasn't," said Gail evenly.

"Obviously. But the indications . . . I mean, you can't help *hearing* things. Well, you're safe, I'm safe, and Sam's God knows where. California, or was it North Dakota? I don't read him. I used to and maybe it's silly of me, but I just don't any more. I wish you'd come see us, Gail. I like your husband so much. He and Peter got along famously. I warned Peter, I said, 'If you try to sell him insurance, I'll break your neck!' Anyway, do come. Young Pete's at the entertaining if destructive stage, which reminds me, we left my sister with him, not that he needs a sitter when we're next door, his lungs are all right."

Gail said she would and presently found herself in the car, driving home. The night was cool and damp, the sky obscured with clouds. And Brad commented:

"The Rollands are all right . . . he's a sound egg, and as for his wife, I always liked Sam's taste in girls."

"She's nice," Gail said. "I never knew her well, of course. As a matter of fact, I met her before I met Sam."

She thought with a sudden desperate longing of Sam, not for him exactly, but for his way of life, his unconcern, his blunt, unvarnished attitude . . . his crazy vigor and lack of veneer. Sam would fight with her, laugh at her, be crazy jealous of any man who'd ever meant anything to her, Sam would wound, neglect, and sacrifice her, but he would never conceal himself behind a mask nor armor himself against her. As for her father, Sam would say, The hell with him, and mean just that.

She thought with a terrifying clarity that perhaps she was truly her father's child. Her mother had desired only love for love, and security. Gail had believed that she too wished security, if without love. But her father had never wanted anything except to be free, and alive, and heedless. Perhaps, basically, that was what she wished, the other desires having been imposed upon her. For certainly, ever since Morrison Rogers's appearance, she had felt trapped . . . not by her father's motivated return but by the Spencers . . . the close corporation, forbearance, and most unendurable, by her own impatient sense of inadequacy and guilt.

X

Toward noon on the following morning the telephone rang and Gail, writing letters in her sitting room, answered. Andrews's voice cut in, he apologized and hung up but Gail heard a click as if someone had taken an instrument from an extension. It was not replaced.

"Gail?" Brad asked. "Everything all right, dear?"

"Did you have a bad time?" she inquired. "Oh, Brad, I'm so glad you called. I've been sitting on the edge of a volcano ever since you left this morning."

"I couldn't call you before, the business has just been concluded. I'd rather not go into details now, so I'll tell you tonight. Wait a moment — what are you doing this afternoon?"

"Lunching with Pat and her mother first, then we're going on to a fitting."

"I'd forgotten. Why don't you meet me at the St. Regis around half past five? Pat and her mother, too, if they can come. We'll all have a drink and then you and I can come home together."

"I'd love to," she said and added, because it was a long time until five-thirty, "Just tell me one thing . . . where *is* he, Brad?"

"In good hands, with a personal courier. By the time I see you he will have been seen off on the Commodore Vanderbilt. . . . Hold on for just a moment, will you?"

While she waited, she felt that someone waited with her, holding his or her breath. Hers, of course, Gail thought angrily.

Brad spoke again. "Hello?" he said. "There's a long-distance call coming through, Gail. 'Bye, dear, I'll see you this afternoon."

She hung up and then went downstairs to the morning room. Alexandria would expect a report however superfluous Gail considered the gesture. She knocked at the closed door, was bidden to enter, and went in to find Alexandria surrounded by mail and papers and Millicent hunched resignedly over the desk.

"Brad just called," Gail said. And stifled the impulse to say, Suppose you tell me what he said!

Alexandria rattled newspapers, pushed the heap of envelopes aside, invited Gail to sit down. Then she asked pleasantly, "Millicent, would you please go upstairs and get me a handkerchief?"

Alexandria's handkerchief was in plain sight on the arm of her chair, a large square of fine, monogrammed linen. Gail's eyes sought and Millicent's eyes avoided it. For if Alexandria wished two or a dozen handkerchiefs that was her affair. Theirs not to question why, theirs but to fetch and carry. Alexandria was entirely capable of barking, "Millicent, leave the room!" in fact she had just done so, if more prettily phrased. Hunt the handkerchief, Millicent, and take your time about it. Alexandria, like everyone else in the world, was unpredictable and inconsistent. Gail thought, She's talked this over with Millicent, worn it to rags by now, why go into this act for my benefit? But Gail had no way of gauging how much Alexandria said or didn't say. She realized that Alexandria considered Millicent a bloodless shadow, schooled to obedience, with unseeing eyes and deafened ears, and that Millicent was aware of, and accustomed to, this attitude. Sometimes Alexandria treated her companion as if she were a dictaphone, sometimes as if she were a mirror, and again as if she were an audience, applauding in the right places. Millicent could be a parrot or an echo, if it pleased her employer. But there were times when Millicent was not taken into Alexandria's confidence. This might, or might not, be one of them.

When Miss Ellis had departed, Alexandria asked impatiently, "Well, what did he say?"

Which was, Gail considered, pretty silly. But she projected herself back, into the third grade, and answered obediently, "Just that everything is all right."

"Come, come," said Alexandria, "surely, he had time to say a little more than that?"

Gail repeated the conversation, practically verbatim.

"So far, so good," Alexandria commented, with her frosty smile, "but I am always suspicious of problems which work out too easily at first trial. I'd advise a cooling-off period before celebration. Don't underestimate your father, Gail."

Gail felt properly flattened. Alexandria's appearance of fragility was charming, and an illusion. She could operate like a steam shovel or a steam roller; not always, of course, Gail reflected, there were times when the methods weren't so obvious.

She said, a little stiffly, that naturally only time could tell but Brad had appeared satisfied with the turn of events.

"Bradford," said Alexandria, "is an idealist."

Gail rose. She must get ready for her luncheon engagement, she said. She and Brad would be home for dinner. She told Alexandria where she would be in the interim, as she had, somewhat rebelliously, learned to do, and went upstairs to dress. On the way she encountered Millicent, the handkerchief waving like a flag of truce and muttering to herself like the White Rabbit. Gail afforded her a swift, sidelong smile which brought a slight flush to Millicent's maiden cheek.

Presently Gail departed to meet Pat and her mother, Pat as radiant as high noon, as effervescent as a bromide but not sedative in effect, her mother placid and admiring. After luncheon, during which Pat never stopped talking, they went to the bridal shop in a big store and Pat tried on her wedding dress. She looked pretty as a pin-up in it but, unlike most pin-ups, almost painfully childish. Gail's throat contracted watching her turn before the mirror, and the elderly fitter, with the middle-aged spread, sat back on her heels, with her mouth full of pins and speaking perilously around them remarked that, as often as she fitted them, she never got tired, there was something special about brides.

Pat's eyes shone, and so did her mother's; in the older woman's the shining was half anticipated grief, half joy remembered and joy prayerfully besought.

Gail's frock was brought out for the fitting. It was simple and in a delicate shade of blue. The hat that went with it was big and demure, with deeper blue flowers. Pat, sitting on a stool in her slip, cried. "You look wonderful! No one will look at me except Bill, and he'll be too scared."

They talked about the wedding, which was to be in Pat's home, and about Evie who couldn't fly in after all. Gail would be the only attendant. And then the rest of the things were brought out . . . not many, all carefully selected. The fitter asked, "Can't this be nipped in, a little? You're so small," and Pat said woefully, "It's disgusting to be insignificant." But she didn't feel insignificant. She knew she was the most important person in the world, except one other. The knowledge illuminated her and Gail recognized it dimly, enviously. She thought, What can it be like, trying on your wedding things, thinking of your wedding day, the day on which you will be married to a man with whom you are crazily in love?

Her head began to ache a little, a dull, persistent pressure, and she was glad when they had finished. Pat must come for final fittings but Gail need not. They said goodbye to the fitter and the saleswoman, and went out. It was a little after five, and Pat said regretfully that they couldn't come with her to meet Brad. They were going to Bill's people for an early dinner. "Not that his father will be there," Pat explained, "or if he is, not for long. That's what I'll be up against; late meals, cold meals, or no meals. Any girl who marries a doctor is a fool." But she didn't look as if she minded being one or as if, at this juncture, household routine mattered.

Gail walked to the St. Regis. She was early and could get a table and wait. But when she came into the King Cole bar, Brad rose from a big table and waved. She had the feeling that he had been waiting for some time, and not alone. Helena Sturm was with him.

She went to the table and sat down, smiling at Helena, and, the greeting over, Brad inquired, "What happened to Pat?"

Gail explained, and the waiter arrived with her drink, which Brad had ordered. She lifted her glass, conscious of a heavy weariness, and Helena said anxiously, "I hope I do not intrude. But Brad insisted."

She looked appalling, her face drawn, her eyes shadowed, and when she spoke her accent was more marked, her voice slurred as if with fatigue. And Gail said quickly, "Of course not . . . I'm so glad to see you . . . How is Dr. Sturm?"

"Much better," said Helena, and folded

her carelessly rouged lips in her secret way, a way which warned, I am sure you mean to be kind but now it is you who intrude, and Gail felt rebuffed and uncomfortable.

They did not stay at the St. Regis long and when they went out a taxi drew up. Gail rarely used the car, by day, because of the parking difficulties. And Brad said, "Get in, girls."

"Please," said Helena, "I can take the bus."

"Don't be difficult." He put her in, and Gail, and gave the driver Helena's address. They dropped her off and went on home, and on the way he asked, "You didn't mind having her? She needed to get out and I thought we wouldn't be alone anyway."

"Why should I mind? I'm sorry I asked about Dr. Sturm. I saw that she didn't like it."

"She's oversensitive and scared," Brad said, "but he is better, for the time being."

"Brad, please tell me what happened today." She felt tense, and coiled. How could he talk about Helena Sturm and her husband, what did they matter, at this moment, surely her affairs were more important, Gail thought.

"Well," said Brad, "there was considerable preliminary sparring. Renton sat in, a good man in any situation. But I'd hate to play poker with your father, darling. However, he knows when a bluff's been called. When he was finally convinced that it was a take-or-leave-it offer and that we didn't care if he left it, he gave in. Renton's secretary went with him to buy some clothes and luggage and we'd managed space on the train."

"Why Chicago?" Gail asked.

"I don't know. He said it was a good base from which to operate. His last gesture was to ask for a compartment. He said he hadn't been comfortable on the trip east and he'd like to depart in comparative luxury."

"For heaven's sake!" Gail said helplessly.

Brad laughed, took her hand and held it. He said, "There was a cancellation, so Renton's secretary got the space and saw him off. He phoned from the station, after the train left."

"I wonder what he plans," Gail said slowly.

"He didn't say. Nor did I ask."

She thought, *How much did he give him?* She must ask, of course, but the question was like a fishhook in her throat. She felt ashamed and nervous. But Alexandria would ask, at once.

They had reached the house and as they went up the steps she said quickly, "Before you see your grandmother . . . let's talk a little, Brad."

He looked at her. "Okay," he said cheerfully, as Andrews opened the door. They could hear Alexandria lecturing Millicent in the drawing room and Brad told Andrews, "Tell Mrs. Spencer that we'll join her very soon."

They went upstairs to their suite and changed for dinner. Dressing, in a most luxurious jungle, Gail thought; nations starved, children died and men plotted, wars flamed and smoldered, the world swung upside down, but Alexandria wore a long frock, Millicent hung more beads about her sagging throat, and Brad put on a dinner coat.

Gail took off her suit and went to wash. She could hear the shower running in Brad's bathroom. After a while he came into her dressing room, where she stood before a long mirror adjusting the belt of a dinner frock made as simply as a sports dress.

"You look lovely, Mrs. Spencer, as usual."

"Thank you," she said. "Brad, how much did you give him?"

The fishhook tore, it brought blood. And Brad put his arms about her.

"Must you look tragic?" he said. "A hundred a week, if he sticks to the terms of the agreement."

"But that's so much," she said slowly, and moved away from him, gently.

"He didn't think so, but Renton believed it a reasonable amount."

"What was the agreement, exactly?"

"In the words of the song, he is to stay out of your life . . ." He looked at her quickly. "That's what you wanted, isn't it?" he asked.

"Yes, of course."

He said, "What troubles me about your father is the terrific waste . . . he has so much intelligence and charm." He sighed. "All wasted," he repeated.

Gail spoke with great difficulty. She said, "You've been more than generous, Brad. I don't know what to say except that I'm grateful and I can't tell you how grateful."

Yet she knew; she was, she thought drearily, too grateful and it was suddenly clear to her that all her life she had suffered under a heavy burden of obligations, first to her mother, now to her husband. By marrying Brad, she had repaid her mother, redeemed her pledge, justified her mother's anxious sacrifice, but there was no way in which she could repay Brad.

He said sharply, "That's not a word which should be used between us; I don't want gratitude." He watched her flinch a little, she was not accustomed to sharpness from him, and went over to her again and took her in his arms. "If there is any gratitude, darling, it should be on my part, I suppose," he told her, "but loving you as much as I do that's all I can feel — just love."

Brad did not go with Gail to Pat's pretty, touching wedding. He had to make a trip to Oak Ridge. Brad and the army got along very well. And he wrote Gail, after he reached Tennessee, "Have a good time and contrive to miss me a little, darling. I'd like to be at the wedding, and discussing with you over the almost inevitable glass of champagne, the union of two agreeable human beings rather than conferring, as I must soon do, upon a method of separating the isotopes of uranium. But a gent who undertakes research at the behest of his government must earn his dollar a year."

Gail went to New Jersey the day before the wedding. She had had a small party for Pat the preceding week, now she must attend the rehearsal and the supper afterwards. She drove herself, in Brad's car, and gave Dink, the ex-GI chauffeur, the time off. It was not unpleasant to be alone on a spring day, driving a good car on good roads. Sam had taught her to drive, when first she knew him, and he had owned a battered Ford.

She thought of Sam, as she seldom did now. She had schooled herself to read his columns with the surface of her mind. But now she thought of him because it was spring, and spring had been fun with Sam, fun, excitement and expectancy, and each day new from the mint. For the first time since she had been an introspective, frightened child, very lonely, despite, or perhaps because, of the close, smothering companionship of her mother, she was wholly indifferent to the coming of the spring. It was like any other season except pleasanter, physically speaking, than winter or the raw days of autumn.

She reflected that Alexandria had not again mentioned Morrison Rogers in her hearing. Yet it was certain that his grandmother had asked Brad about the meeting, but not in Gail's hearing; nor had Brad reported any discussion.

The party was pleasant, as was Pat's big old house. Bill was more subdued than Gail had ever seen him, hence more likable, his parents were attractive, Pat's parents hospitable, and Pat herself like a blown flame. After rehearsal they had an informal supper and finally Gail went to bed, in a small pretty guest room, and lay awake listening to the wind in the young leaves and hearing a sleepy bird song. It was the first time since her marriage that she had been away from Brad. She missed him mildly, yet she was glad to be away; it was wonderful to lie there, feeling free, feeling alone, a separate person.

The wedding was in the afternoon and Gail went into Pat's room shortly before she was dressed and stood watching Pat and her mother. They were charming, they brought the tears to her eyes . . . the older woman, handsome and severe, in the dove-gray frock, the girl with her radiance and a mist of white around her.

Then she was alone with Pat for a moment and Pat said hurriedly:

"Look, while Mother's answering the phone — I meant to tell you last night but with all the excitement, I couldn't . . . Gail, *Sam's coming!*"

"Sam!"

"He phoned, after you got here yesterday, and wanted to know, could he come. Said he saw it in the paper. What could I say, Gail? We always got along and Bill likes him."

Pat was half in tears, not because she thought the situation very serious, but because at this moment the balance between tears and laughter was very delicate indeed.

Gail said, "You did all right, Pat. Don't worry so. How can it possibly matter?"

"But if you're embarrassed —"

If she was, she looked the reverse. The plain pale-blue frock became her as the spring becomes a garden. She looked cool, unruffled and lovely.

Pat added, "But you don't have to say more than hello."

"I'll say good-bye too," promised Gail, smiling. "I saw him in Arizona, you know."

"I didn't. For Pete's sake," cried Pat, "what happened?"

"What would happen? We ran into him, we had a drink, and that was that."

Pat put out her arms, cried, "Oh, I forgot my dress!" blew her friend a kiss, and said, "Here comes Mother."

The wedding was in the big living room of the frame house set back in apple and elm trees. The room was bare of furniture for the occasion, and spring flowers banked an improvised altar. The piano had been moved to the hall, Pat's young aunt played, and Pat came down the stairs. There were not many people at the wedding itself. The sun came in, and Pat's voice spoke, clear and sweet, and someone, not her mother, nor Bill's, wept audibly and a man said irritably, "I hate weddings."

Gail saw Sam instantly; it was impossible not to see him, he was so tall, and there were so few people. Later, when other people had come and both living room and dining room overflowed, he came to speak to her. He said, "You're looking very bridal yourself."

"Thanks." She smiled at him, and he asked, "Where's Brad?"

"In Oak Ridge."

"You going on home," he inquired, "after this is over, or off with the gang to dance? I heard rumors about that."

"I'm driving back, Sam."

"Alone?"

"Yes."

"Not alone," he said, "give me a lift, will you . . . and have dinner with me, before we get to town?"

She hesitated. If she said, No, he would think her afraid . . . If she said, Yes . . . ?

"All right," she said, after a moment.

They had dinner in a place on the other side of the Hudson usually crowded and noisy but almost deserted when they reached there, early. The lights of the town shone high and wonderful across the dark flow of water, and, as Sam said, at least there was a place to park the car. "Quite an impressive job," he added, "and I must say, considering who taught you, you drive very well indeed."

On the way to the restaurant they had

talked of nothing save the wedding and of Sam's experience; the first swing round was over, he said, he would catch his breath and move on, this time, New York and the New England States. It had been quite an eye-opener, the West and the South, but there was a lot more ground that he must cover.

He had a cocktail and over the rim of his glass he said, "Change your mind and join me?"

"I've had champagne . . . I don't mix my drinks."

"To you, then. How happy are you?"

"Very," she said quietly.

"Your enthusiasm overwhelms me. What exactly is Brad's job? I never really knew."

She said, "As far as I am concerned, only Einstein could explain it. You know as much as I . . . that he is doing research for the government, but in his own laboratories."

"Do you know someone named Helena Sturm?"

She answered, startled, "Yes, she's one of Brad's assistants. Why?"

"Oh, no special reason. She was at the Stork last night, with a group. Someone pointed her out to me . . . and told me a little about her . . . but not enough . . ."

"How do you mean, not enough?"

"I've always been curious. The man —

someone brought him to our table — is a surgeon. He knew her husband. He spoke of her in connection with Brad."

She asked coolly, "What connection?"

"Are all wives suspicious? Nothing, really. Merely that she was an attractive woman, that she wasn't seen around much, so he was surprised to see her last night, but that she was with a group of Europeans, very gay, astonishingly rich, which might have explained it . . . old school-tie friends or something . . . and that there had been some speculation about her and Brad and people — her friends, I gathered — had thought, how suitable, two brilliant scientists and one of them a woman . . . only, of course, I introduced you to Brad and upset an applecart . . . perhaps two."

She said, "Helena Sturm is devoted to her husband."

"I heard about that, too. It appears that people, in their realistic way, had believed her husband was not long for this world."

She said evenly, "I'm glad she was there last night. She doesn't go out much, she stays very close to her home . . . She should have some recreation."

He asked abruptly, shortly before they left, "Will you tell Brad you saw me?"

"Naturally."

"Why naturally?" he asked irritably. "It would be natural if you didn't. Is he staying away long?"

"I don't know, as he didn't when he left."

"Odd," he commented, "to know an atom is your rival; if it is an atom —"

Gail raised her eyes. She said, "Not any odder than anything else, Sam."

"Most women," he reflected, "could more easily cope with, say, other women — you can buck emotions, perhaps, but the worship of pure science . . ." He shrugged. "That's something that eludes you . . . or so I would think."

He looked at his watch and said cheerfully, "I have a date — big, blonde and beautiful. Are you interested?"

"No."

"Liar," said Sam cheerfully. He beckoned to the waiter. "Let's go," he suggested, "time's awasting. How about dinner another night or driving me out into the country one fine day. Or can you get past the guards?"

"You're being somewhat offensive," she said.

"Don't come all over dowager," he advised; "you had a touch of it in Arizona, if I remember correctly, and it's apt to grow on you. Why not?"

She said, "I'm sorry, Sam, but I haven't time. Mrs. Spencer is going to the country this weekend and I'm going with her."

"What part of the country? There are forty-eight states, all with some rural portions."

"Connecticut," she said, "near Ridgefield."

Sam rose, towering despite his stoop and poor carriage. He said, "You mad fool, such abandon, such moonstruck nights and wild delirious days. You and old lady Spencer, surrounded by ancient retainers, rats in the wainscoting, and silence. Or does she read aloud, nights?"

Anger struck through her like an arrow but reached no mark. Suddenly she was not angry. She began to laugh, without volition, and he tucked her hand in the crook of his arm and said, "That's more like it!"

"Well, frankly," she admitted, "I don't look forward to it."

"Duck out, have a date, have a migraine, have a mild leprosy — and stay in town with me." He walked her out to the car, rapidly, watched her get in, and leaned there at the open door. He asked, "Wouldn't a discreet nostalgic affair interest you at this point? I've always liked married women."

Gail stopped laughing. She said crossly,

"Get in, Sam, or you'll be late for your date. And don't be such an idiot!"

Coming into the house, she found Alexandria in the card room, with two of her antiquated friends and Millicent tremulously making a fourth at whist, the game Alexandria preferred. Andrews informed Gail, when he let her in and took her suitcase, that Mrs. Spencer had asked if she would join them. She did so, obediently, conscious that she must look terribly alive to the four women sitting grimly at the table, in the elegant little room where a small fire burned on the hearth despite the warmth of the night. But their blood was thin and chilly, even Millicent's.

Gail knew Alexandria's friends, aging and smart in their muted colors and made-to-order frocks, but their expressions were bombazine and jet. Millicent gave her a faint twinkle of resignation. The end of the rubber had been reached and Alexandria made figures on the score pad with a gold pencil. She said, "Do sit down, Gail. Andrews will bring refreshments in a moment. And tell me about the wedding. I expected you a little earlier."

Gail made no explanation . . . neither, I stayed at Pat's later than I planned, which would have been a lie, nor, I went out with a group afterwards, which would have been another, nor the truth, which was no business of Mrs. Spencer's. She described the wedding, helped Andrews serve thin sandwiches and fragile slices of cake, and inquired the ladies' pleasure . . . mild highballs, port? . . . and as soon as she could she went upstairs. She wrote to Brad before she slept. She said, among other things, that it was a lovely wedding, that Sam had turned up there and she had driven him back to town, stopping to dine on the way. Her duty concluded, she added, not without faint malice, that Sam had seen Helena Sturm at the Stork the night before, she had been pointed out to him . . . "Erich must be better," she went on in her round pretty hand . . .

She sent him her love, hoped his work was progressing, and reminded him that she would be in the country for the weekend.

Then she went to bed. It was a long time before she slept. She thought, All the time I was with Sam I didn't feel anything . . . that is, nothing special . . . Oh, he made me angry, he needled me and all that, but —

Still she had been careful not to dance with him nor touch his hand; once he had touched hers, taking it in his own, tucking it under his arm, holding it there . . . she remembered that, a little too clearly.

★ ★ ★

They drove to Ridgefield in the big car with Alexandria's chauffeur upright at the wheel. Andrews and his wife had gone ahead by train, and together with the caretaker, his wife and a local cleaning woman would "do" for them. Alexandria's maid and Millicent were in the car.

The main street of Ridgefield is very beautiful, the trees are rooted in age and the grass grows wide and green and there are great houses, set close or far back. There is peace there, and quiet. But the Spencer house was out of the village on a winding road, set in many acres and commanding a view. It was not a house from which people had seen battles, neither colonial nor of the early eighteen hundreds. It was of the nineties and it was terrible, a vast pile of stone with cupolas and monstrosities of architecture and a porte-cochere. It was furnished massively and stained glass glared here and there at the unwary newcomer.

The grounds were beautiful, past the tended gardens, a fat greenhouse, lawns, flower beds and stone animals, for beyond them were the fields striped with stone walls, the woods coming into spring, and alive with wings, the little hills, the brooks flowing free . . .

Evidently there had been a little too much nature for the Spencers to "improve" it all.

Dinner and stately conversation by the fire was much as it would have been in the Fifth Avenue house. Here, as there, Spencer portraits leered grimly and the atmosphere was no more lavender and old lace than in the city. Mr. Spencer had built and furnished this house, and it stood as a monument.

"It's hideous," said Alexandria, with satisfaction, "but it would be worse done early American, in chintz and antiques. It's at least true to the period. If it had been a little earlier, it would have been full of red velvet and wax fruit under glass; as a matter of fact, the Victorian has once again come into fashion. But I like it as it is. Bradford thinks it's quite dreadful but he's fond of it."

Gail slept in Bradford's vast room, in a massive carved bed, surrounded with what looked like singularly uncomfortable furniture. But there were snapshots and photographs of him about the room, from which he looked out at her, as a rather appealing if undistinguished little boy, and some mementoes of his preparatory school and college days; and a case of battered books, one of Cooper, and here and there the oddest finds, fairy tales, *The Water Babies, Back of the North Wind,* and a volume or two of poetry, which she took in her hands and which fell open easily, as used books do.

The next day, after a stupendous breakfast, she made dutiful rounds with Alexandria. Millicent following with unnecessary extra wraps, wore stout country shoes and tweeds. But Alexandria wore city black, high heels, and used a cane. The garden, the empty stables, the gardener and caretaker's stone cottages, the greenhouse, gay with spring bloom . . .

After luncheon, when Alexandria slept, Gail went out alone and walked. She walked in the wet fields and beside the ice-cold brook; she picked some violets, they were wet and dark, had no scent, and wilted almost instantly. She sat on a fallen log and listened to the birds busy about their business of building and singing . . . and walked along a little ridge and looked over more fields. The air was sweet and cool and the sun a warmth in her flesh, and a delicate blue sky was bent like a bow over this little portion of earth.

The caretaker's dogs came tearing after her, a red setter, thin and friendly, a fat little cocker, the color of maple syrup, running on short, feathered legs.

She saw a snake slide into the sun from a

stone wall and turned away, shuddering; and a little later a black and white cat sleeping on another wall made her pause and smile.

Everything was here, the snake warming its cold blood, the cat replete with mice, the newborn insect, the burrowing mole, the flowers springing from the ground, pushing through the damp, dark leaf mold, the water released from ice, the leaf released from the bare, dreaming tree . . . There was nothing the matter with the country, she thought, turning back, reluctantly, to the frowning, too substantial house, except some of the houses and, probably, some of the people.

But it was not her cup of tea; she could admire it, she could appreciate its beauty, its peace and its contrasts, but she was a cockney, a child of the city. She remembered her months in the small town, the occasional picnics, the lake, the trees . . . She had not been happy there, but when she had come to New York she had been happy, no matter how frightened or anxious. Streets and noise and people . . .

Brad telephoned that night. He had not yet had her letter but by the following night he had, and called again. He was glad she'd had fun at the wedding, he said. And she asked, sitting at the telephone table in the hall — as there was no extension save one in the kitchen, and conscious that Alexandria was listening from the living room, "You didn't mind?"

"About Sam? Of course not . . . how is he?"

"As usual," said Gail. She thought, How foolish to have asked, perhaps he hadn't minded, but now perhaps he will. I underlined it, I suppose.

On the next day they returned to the city. Mrs. Spencer would not be in residence in Ridgefield until somewhat later, at which time, as had been arranged, Gail would remain in town with Brad, except for weekends and during the times when it would become too hot; "better for her to be in the country then," Alexandria had decided.

A little after eleven on the night after their return Gail was writing to Brad. She, Millicent and Alexandria had gone to a movie at the Normandie. It was a western, a form of entertainment to which Alexandria was addicted. Gail was describing it to Brad when the telephone rang and she schooled herself not to answer it. That was Andrews's obligation, while he was on duty, Alexandria had once informed her, "so uncontrolled," she had said, "all this rushing to the telephone!" and after a while, Andrews knocked on her door. "A call for you, Mrs. Spencer," he said.

"Who is it?" she wondered aloud and Andrews said, "He didn't give his name. He said it was urgent."

She picked up the instrument on her desk and spoke into it and Sam said, "Gail? Get down to my flat as soon as you can."

"Sam?" She stuttered a little, in her astonishment and fear. "Why? What are you talking about?" She recovered, adding, "Are you drunk?"

"No. But there's a man here who is. He claims to be your father. *Now* will you get down?"

She said faintly, "As soon as I can."

She snatched at her coat and at a handbag. Fortunately she had not undressed. She flew downstairs and heard Alexandria call to her.

She did not answer. Let her sit up, let her formulate her questions and answer them herself. Gail would deal with all that later. There was no time now.

Hatless, her face white and strained, her heart heavy with apprehension, she went to the curb and waited for a taxi.

XI

Gail told the taxi driver to wait, and went up the brownstone steps and rang Sam's bell. Her heart shook, her knees were water. The lock clicked sharply, she went in and up the narrow, familiar stairs. She thought, How many times have I climbed these? A fraction of her mind was stubbornly preoccupied with the past; with the remembered sense of anticipation that once she had known, the enchantment and excitement. She had climbed these stairs to reach a precarious, unsatisfactory happiness, marshaling her resolution on every tread, setting up her defenses. In the apartment, two flights up, she had experienced anger and delight, she had quarreled, kissed, and become reconciled.

Sam spoke from above her. "Gail?" he asked.

She said, almost inaudibly, "Yes," reached the landing and saw him standing there.

He said, "You took forever. It doesn't matter. He's out, cold."

"What happened? How did you . . . ?"

"Come in," he said, "we can talk and he won't hear anything. What a capacity! I

250

gather that he's been fried for about three days."

The living room was as she recalled it; the untidiness, the books, overflowing shelves and tables, heaped against the walls; her photograph on the littered desk; the smell of cigarette smoke clinging to the shabby curtains.

Morrison Rogers was asleep on the big couch, his face relaxed and quiet; an old face, battered, and, even in unconsciousness, guarded and bitter. His breathing was loud in the room and he smelled of stale whisky. His clothes were rumpled, his coat hung over a chair, his collar was loosened.

"Give me your coat. Sit down," said Sam. He took her coat, lighted two cigarettes, handed her one. He added, "We can talk this out. He won't come to, for a while."

She said dully, "I don't understand. Where did you find him, how did you know who he was?"

"All in good time. I found him at Ricky's."

She knew, the bar on Third Avenue, the hangout for newspapermen, for Sam's gang; the place she had often telephoned when Sam had failed to show up for an engagement or when she had to reach him quickly and he wasn't at the office or in his apartment.

"What was he doing there?"

"What do people usually do in a barroom? He was drinking and had been for several days. I drifted in tonight looking for a couple of guys. They weren't there. Jake was, a rewrite man on the *Planet*. We had a drink, and he went out. The place was quiet. I saw a man alone at a table, drunk as a hoot owl but still going strong. When he wasn't quoting Shakespeare, he was building a small bonfire in a big ash tray. Bits of paper. I asked Ricky what gave. He said the guy had come in during the early afternoon. He could pay for what he drank, and he wasn't disturbing anyone. When he appeared, the place was nearly empty and he entertained Ricky. Some life he'd had, Ricky said admiringly. Anyway, he hadn't thrown him out. I went over to his table. Maybe there was copy here. I know pretty much about what kids are thinking and planning, here was a chance to talk to someone on the sidelines. Maybe, I figured, a veteran of the first war. What had happened to him meantime, what did he think about, what was happening now? I wasn't very serious about it, just bored."

"Sam, get to the point."

"There isn't any point. I bought him a drink and we were pals. He discussed the state of the world for some time, quite brilliantly. He said he'd worked on a newspaper once, in Spokane. He told me his name, and it rang a bell. You'd told me about him, remember?"

"What else did he tell you?"

"His version . . . old, friendless man, who rediscovers his only child only to be repudiated by her and pensioned off by her capitalistic husband who forced him into signing an agreement. That was his copy which he was burning in the ashtray. He said he had made up his mind to go to a newspaper and sell his story. He would be happy to sell it to me."

She said, white, "He promised not to come back here nor to get in touch with me. Brad was more than generous."

"That's what I told him," said Sam. "If someone would guarantee me a hundred bucks a week, I'd never beat feet again. I'd sit down in some shack on a Florida key, go fishing, and write the great American novel."

"Why did he come?" she wondered drearily.

"He'd blown the dough, next week's installment wasn't due, he couldn't draw ahead, besides, he found himself in New York when he should be in Chicago if he intended to get what was coming to him. He admitted that it had served him for room and board and occasional drinks. But he'd got into a poker game, given his IOUs, and then thought the arrangement over. His original idea was to come here, see Brad, and demand an advance. He thought better of it on his arrival. The next idea was the newspapers. He admitted that he doubted if Brad could be scared into increasing the allowance but he figured the newspaper would pay him enough so that he wouldn't need the allowance. Which leads me to believe he's never worked on a newspaper. There isn't a story big enough to provide a life annuity."

She asked, "Sam, what am I to do? If Brad finds out he won't give him another cent. And then he *will* go to the papers."

"Do you care if he does?"

"Naturally I care. Brad says he wouldn't. I don't doubt it. But I have to live under the same roof as Alexandria Spencer."

"Okay . . . how much money have you on you? I'm broke, as usual."

"A little over two hundred."

"That will do it," said Sam. "He can sleep this off here but if in the morning he's in bad shape I'll get a doctor around to help sober him up. I've done the guy a couple of favors, he won't ask questions. I'll sit right on Pop's tail, take him to Chicago myself and replant him in whatever place he's been living; I take it that it's a small, cheap hotel. I'll tell him that no newspaper would touch the yarn and that if he knows what's good for him, he'll stay put, draw his hundred a week, and no questions asked. It won't be hard. Don't worry, darling."

"It isn't for myself," she said brokenly, "but Brad's been so good . . ."

"Hard to take, isn't it?" he asked shrewdly.

"What?"

"Brad's — goodness."

She began to cry, helplessly, her head bowed in her hands, her shoulders shaking, and Sam rose and lifted her from the chair. He sat down in the old easy chair with her in his lap. He said, "Go ahead, Rusty, cry here."

Over her bent head he watched Rogers stir, and heard him speak, incoherently, saw his eyes open and, after an effort, focus.

Sam smiled a little, waiting. He did not move.

"Well, well," said Rogers, not too thickly, "what have we here?"

Gail sat up, and mopped at her eyes with a fist, like a child. Her hair was tumbled about her wet, flushed face and she drew her breath sharply, catching it.

"A chippy," said her father, "off the old block. And I didn't even know you'd met!"

"We're old friends," said Sam equably.

"How nice," said Rogers. He sat up, with an effort, and looked around dizzily. He said, "If this is Upper Fifth Avenue, I'm a missionary. How'd I get here?"

"I brought you, with assistance, in a taxi, more than an hour ago. A poor abode," said Sam courteously, "but I call it home."

"How'd *she* get here?"

"I sent for her."

"Where's her devoted husband?"

His words came slurred but clear enough; and Sam answered, "Out of town, Mr. Rogers."

"How very convenient." He looked at Sam and then at Gail, who had gone back to her chair. She couldn't speak. Her throat was a hard tight knot and she felt physically ill.

"Hardly my idea of a love nest," said Rogers. He lay down again, and spoke, his regard turned from them, "And it puts me on the spot. This might interest the Spencers but, on the other hand, you wouldn't take me to your newspaper as you promised, if I reported this happy ending."

Gail looked at Sam wordlessly.

"I had to promise something," he told her irritably.

"Maybe," suggested her father, "he wanted to get a bit of his own back."

"Shut up," said Sam violently.

Gail spoke slowly. She said, "You would have taken him . . . No, you couldn't afford that. But you know everybody, you could have given him a lead, elsewhere."

"So what?" said Sam. "Perhaps that was my idea, originally. I wouldn't mind seeing the Spencers squirm. Provided, of course, that when your parent sobered up he still looked at the matter in an impractical light."

"Why did you call me, then?" she asked.

"I'd thought it over," said Sam. "I thought, perhaps, we could make a deal."

Rogers sat up again. He swung around, his feet to the floor. His face was pasty white, and the sweat stood on his forehead. He said, with an enormous effort:

"A man after my own heart . . . a heel and a bastard. Why don't you make the deal? You're not as unlike me as you hoped, are you?"

He shuddered visibly, made an uncertain gesture with his shaking hand, added unevenly, "I need a drink," and lay down and was silent.

"He's out again," said Sam unnecessarily.

Gail got to her feet. She asked, "What kind of deal, Sam?"

"You know." He rose and took her in his arms and she did not resist him. She stood there, very quiet, completely unresponsive as he kissed her roughly, urgently. He said, "Forget it. I was out of my mind. I'll see that he gets on the train. I'll go with him."

She said, "I don't care what you do or don't do." She felt his arms slacken and moved away from him and emptied her handbag of money except for some dollar bills and change. She put it on the table. "You can give him his lead, if you wish. And the money. And when Brad comes home, I'll tell him exactly what happened."

"And will he believe it?"

"I haven't lied to him. He knows that."

"We're washed up, then?"

"We have been for a long time."

"I don't think so. I think you are still in love with me. It would have been very simple, Gail. Your time's your own. Brad is engrossed in his work and — his other interests."

"What other interests?"

He said, "I liked the guy, I thought he was getting a bad bargain. I thought he deserved more than a woman who'd marry him for what he had. But you were second choice, after all."

"What do you mean?"

"Look at it logically. What's hurt, under the circumstances, except your vanity? After the night I saw Helena Sturm in the Stork I made inquiries. I know a lot of people, including some she knows. Wasn't it obvious they'd speculate? Brad's vulnerable enough, I dare say, and he was with her every day . . . she's damned attractive, Gail, when she lights up. She would, for a man who aroused her . . . But Brad couldn't marry her, as she had a husband, and she couldn't leave a husband who had been through that particular hell . . . even if as a husband he —"

"Stop it, I don't want to hear."

Sam said inexorably, "Sturm's insanely jealous of his wife . . . perhaps he has reason. They say, after Brad's marriage to you, the talk died down."

"I don't believe it. I don't believe that Brad and Helena Sturm were ever in love."

"Maybe they weren't, maybe it was something else, there are two sides to every moon, and at least two names for everything. Pretty it up, if you insist. We would have gone along all right together . . . in marriage, which I suggested, remember? Or out of it, which I also suggested, a long time ago and again tonight. You could have had your cake and eaten it with all due discretion . . . Okay, so I was willing to cross you, because I was sore, because I find I'm not as good a friend of Brad's as I believed, because a Spencer scandal would have been entertaining. But maybe I didn't think you'd give me that choice, maybe I believed you'd make the deal with me, knowing all the time it was what you really wanted — not needing to make a deal and knowing that too. But you enjoy being sacrificed, you might have enjoyed this too if you could figure it as a sacrifice. You've never been very realistic."

Rogers turned over, an arm trailed down, he groaned, and made an animal noise in his throat.

Gail said, "I hope I never see you again, Sam."

"I don't promise. I'll make the noble gesture, however. I'll convoy your old man to Chicago, and throw the fear of God, cops, and the law generally into him, and when he realizes that a steady source of income may be lopped off, I imagine he'll play ball, for a while at least."

"It won't be necessary," she said. "I've been under obligations to too many people. I won't add you to the list."

She went to the telephone and, while he watched, startled, she dialed her own number. After a long time, and constant ringing, Andrews replied sleepily. At night, the telephone in Alexandria's room was switched off.

"Andrews?" she said. "I'm awfully sorry to wake you but my father has been taken ill, and I'm bringing him back for the night. Would you get the small room ready, and help me with him when I come? I'll get a cab now."

"You're out of your mind," said Sam.

"I don't think so. I'll put him on his train," she said, "it's time I took a little responsibility."

"Where will you get a cab this time of night?"

"I kept mine, it's waiting." She picked up the money she had put on the table and went over to the couch. She took her father's lax hand, slapped it sharply, slapped his check, and spoke clearly, evenly. "Wake up," she said, "wake up . . . we're going home."

He stirred and mumbled and did not wake.

Sam said, "You can't, you know."

"I'm afraid you'll have to help, then," she said, "much as I dislike it. He is heavy, but between you and the cab driver . . ." She thought a moment and added, "Or I could call an ambulance."

"Oh, hell," he said, "go down and get the driver; I'll do what I can."

Gail went downstairs and out where the cab waited and the driver said cheerfully, "I was wondering about you, miss."

But not especially about the fare she'd rung up, for he knew the house from which he had taken her. He had no idea who lived there but it was a solid structure.

She said, "There's an elderly man up the stairs, two flights, in a friend's apartment. Do you think with help you could get him downstairs, and into the cab? I want to take him home. He's ill."

The driver was a big man. He said, "Okay," got out of the cab and followed her. When they reached the flat Sam had managed to put Rogers's coat on him, to button his shirt and tie his tie. His eyes met the cab driver's in comprehension and the driver shook his head. He didn't like drunks riding in his cab. Too many risks. On the other hand, you had to maintain the fiction for the lady's sake. He was a chivalrous soul. He said, "All right, chum, let's go."

Rogers was tall and thin, but there was no life in his body and the two men struggled down the stairs with him, with difficulty. Gail threw her coat about her, took her bag and her father's top coat, and followed.

They got him into the cab and propped him up and Sam asked, "Can you manage?"

"From now on." She did not offer her hand, she merely looked at him and said, "Thanks," a little too smoothly. She got in, the door slammed, and the gears ground. She did not look back.

It was not a long ride; at that time of night the streets were not crowded, the theater business was over. But it seemed as long as halfway across the continent. The cab rounded corners, Rogers swayed, and Gail put her arm around him and braced him as firmly as possible. It was a very hard thing to do. The smell of liquor made her sick, the sound of his breathing frightened her, the weight against her was distasteful, it made her flesh creep. But this was her flesh, too . . . and this breath was, in a sense, her breath.

When the cab stopped in front of the Spencer house, she spoke to the driver. She asked, "Will you get in here with him while I fetch someone to help — and then will you help us get him upstairs?"

"Sure," said the driver, curious and friendly. He thought, He certainly tied one on.

She used her door key as she told Andrews she would and he was waiting for her in the hall. She said, "I'm sorry about this,

Andrews, but it can't be helped. The driver will help you get him in — we both will." Andrews was an old man, she thought, alarmed, and the stairs were long.

You couldn't get a dead weight like that upstairs and be noiseless about it, no matter how you tried. The light switch clicked in Alexandria's room and she called imperiously, "Who is it?" and Andrews made a small resigned sound.

"Get him in his room," said Gail quickly. She gave the driver two bills, a twenty and a five. She said, "Thank you, for everything," and knocked on Alexandria's door.

"Come in," Alexandria said. She was sitting up in bed. She stared incredulously at Gail. "Where have you been?" she demanded. "What was the noise I heard . . . and the voices?"

Gail closed the door. She said, "It's my father, Mrs. Spencer," and neither noticed that she had reverted to the old and easier form of address.

"Your father!"

She said, "I brought him here. There was nothing else I could do. The cab driver and Andrews are putting him in the small room beyond mine. In the morning I'll call a doctor . . . and as soon as he is able, he will leave."

"Where did you . . . ?" Alexandria broke off. She asked, "Is he ill?"

Gail looked at her with level eyes. She said, "He is very drunk. But he won't disturb you, I'll stay with him and see that he doesn't."

She went out and closed the door while Alexandria was still talking. But Gail did not listen or reply.

She met the cab driver coming out into the hall and he said, "Well, thanks, miss. I said I'd stay and get the old — the gentleman undressed but the other old fellow said he could manage."

"He will," she assured him and went downstairs to let him out, to lock the door and attend to the lights.

Then she went back up to the little guest room.

Andrews said, "I took the liberty of fetching some pajamas." They were his, she saw, not Brad's. And her father was in the narrow white bed in the quiet room. Under the shaded lights his face looked younger, less embittered.

She said, "I've explained to Mrs. Spencer. I wonder if I should call a doctor now?"

Andrews said, looking old, but competent in his hastily assumed attire, "I don't think you need, Mrs. Spencer. I believe he'll sleep for the rest of the night." He hesitated. "I have had some experience in these things," he added.

Her mind fled, shocked, to Brad's grandfather. Was it possible? she wondered. Brad wouldn't know, he didn't remember him. And Andrews had been in the Spencer service for a very long time.

She said, "I'll stay with him."

"There's no need," Andrews said, "let me instead."

"No, you must get some sleep."

He said, disturbed, "And you, Mrs. Spencer. If you were to leave the door open between this room and your bathroom, you could hear him . . ."

She smiled faintly. She said, "Thank you, Andrews, you've been very kind."

But he lingered at the door. He said, "If you need me, will you call?" and she promised.

Gail went back to her room, took off her things and put on a robe and slippers. She could not sleep, tonight, and doubted if she would ever sleep again. Later she would think of Sam, of Brad and Helena Sturm, and even of herself, but now she had a more immediate problem.

Very early in the morning Andrews came in with a cup of tea. He was not surprised to find Gail sitting beside Rogers's bed, half asleep. Roused, she opened her eyes and tried to smile, and he set the cup down and said softly, "If you would drink this . . ." and then, "I took the liberty of calling Dr. Evans."

A youngish man, not Alexandria's throat-clearing, stuffed-shirt specialist, but a friend of Brad's. Gail knew him slightly.

Andrews said, "I think Mr. Rogers will be ill when he wakes, Mrs. Spencer. I explained to Dr. Evans — and he told me he would be here as soon as possible, and would bring a nurse."

She drank the tea for its warmth, and Andrews added, "I can stay here for a while, Mrs. Spencer. It isn't time for Madam's tray yet and one of the girls will arrange it for me."

Gail nodded, she was numb with fatigue. She went into her room, undressed, and got under a very hot shower and then turned on the cold until it stung her and she felt momentarily rested and alert. She was starting to dress when Alexandria came in without knocking. She wore a voluminous robe, her hair was not dressed for the day, her little face was guiltless of rouge or powder, and she looked every year of her age.

She said, "Perhaps you are willing to afford me a more complete explanation?"

Gail did so, in very simple words. She said, "A friend of mine telephoned me last night. He is a newspaperman. He went into a bar and my father was there. He had not known him but when he learned his name he realized who he was. He took him home, to his apartment, and called me from there. I went down, and between Mr. Meredith and the taxi man, whom I had kept waiting, I brought my father back here. As soon as he is able to travel I'll see that he gets back to Chicago."

Alexandria said, "I knew he'd break his word." Her face was alive with malice. "Do you intend to keep this from Bradford?"

"No. I'll telephone him as soon as I've seen Dr. Evans."

"Dr. Evans?" Alexandria, standing, steadied herself with one hand on a chair. "Why?"

"He is bringing a nurse."

"For a drunken man?" said Alexandria contemptuously. She knew, however, a good deal about men who drank, who required doctors and nurses and the fiction of a severe attack of indigestion.

Gail said, her mouth stiff, her words brittle, "He'll need attention, Mrs. Spencer. I am sorry it had to happen this way."

"Sorry?" said Alexandria. "And you expect Evans not to talk, nor the servants . . . nor your friend, whatever his name is . . . to say nothing of the cab driver?"

"I don't know about the cab driver," Gail said wearily, "it's probably all in the night's work for him and not the first time he's brought a drunken man home. I don't know about Sam Meredith either, but I can't see what end it would serve for him to gossip. As for your servants, they've been with you a long time . . . and the doctor is or should be bound by his professional ethics."

"You had no *right* to bring your father here," said Alexandria.

Gail looked at her. She said slowly, "You dislike me, Mrs. Spencer, you always have. It's natural, and I don't blame you. But this situation isn't my fault, unless it is my fault that I had a father in the first place. And I must remind you that I have every right to bring my father here, unpleasant as it is. For this is Brad's house and I am Brad's wife and it is my home."

For a moment Alexandria looked at her, stricken and uncertain. And Gail thought, Why, that's what she's been afraid of all along, that I would be free of the spell someday, that I would stop leaning over backwards, that I would assert myself, and she would be helpless. It was like Alice;

Alice crying, "They're nothing but a pack of cards." She felt sorry for Alexandria for the first time. She said gently, "I am sorry . . . sorrier than I can ever say. He won't trouble you in any way. I'll see to that. Please go back to bed and let someone bring you your tray. I'll call Millicent, for she'll have to know."

Alexandria did not speak and Gail put her arm about her and took her back to her room, and helped her into bed. She took the thin, dry hand in hers. She said, "Brad will advise me. Please don't be so upset."

Alexandria's sunken black eyes flashed with some of their old spirit. She said, "I'm not upset, and I knew something like this would happen. I did not trust that man. But for the first time since you married him I realize you are my grandson's wife, and this is your home. And I live in it on sufferance and because my husband wished it."

"No," said Gail, "because Brad loves and needs you."

She went out, closing the door softly, she could not bear to see Alexandria cry, her face broken into lines of bereavement and insecurity. And there was nothing she could do, save repeat the empty assurances. Alexandria was not weeping because Gail's father had, like any bad penny, turned up again. She wept only for her lost authority.

Gail went to knock on Millicent's door, and then to leave her, goggle eyed, snatching at her clothes, rising, as she put it, to meet the emergency. And presently Dr. Evans arrived, with a male nurse, and went into the small room and released Andrews.

Gail went to her room to wait. She fancied that the tea sloshed around emptily in her stomach and her nerves were taut with anxiety.

Later she talked to the doctor. He was a fat, brisk, competent man who minced no words. After the situation was discussed, "How long has your father been an alcoholic?" he asked.

"I don't know. I haven't seen him since I was four, until recently."

"His heart's not very good," said Evans. He frowned, a little. "I suggest you let me put him in a private hospital which is prepared to deal with these cases. We could get him over the hump here, but the treatment isn't too pleasant, you know. The nurse is efficient, I have employed him before this, he would go along. Would you do that, Mrs. Spencer? Would you leave it to me, as Brad isn't here? Have you told him, by the way?"

"Not yet . . . I waited until I'd seen you."

"Tell him to get in touch with me. And

don't worry. I'll make all arrangements, and send a private ambulance . . . we should have him in the hospital within two hours."

When, finally, she reached Brad it was the greatest possible effort to speak to him. So she said as little as possible and Brad listened. He said, "I'm sorry, darling. I'll get home as soon as I can. It's out of the question for another forty-eight hours, I think, unless you find you can't manage."

"I'll manage."

"Let Evans assume the responsibility, and take it a step at a time, dear. We'll talk it over when I return. Meantime I'll get hold of Evans." He added, "What a stroke of luck that it should have been Sam who found him," and Gail laughed and he asked sharply, "Are you laughing, Gail?"

"I suppose so," she gasped, "or else I'm having hysterics. Don't worry, Brad, too much."

The ambulance came and Morrison Rogers departed. Alexandria kept to her room and sent for her own physician. She had had, she said, a shock; she was tired and wished to rest. Millicent stayed with her, reading aloud, measuring drops, coaxing her to eat from a tray, emerging only to order her own trays, and leaving Gail to have her meals alone. Andrews's was the only comforting voice in the house, reassuring Gail, that she was not to fret, that everything would be all right.

On the third day Gail went to the hospital in which her father was recovering. She had expected Brad in, but his plane had been grounded the night before because of weather. So she went alone, bracing herself for the encounter. She found Rogers looking white, thin and drawn, but with clear eyes. He was shaved, and neat, and quite unresigned.

He said, as the nurse left the room, "I suppose I'm to thank you?"

"Not necessarily."

"I don't remember a great deal, but any gutter would be more amusing than this place." He shivered. "So now I'm to go back to the gutter?" he inquired.

"Why did you break your word?"

"Did I give it? Oh, I signed a paper but better men than I have signed papers . . ." He grinned at her, dimly. "Gail, a little money is worse than none."

"A hundred dollars a week is not a little money. Men support families on that amount, and not as many men who'd like to —"

"All very true," he conceded, "but for me, it's either too little or too much. When I have nothing, I expect nothing. I live by my wits, a feast today and to hell with tomorrow's famine. But when I have a little, or a hundred a week, I want more . . . I begrudge the necessity for keeping up appearances, a decent roof, respectable clothes, three meals a day; a man on a hundred a week is expected to have these things but, damn it, he has to pay for them and there's not enough left over for amusement. Well, the agreement's gone by the board . . . I'll get along on my own . . . as far as your worthy husband is concerned. And no hard feelings. But how about you? We could make an agreement. I dare say he's settled something on you or that you have a handsome allowance. Lump sums, my dear, one at a time . . . when one's gone, then another. I might not need a retread for weeks . . . or I might need it day after tomorrow."

"No," she said steadily.

"I remember a little," he said. "That wasn't the first time you'd been in that apartment, nor the first time you'd cried in my good Samaritan's arms." He laughed. "Sam," he said. "I remember that now. Samaritan. Not bad."

"Brad knows all about Sam Meredith."

"Does he, indeed? Perhaps I'll be able to add to his knowledge?"

Brad walked in, without knocking. He asked, "Whose knowledge?"

Gail rose. Her hands were shaking. She locked them, one within the other. She said, "Go on, answer him."

"I'll leave that to you," said Rogers.

"She doesn't have to," said Brad pleasantly. He put his arm around Gail and kissed her cheek. He said, "Sit down, and we'll talk this over."

"I am purged," said Rogers, "figuratively and literally. I am weak, physically and morally. At the moment I am willing to take the pledge. But the moment never lasts. What do you propose doing with me?"

"Dr. Evans thinks you can be cured," Brad said.

"How optimistic. And suppose I don't want to be?"

"It would then be a waste of a physician's time and my money to try," Brad agreed.

"And if I say I would like to be myself again . . . or the self I dimly remember?" Rogers asked cautiously.

"Dr. Evans has a friend," said Brad, "who is chief of staff of an extremely good sanitarium, in California. You would go there, when you are able to travel with your nurse. When you are well again, you may choose your own place of residence — here," he said casually, "or the West, anywhere you wish. It seems to me that you would then be able not only to live on, and up to, the terms of our agreement but you might even find something with which to occupy your time."

"A dreary prospect," said Rogers. "I'm a periodic drunkard, you know," he added carelessly. "I have my ups and downs. Your suggestion sounds like the strait and narrow path, also very level, difficult for one of my temperament. To become a sober, useful citizen at my age is a somewhat gruesome prospect. But I see no other way out," he said mildly, "as I can intimidate neither of you." He held out his hand. He said, "I like you, Spencer, rather more than I like my daughter. She frightens me a little."

"I don't mean to," said Gail unhappily.

"I don't blame you," her father said. "There's no reason why you should yearn over me, or I over you, for that matter. I don't enjoy this situation nor do I like what's happened to me in the last few days. Make the arrangements, Spencer . . ." He closed his eyes. "I think I'd like to sleep, if you don't mind," he said.

They returned to the house and on the way were silent. Just before they reached there Gail said, "Your grandmother is very much upset, she has made herself ill. I shouldn't have brought him to the house, Brad, but I didn't know what else to do."

"You did the right thing," he said, "and Gran will get over it. I dare say it upset her more to have you make your own decisions than what had caused you to make them."

"Yes, I know. There's something else I must tell you."

"No need," he assured her.

But when they reached the house she asked him to come with her to their suite before he saw his grandmother. He had not seen her, he had simply dropped his bags at the house and followed Gail to the hospital.

In their sitting room she lighted a cigarette and stood at the windows, the soft spring light in back of her. It was a good sunny day, warm and wonderful.

She said, "Sam had plans, Brad. He thought if he covered up for me in this matter that I would have an affair with him. I don't know how else to put it. And he promised my father that he would take him to the right newspaper person, someone unscrupulous, who would break the story. He half meant it. Then he thought he could frighten me into making a deal. That's what he called it. He believed I was still so much in love with him that I'd seize on it as an excuse . . . and tell myself I was forced into it."

"And are you still in love with him?"

"No. No, I'm not. Believe me, Brad."

Now was the time, now she could ask, And were you, are you in love with Helena Sturm? Did you marry me mainly to detract attention from and to protect her? But she could not ask it. It wasn't, she found, her business.

"I believe you." He smiled and said, "Now suppose I go in and tackle Gran?"

XII

When Brad had left the room, Gail stood irresolute. She thought, I should have asked to go with him; no, gone without asking. This is my affair, whether I like it or not. But she felt physically exhausted, unwilling to face Alexandria's sharp black eyes and complacent spoken, or unspoken, I told you so.

She went to her desk, sat down and turned the leaves of her engagement book, trying to shut her mind to speculation and anxiety. She was due, she saw, at a committee meeting tea this afternoon, during which plans for a large charity entertainment would be formulated. It would not be the first she had reluctantly attended, listening to the preliminary gossip, discussion, arguments. The Old Guard would ram its ideas through, the younger women would protest and be silenced, the climbers would eagerly agree and dream of their names and their photographs in the press.

Since her marriage Gail had been asked to serve on several committees. The idea did not appeal to her and she had asked Brad if she must, and been told that, naturally, she need not, it was up to her. But Alexandria remarked that Gail had no choice.

"Sooner or later," she said, "you will, I trust, take over my responsibilities." She had listed the organizations in which she was actively interested, "all," she concluded, "sponsored by the Spencers since their inception."

Gail had said that she didn't know how, she had had no experience, and Alexandria had silenced her with a silky "Surely you can learn?"

Alexandria believed that to be a Spencer by birth, or to become one through marriage, entailed certain civic and philanthropic obligations. But Gail felt herself a Spencer only on sufferance, relegated, properly, to the background, and assumed, moreover, that even were her personal interest aroused, any deviation from Alexandria's ideas would be criticized. But she had outwardly conformed to keep the precarious peace, attending meetings and benefit parties, and appearing, early in the spring, at a fashion show, conscious that her coworkers regarded her as an outsider. She had overheard two recent Social Registered brides discussing her. "Of course," said one, "she models the clothes divinely. Why not? She was a professional."

But several of them had been professionals also, some for fun, some for bigger game, some because a living must be earned. Yet their position apparently differed from hers.

In a way, it was an amusing switch. If Gail's provocative figure and face no longer appeared on magazine covers or posing against a backdrop of cacti and swimming pools, she still looked from the advertising pages, the proceeds given to charity, or from the rotogravure sections . . . not as Rusty Rogers, who earned her living, but as Mrs. Bradford Spencer, who sponsored, gratis, this or that product for the benefit of this or that charity.

She had not, she saw, set down the hour of today's engagement so, still determined to occupy herself with trivial things, she looked in her address book and dialed the number of the committee chairman at whose home the tea would be given. She reached a wrong number, apologized, hung up, and after a moment dialed again. But the same voice replied, with comprehensible exasperation. It was a practical demonstration of the fact that you can make the same mistake twice.

Gail sat back and looked at the black and white face of the dial. She dialed again, singularly concentrated upon the simple procedure, and was rewarded by the fruity voice of Mrs. Parkinson's butler, confirming the fact that she had made contact with the Parkinson residence. Mrs. Parkinson was not at home, he informed her, but the hour set for the tea was four o'clock.

Gail hung up and sat back feeling curiously limp. It was extraordinary how much significance she attached to a footling, routine error. Anyone could be forgiven for dialing, say, the numeral three instead of eight . . . anyone in a hurry or preoccupied. But she hadn't been in a hurry, and to do this twice was more than woolgathering.

She rose, no longer irresolute.

Walking down the hall, raising her hand to tap on Alexandria's closed door, she remembered telling Sam that it was time she assumed responsibility. Brave words, spoken in anger and shame. Yet, bringing her father to the Spencer house and then turning the problem he represented over to Dr. Evans and Brad had been as far as she had gone, and it was not far enough.

"Who is it?" asked Alexandria.

"Gail."

"Come in."

Alexandria was sitting in a big chair by the windows, and Brad was across the room, on the end of the chaise longue. Evidently Gail had interrupted an argument, for Alexandria was flushed, her lips set in a thin, rouged line, while Brad wore his look of conscious patience. But he smiled at Gail, said, "Hello, darling," and made room for her beside him.

Alexandria said briskly, "I'm glad you came. I was about to ask Brad to fetch you. He's told me of his plans for your father. I dare say they'll serve but, frankly, I think it's throwing good money after bad."

Gail said, "I think so too, as things now stand." She addressed her husband directly. "At first it seemed a wonderful solution," she told him, "but it isn't, really."

"Why not?" he asked quietly.

"It's too easy." She looked at Alexandria. "I remember you once said you always suspected a too-easy solution. This was one — once we had his consent, which wasn't hard. He's at the end of his rope, ill, and I think, afraid. The rest is a matter of financing, sending him west with a nurse, putting him in an expensive place, and leaving it up to the doctors."

"What else can you do?" Alexandria asked sharply. "Not that I'm credulous enough to believe that he can be cured; yet, as long as he remains under supervision, he's harmless, I suppose."

"Dr. Evans believes he can be cured, if he wishes to be," Gail said.

"Never . . . at that age."

"I don't know that I'd want to be," said Gail slowly, "in his case. Call his drinking anything you please, an escape, an excuse, an illness . . . what incentive has he? Who cares whether he's cured or not?"

Alexandria lifted her eyebrows, but Brad's hand closed over Gail's and held it. He said softly, "Good girl."

"What do you mean," demanded Alexandria, "who cares?"

"We don't," Gail said stubbornly, "none of us . . . except in so far as it would save us embarrassment." She looked at Brad. "I don't mean you," she added.

"Never mind me," he said promptly. "I've told you I hate waste. But you've been arriving at some conclusions. What are they?"

"I've let you do it all, Brad," she said evenly, "and you've been fine. But your first attempt failed and this one will too, because he can't achieve anything alone."

"Alone?" repeated Alexandria querulously. "With the best medical attention in the country?"

"He'll still be alone."

Alexandria laughed shortly. It was like a

small, sharp bark and devoid of merriment. She said, "I never expected to see you turn sentimental."

"I'm not sentimental," Gail began hotly, but Brad said, "Wait a moment, Gail, what, exactly, do you want to do?"

"First of all I want to pay for his care," Gail said. "I know that's quibbling, because it would come out of the money you gave me, Brad. Still, I'd feel better about it. Secondly, isn't there a nearby place to which he could go — where I could see him — so that he'd come to feel that someone took an interest, beyond the obvious one?"

"There are a dozen such places," Alexandria answered promptly, "within one to three hours of New York. But if he were admitted to one and you went to see him there, you'd defeat the entire purpose. Someone's bound to talk."

"I spoke to Dr. Evans," Gail said, "that first morning. Alcoholism is a disease, not a disgrace. What if people do talk? Oh, I admit I was afraid of that originally." She turned to Brad. "I felt so insecure myself," she said, "not through any fault of yours or anyone's. Just my own. But now I realize that whatever people say it can't reflect upon you or your grandmother, unfavorably. How could it, when you accept the situation and do everything in your power to correct it? As for me, my father can't affect me, either. I'm responsible for and to myself."

"Fiddlesticks," Alexandria remarked. "You talk as if you had succumbed to some particularly sloppy form of so-called religion."

Gail didn't answer. She asked, "Brad, what do you think? It's not that I've discovered any filial feeling. I haven't. It goes beyond that."

"You must do as you wish," he said, "and there's a very good sanitarium in Connecticut. I know the medical director."

"Oh, fine," said Alexandria bitterly. "A short run from Ridgefield! And I know Dr. Manners, too. He's dined here."

Gail braced herself. She said, "I'm afraid I must ask you to keep out of this, Mrs. Spencer."

"Sooner or later," said Alexandria, rallying, "you were bound to become insolent."

"Gran!" said Brad sharply.

But Gail broke in. "Never mind, Brad," she said, "and I don't think that's the word. I think you mean, sooner or later, I was bound to assert myself. Perhaps you consider that insolence, Mrs. Spencer. I don't. I'm sorry to cause trouble, especially for

Brad. For years I tried to put my father out of my mind, refusing to acknowledge that he existed, hoping that he didn't and resenting him, because of my mother and myself. Well, he does exist and I don't resent him because he has as much right to exist as any of us. I don't like what he's done with his life. I suppose it's partly selfish, wanting to see him correct it . . . as far as it can be corrected. Partly because of you and Brad," she added, "for very different reasons. But mainly because, whether I like it or not, I'm in this, up to my neck."

"I wash my hands of the matter," said Alexandria clearly. "Brad chose his profession without consulting me, and I put nothing in his way . . . not that I could have," she remarked. "He married you without asking my advice. He was in a position to do so. If he chooses to abet you in this astonishing role of ministering angel, that's his concern and yours. Don't bother me with it, further. But," she warned, her black eyes bright, "if I am any judge of character, you won't find your extraordinary parent easy to manage. He's quite a realist, in his own way."

Brad rose. He said with finality, "Well, that's settled, then. I'll telephone Dr. Manners, and also Evans."

He looked at his wife. "What's your next step?" he asked.

She said, "I'll talk to my father today."

She did so, after luncheon, at which Alexandria did not appear, but sent Millicent down, probably to report any discussion which might take place. None did. Brad conversed amiably about Oak Ridge, the people, the climate, the astonishing setup. And after luncheon the car came around and took Gail to the hospital before going on to the laboratory.

"Good luck," said Brad, as Gail got out, and she stood a moment in the sunlight, looking at him, wishing cravenly that he would come with her. He would if she'd ask. He seemed to read her mind, as now and then he was able to, and added, smiling, "You'll do all right alone."

Getting out of the elevator, she was conscious of a steadying sense of accomplishment. Every step had been difficult, but she took each on her own. Brad had backed her up, but had made no suggestions.

Rogers's nurse was sitting in the corridor. He rose as she approached the desk and she asked mechanically, "How is Mr. Rogers?"

"We're fine," he answered, in the irritating plural. "He has a visitor, Mrs. Spencer . . .

Dr. Evans left no orders about visitors and Mr. Rogers was insistent I contact the gentleman."

Apprehension was cold in her flesh. "What visitor?" she asked.

"A Mr. Meredith."

"I see." She hesitated a fraction of a second. She could go away and return later. But then she would never find out why . . . for neither her father nor Sam would tell her.

She nodded, went down the corridor, and knocked at the door.

Sam was sitting by the bed. He rose, looking concerned. She was evidently the last person he or her father expected. Rogers's face was a study in amazement and almost childish guilt. "You know each other?" he inquired politely. "Oh, of course. How stupid of me . . . Gail, my dear, do sit down. I hardly looked for you, twice in one day."

"That's evident," she retorted, and remained standing. She asked, "Sam, what are you doing here?"

"Your father sent for me."

Rogers said, "I retain the most curious recollections, in this instance, the name of my — rescuer. He's in the telephone book, too."

"Why did you send for him?"

"To thank him, naturally, when I was

more or less in my right mind."

Sam looked disconcerted for the first time since she had known him. He said hastily, "That's right, Gail."

"And I thought," said her father innocently, "that I might patch up what appeared to be a misunderstanding between you two young people . . . all my fault, and it seemed too bad, as you are friends of such long standing."

"Let's not play games," Gail said. "What did either of you expect to gain by this?"

"Don't be belligerent, it doesn't become you," Rogers said acidly. "Perhaps I wanted to keep Meredith apprised of the situation . . . just in case anything went wrong. The power of the press, you know, to say nothing of its freedom."

"Don't mind him," said Sam, "he can't help talking like a ham actor in the role of conspirator. But it's like this — he seems to think that the Spencer interests are determined to shove him into a loony bin and he wanted . . . outside advice and interest."

Gail looked at her father without speaking, and he said uneasily:

"Well, what of it? I have to protect myself. A lot of superfluous or unwelcome people have been rockabyed into lunatic asylums, given enough money and influence back of the move. How do I know this place in California is what you say it is? It's a long way off."

"He's got something there," said Sam.

"You know Brad," Gail reminded him, "you were his friend. You know me."

"I thought I did."

She went on, "Do you seriously believe either of us capable of a thing like that?"

"Nope. But it was a way . . . to keep in touch."

She said, "There's no way. And I told Brad about the other night. I told him all of it."

Sam shrugged. "Well, as I've said before, you can't blame a guy for trying."

The door shut quietly.

Gail sat down, as she found herself compelled to do so. And her father said, "A dirty trick, wasn't it? But then, my mind works that way. And I thought, Suppose they railroad me. I haven't a chance. I couldn't even jump out of a window or off a train: Not that I'd want to . . . distasteful as most of my life has been I'm too egotistical to relinquish it, God knows why."

She asked, "Do you believe that Brad would do such a thing to you?"

"No. I like your husband, in an impersonal sort of way. I believe he's an honest man. But I wouldn't put anything past that harridan of a grandmother — and I'm not so damned sure of you. So I sent for Meredith. Let's not fool ourselves. He'd be delighted to get something on your husband . . . and you too, I dare say. A legitimate beef, very humanitarian. Poor old man, whose worst fault is elbow-bending, homeless and friendless, craving affection, bought off by rich family with mere pittance and, once lapsed from grace, shunted into the limbo of the lost. A pretty picture, which seemed a form of insurance against — incarceration."

"You mean that?"

"I got scared," he answered with the utmost and, she felt, most sincere simplicity.

An impersonal feeling of pity stabbed her, not alone for this man whose face was still a stranger's, who meant nothing to her emotionally, but for all men, for everyone in the world, everyone who must sometimes be alone and afraid.

She said gently, "It would not have happened, ever. And I'm here to ask a favor."

He asked warily, "What kind of favor?"

"Instead of a sanitarium in California, would you consider one nearby, in Connecticut?"

"Why," he asked, astonished, "what difference could it make, save in train fare, which is of no consideration?"

"I'd rather you were where I could see you."

His face came suddenly to life; it was young, it was interested, it was sharp with curiosity and unbelief.

"You?" he asked. "Why? Duty, a tract, a pound of tea? Do you think of yourself and of me in such terms: the good child, the erring parent?"

She hadn't thought she could laugh, but she did, and to his further confusion. He grinned after a minute. "It is a note of comedy, after all. I meant it, however, as satire," he admitted.

She said, "You and Brad's grandmother are somewhat alike."

"God forbid," he said piously. "Skip it. What's come over you?"

"I don't know."

For the first time he regarded her as something other than an instrument, a pledge of subsidy, or a possible danger, and she added quickly, "It isn't duty. Perhaps it's paying a debt. After all, you were responsible for me."

"Involuntarily, I assure you. A crass error, I did not plan a family. I am far from being a family man."

"Nevertheless, here I am. And in my turn

I have some responsibility toward you. Not just financial. I didn't want it that way. I didn't care what happened to you as long as it didn't affect me. I still don't want to care but, somehow or other, I do."

"You're a curious girl," he said, "and, I may add, not my type. Perhaps you are like me, hence incompatible. You aren't like your mother . . . she suffered and worshipped and clung and enjoyed poor health, poor spirits, and being kicked around. Oh, don't protest. Look back, intelligently, and you'll see it's basically true. You're too self-assured . . . or is that just a front? Your emotions aren't easily discernible. I've seen them exposed just twice . . . when we met for the first time in years and the other night, in Meredith's apartment, when your weakness had nothing to do with me."

She said, "I was in love with Sam Meredith, and he with me. Sam didn't want to marry me although he finally suggested it. I refused. I had by then met Brad, through Sam. And I wanted what my mother had never had, freedom from too much loving, and a complete security. Brad knew this when he married me; he knew about Sam, he does now. He knows also that I promised my mother that I'd manage my life better than she managed hers."

"Such candor should be rewarded," said Rogers. He looked at her somberly. "Never again mortgage your future . . . never be trapped into obligations. Your mother was a good woman and most uncomfortable to live with . . . she was smothering, devouring, hell bent on sacrifice. I couldn't take it. You couldn't either."

Gail cried, "I did, I loved her!"

"How much? I wonder. Or was it yourself you loved . . . plus your sense of guilt, the belief that if she hadn't been burdened with you she might have been happier, lived longer? Don't deceive yourself. She could inculcate guilt, very subtly. I couldn't take that either. I was a bad husband, granted, but believe me, she didn't want a good one; she didn't even want to be happy. She liked the stake and the flames."

Gail was silent, remembering many things, and her father went on:

"I fell in love with her because she was pretty, appealing, and besotted about me. It didn't last, with me. Many years later I fell in love with another woman. No, let me make a distinction. I have fallen in love with several but I loved only one. She would have nothing to do with me, which was sensible of her. But for a brief time I had a glimpse of what happiness might have been — such a glimpse isn't conducive to peace of mind unless you're a far stronger person than I."

She said, "I'm sorry," inadequately and he murmured, "You needn't be." He closed his eyes a moment, and was old again and growing tired. And without opening them wide asked, "Well, what about this place in Connecticut?"

"You'll go, then?"

"Connecticut, California, Timbuktu? What does it matter? Don't think I haven't tried reformation before, if not on a luxury scale. At one point I voluntarily offered myself as an experiment. In a word, I asked to be cured; and was."

She asked eagerly, "You did . . . then, you'll try again, you'll co-operate?"

"That time," he said, "I co-operated to beat hell. Well, nothing came of it. A cure won't stick if you don't want it to. I had an incentive to be cured but the incentive was removed. *She* removed it, *and* herself."

"I don't expect or want promises," she told him. "Just, that you'll try and that you'll see me while you're trying."

"I don't get you," he said wearily. "You owe me nothing. You once believed that, didn't you? Well, believe it again. I put myself in the picture with one object in mind — blackmail. At the time you subscribed to this notion. I didn't ask to be received with open arms, merely with an open purse. You didn't like me then; I doubt if you do now. So what's in it for you?"

"We might learn to respect each other," she said.

"All right," said Rogers, "make your plans, I'll try, although I don't relish the idea. But the first thing we have to learn is to respect ourselves and in my case that's a tough assignment."

Gail drove her father to the sanitarium in Brad's car. Her own, ordered for her, had not yet come. Brad did not go with her, nor the nurse. And her father asked as they drove along the Parkway, green with young summer, and crowded with cars, "Aren't you afraid?"

"No."

He smiled. He looked a good deal better. He had already met Dr. Manners, in town. He said, "I like Manners. But he won't like me, I'm too apt to match wits with him."

"Must you be difficult?"

"I dare say. It's a very different setup from the one I experienced," he told her. "A room of my own, a good bed, good food, books, the radio with which you handsomely provided me . . . consultations, lectures, and

297

suitable exercise, and occupational therapy. I'll make you a footstool," he said, "and that's a threat."

"I'm not to see you for a little while," she said, "then I'll be allowed to come. I won't be far away. Brad wants me to go to Ridgefield and stay, when it gets warmer."

He said, "I think perhaps Brad deserves more than you are willing to give him."

"Not willing," she said, low and flushed, as if he'd betrayed her into a confidence, "but — able."

He said suddenly, after they had left the Parkway and were taking the winding roads which the map Brad had given her indicated:

"It's pretty here . . . I don't know this state very well. Do you know, I'm grateful to you, Gail. You've given me an interest."

She took a corner a little sharply and asked, "What do you mean?"

"In you, in your husband . . . as a problem . . . impersonal enough, like doing a jigsaw puzzle or a crossword . . . looking for the right pieces, the right words to make the pattern come clear. It's a long time since I have been interested in anyone but myself."

The sanitarium was a pleasant place, not too big, with the main house and cottages set in tumbling little hills, surrounded with woods, and the garden of early summer. But after they were received and sat in Dr. Manner's quiet office, she could sense some of her father's assurance leaving him and he became exceptionally silent. And when, finally, they said good-bye he had the strangest look, that of a child going to school for the first time, faced with the discipline of the group and of strangers. Gail held out her hand, he took it, and held it, and said, quite urgently, "You'll come see me?" and she promised, "I'll come."

She drove back to town before evening fell, for she and Brad were going to the Sturms' for a late dinner. She had no desire to go, but Brad asked very little of her. She felt a little ill, and wondered, as she had for some time, whether or not she was pregnant. The possibility had never been distasteful to her, and was not now. But it frightened her, as if another link had been forged. She told herself, But if it's so, I'd be glad. Yet she hardly thought of herself in connection with a child, except as the instrument of conception and delivery. She thought of Brad. It would, she believed, make him happy, it was something that she could do for him.

He came in late while she was dressing and she told him about the trip. "I was a little uneasy, once we'd started. I thought maybe I should have brought the nurse . . . but I can't stand that little man," she admitted. "I thought what if he gets the wheel, or makes a scene or forces me to stop and let him out . . . oh, all sorts of crazy things."

"But he didn't."

"No, and when I left him I felt as though we'd already made progress. He approved of the place and his room; the nurse who talked to us is very attractive," she said, smiling, "and he liked Dr. Manners and the assistant. And he wanted me to come see him. I believe he really wanted it."

He said, "I think you are going to like your father, Gail, one day. Not perhaps as your father, but as a person . . . with no strings attached."

Going to the Sturms' she wondered why the occasion seemed so repugnant to her. She was sorry for Erich and for Helena, she admired them, but did not know either of them and in her brief encounters with Helena had been kept at arms' length. But ever since the night Sam had spoken of the gossip about Brad and Helena . . . I *can't* be jealous, she thought, you aren't jealous unless you're in love. But that was all mixed up. She did love Brad, he commanded her affection and her respect . . . every day a little more. Their relationship was serene and satisfactory. They were honest with each other, which people in love are not, as a rule. Yet, he was in love with her.

If I'm jealous, she thought, I've no right to be.

When they reached the Sturms', the little aunt opened the door. She looked completely distracted. She cried, "But Helena isn't home . . . I thought perhaps you were bringing her from the laboratory, Mr. Spencer."

Erich came wheeling up, in his chair. He asked, "Did you leave her there?"

He had left there, said Brad, astonished, but, then, he had gone early and not directly home. He went to meet someone, in from Washington, at the Carlyle. Helena often worked late, there was no reason for alarm.

Erich made a wide gesture. "All very well for you," he said, "but *I* am alarmed. I sit here all day, thinking of her. You, Spencer, you are with her . . . you know what she does, where she goes, you know her work . . . I am not even permitted to know that . . . except in the barest outlines."

Brad looked at Aunt Elsa, marking the white line about the big man's mouth and the blazing unhappy eyes, and Elsa nodded and scuttled off to come back with sherry and biscuits, and to flutter about Gail.

"If she doesn't come soon," said Brad, "we'll telephone."

"It is maddening," Erich said, refusing the sherry, "all day long, to wonder and never to know. A woman must feel like that about a man whose business takes him away from her, brings him together with other women." He looked at Gail for a moment. "I sit here like a log, all my skill, all my knowledge, useless — not quite a human being, no longer a man. My wife goes out, and works to support me . . . and sometimes it is very dark . . ."

His voice trailed off and Brad spoke quietly. "You are agitated, Erich," he said, "but Helena will come soon, and it will be all right. Suppose I wait here with you? She will be tired when she comes. Gail will go on home and we will have our party another time."

Aunt Elsa said tremulously, "Such a nice dinner, I have prepared it myself."

Gail rose. She said, "Please let me help with the table, and in the kitchen."

They went out to the tiny kitchen and Aunt Elsa said nervously, "It has been coming on again like this for several days. Helena wished to postpone the dinner, but he would not hear of it. He grows angry, shouts, accuses . . . and there is nothing we can do."

The kitchen was full of good, homely smells. Gail's stomach turned over and she felt faint. She asked, "May I sit down a moment?"

"My child," said Aunt Elsa, "you are ill, no?"

"No," she said. "I — I had a long drive today, and perhaps I am tired. If I could have some water . . . ?"

Drinking it, she heard Erich's voice, raised, and Brad's lower, even tones and then the telephone, and after that silence and then a most dreadful sound.

She ran into the living room, the older woman following. Erich was throwing himself from side to side in the chair, he was cursing interminably, in German.

Brad said, "There's been an accident at the laboratory. No, she isn't badly hurt. They've called a doctor. I'll go there at once." He looked at Gail, and she saw the conflict in his mind; he was afraid to leave her, yet someone had to stay. Elsa had gone wholly to pieces, sitting, shaking and weeping, in her chair. And Brad said, "You'll have to stay, darling. Make her give you the doctor's telephone number. Call him at

once. I will bring Helena back here or phone
. . ." He bent and kissed her, hard, quick,
gripping her shoulder. "I count on you," he
said.

Gail spoke to the weeping old woman as
Brad's feet sounded on the stairs. "What is
the doctor's number?"

"There . . . in the black book by the telephone . . . inside the cover," Aunt Elsa said
with difficulty.

Gail knelt down beside Erich Sturm. She
put her hands on his dreadful hands and
looked into his dreadful eyes. She said,
"Helena is not badly hurt. Brad will bring
her home . . . believe this."

For a moment he was quiet, looking at
her. He said, "You are his wife, aren't you?"
and then the cursing began again, the shaking, the agony, as if he were trying to wrench
the spirit from the bondage of the body.

Gail rose and went to the telephone, not
turning her back on him; she found and dialed the number. The doctor was in, and answered. She told him who she was; and the
circumstances.

"I'll be right there," he said, "make him
take the sedative . . . the aunt will know . . ."

Gail spoke across the contorted figure in
the chair. She said, "The sedative, Aunt
Elsa."

304

But when the old woman, pulling herself together, brought the capsule back in her shaking hand, Erich Sturm struck it from her hand together with the glass.

"Bring another," said Gail, "and give it to me."

She knelt beside him, with the capsule in her hand and the fresh glass. She said, "You must take this, Dr. Sturm. Helena is going to need you. She's been hurt. She will need your care and your knowledge, she will need you."

He took the capsule and swallowed it, without water. He said after a moment:

"I thought when I saw you that she would . . . I thought she would tell herself it was no use . . ."

"Erich," said the old aunt. "Erich!"

"Go on," said Gail. She thought, No matter what he says, if he will just go on, talking rationally . . . or as rationally as possible.

"If she had just wanted to sleep with him," said Erich, "I could pretend not to know. I understand these things. She is a young woman, desirable and passionate. I could endure what she gave of the body. But never what she gave of the heart. You understand that? Perhaps he was a little in love with her. Not enough. I watched her suffer, because she knew it was not enough. I watched her suffer after he married. You came, and I watched you." He looked at her with the singular piercing eyes, so alive, so wretched. He said, "I think you are pregnant. Are you?"

"I don't know, Dr. Sturm."

"I think so. I delivered many women, before I specialized. You have the look . . ."

Elsa spoke with an inconsequential eagerness. "She was faint, just now in the kitchen smelling the food."

Sturm said, "When, after Helena saw you for the first time, she told me, 'She does not love him, she has married him because of the money,' I was not sure. I waited until you came here. I saw she was right. You had not . . . the radiance, the outgoing, the wonder that is in women who love and are loved. I know what that is, I have experienced it. Do you think I could forget it? Yes, she was right. So I knew that sooner or later he would turn to her, because she has loved him a long time, because she is good, and faithful." His face was twisted and she forced herself to look at it, to keep her hands on his. "Yes, he will turn to her and she will be there."

"No," she said. "No, you are imagining things."

"I am not a child nor a fool," he said, and the black eyes burned in the white face. "I know what it is to have been loved by her. She loves me now, as a child, as a brother, as a comrade, as a ghost. To be loved as a ghost is the worst . . . she does not need me. She needs a *man*," he said.

"Brad loves me," said Gail.

"How long can that last? You sleep in his bed, you bear him a child, you are agreeable, you are beautiful, you are kind. Who can be nourished on these things? I am not, and I am half a man."

He was silent, his battered hands moved under hers. He said, "Perhaps she is dead, and then will love no one. I have wished her dead . . . I have not the strength to kill her . . . I cannot even destroy myself. If she were dead she would lie alone, loving no one, her heart would be quiet and her soul would escape and I too would be at peace." He looked down blindly and she saw at once, with a most dreadful wrench of terror, that he no longer saw her. He said, "Helena . . . come closer to me . . . come very close."

Aunt Elsa screamed. "Get up," she begged, "quickly, quickly . . ."

She ran to the door and opened it, crying for help, her English deserting her, and Gail, held in the nightmare bondage of fear, tried to move. But Sturm's shattered hands were clumsy fists, smashing at her, at her head, at her face, the twisted fingers trying to unclench. She heard his heavy breathing, the terrible sounds . . . She heard people running and somehow stumbled to her feet, seeing nothing . . . The hands could not hold her, they were without strength, but they could manipulate the chair. She took a step and another, and then fell, in the path of the wheels.

XIII

Gail lay quiet, her eyes closed. She thought, I have had a nightmare. Part of the nightmare was dream and part awakening. The dream was darkness and escape, the waking was a confusion of sounds, of running feet, of voices. She was conscious of arms lifting her, and that Brad was there. She had asked, "Brad?" and he had answered. Then someone had spoken with authority, raising her a little . . . "Drink this . . . can you drink this?" but her teeth had chattered against the rim of the glass, something cool had spilled idly down her chin and breast . . . something hot and hurting had been squeezed from her eyes. Someone had wept, aloud. Another or herself? Lights, and her eyelids, lifting and faces crowded above her, ballooned and wavering, out of all recognition. And then the same decisive voice, stating, "She will sleep now."

A bee stung her and she whimpered.

Now the nightmares, the dream, the partial awakening receded. She was conscious of her body, aware that it ached, a little; and that it lay on softness.

She opened her eyes. There was very little

light. The room in which she lay was small, and unfamiliar. It smelled of something she could not identify . . . sweet, dusty . . . and also of soap and of fresh air.

Someone moved silently about the room, and Gail could not turn her head, it seemed too great an effort, but she spoke and was astonished by the sound of her own voice.

"Brad?"

"He will be here presently. You must not talk."

She focused her eyes, concentrating. She saw Helena Sturm's small pale face, yet not so pale as she remembered it. There was an angry mark on one cheek . . . and something else was wrong . . . something she could not define.

Now she remembered, and shrank within herself. She asked, "Helena? You're all right?"

"It was nothing," Helena said, "a minor burn . . ." she raised her right hand, and it was bandaged . . . "a little, also, on my face . . . and my hair and eyebrows singed."

"Erich?" Gail whispered.

"He is all right. Try to rest, you are not to talk."

Gail's mouth was dry, and words were cotton. Her head ached. She closed her eyes again and slept.

When she woke it was day, and the sun

pressed, golden, against the drawn shades, struggling into the room in a diffused watery light and Brad said, "Hi!" and then, "No . . . lie still."

"I'm fine," she said wonderingly; and was. Her head was clear and her eyes. And what she remembered no longer terrorized her. She said, "Please tell me what happened — after I fainted. I suppose I did faint?"

He looked very tired but his smile was reassuring. He said, "Yes, several times . . . you couldn't seem to make up your mind. We're going home very soon. Evans will be here any minute now . . ."

"But I'm undressed!" She touched the old-fashioned white nightgown, long sleeved and frilled. "Who undressed me?"

"Aunt Elsa and I . . . that's her nightgown."

"I'll dress," she said, and tried to sit up again, dizzily. But the dizziness cleared.

"Nope," said Brad, "you're going to be carried downstairs."

"That's silly," said Gail, with some spirit.

He said, "You have had a bad emotional shock, coming, I suppose, on the heels of several shocks. So you're going to a hospital for a few days to rest."

"I don't want to go to a hospital," she said childishly, "I want to go home."

"We'll ask Evans," he promised easily.

"There's nothing the matter with me!"

"You're going to have a baby," he said gently, "did you know that?"

"Oh." She felt the foolish tears smart, back of her eyes, and the color rose from throat to forehead. She said, "I didn't know . . . that is, I wasn't sure, but I was going to tell you, and to ask Dr. Evans to recommend someone . . ."

He said, "He will. Meantime, easy does it."

"Are you glad?" she asked, after a moment.

"If you are." He made a distracted gesture very unlike him and she put up her hand and he took and held it. "If I hadn't gone last night . . . but I thought . . . I didn't know what to think . . . there was no one in the lab but Helena. The people still in the building heard the explosion, rushed in, and whoever telephoned here was half hysterical."

"Explosion?"

"It wasn't bad, there was little or no damage. Helena's burns are superficial, if painful. I got there just as she was leaving, having directed everyone and everything, under her own power. She was coming home. If only I had stayed. I blame myself, bitterly."

"No," Gail said, "you couldn't have

stayed. Suppose the explosion had been a bad one? I don't know about these things but surely much of your work would have been destroyed. And, there was Helena."

"You believe yourself less important to me?" he asked gravely.

"I should be." Her eyes widened. She asked, "Erich? He wouldn't take the capsule . . . the first one. He did, the second, I gave it to him."

"Too mild to be effective in the circumstances. I didn't dream, when I left, that he would completely blow his top."

"Who came?"

"The people downstairs, and then Sturm's doctor."

"Where is he? Erich, I mean?"

"He is here," he said sadly, "for a little while. He is cared for, darling. And Helena must do what she now knows is right."

But her thoughts had veered away again. She said, "I hurt . . . Brad, you haven't told me all the truth, have you? I lost the baby?"

"No, dear, but there was danger of it, and still is. That's why you are going to the hospital."

Aunt Elsa came tiptoeing in. She said anxiously, "Dr. Evans is here."

Evans came in and stood beside the bed, his finger on Gail's relaxed wrist. He asked,

"Feeling fine, are you?"

She said, "I'm hungry."

"That's easily remedied. And after breakfast, blankets and a couple of strong gentlemen and the hospital."

"Must I? Can't I go home?"

"Not for a few days." He looked at Brad and Brad smiled at his wife and went out. Evans sat down and regarded Gail. He said, "You had a rugged time last night. Did you know you were pregnant?"

"I wasn't sure."

"What's wrong with your calendar?"

"It isn't always reliable. But, I hadn't felt awfully well. I was going to your office this week."

"Well, it's early in the game," he said, "and you're a healthy young woman. You were frightened last night and small wonder. Tired too . . . the business with your father took more out of you than you realized."

She said, "It seems stupid. Women can go through earthquakes and tornadoes and fires and floods and not —"

"Not all women . . . and this was a different kind of fear; besides, you fell."

She said, "My foot hurts, too!"

"The wheel chair," he said briefly. "Try not to think about it. You're going to be all

314

right. Concentrate on getting well and going home. After that you'll have to be careful, for a while. No jumping off heights or dancing the samba for a time." He rose. "I smell coffee, and I'm going to beg a cup . . . two . . . one for you, one for me," he said.

Brad brought her tray, coffee, fruit juice, toast, and watched her while she ate. But after the first few minutes she was no longer hungry and said so.

Blankets, the stretcher, the men to carry it. She asked, swaddled and lifted, "But Helena?"

"You'll see her later," Brad said.

"And you?"

"I'm coming along," he told her, "as supercargo."

She saw no one as she was carried out, only the stretcher bearers, Brad and Dr. Evans, but she could hear, stifled, muffled, the sound of a desperate weeping.

She was in the hospital only a short time. The nurses waited on her, the room was full of flowers. Evans came and brought the obstetrician, a sandy, middle-aged man, with direct, bright eyes and a therapeutic briskness. He sat down and entertained her with long, irrelevant stories, interspersed with sudden leading questions. She liked and trusted him.

She was allowed no visitors, except Brad, and when she went home again they carried her upstairs and she was informed that she must stay there another few days, up and about, regaining her strength.

Alexandria was admitted and looked at her sharply, sitting by the window in a big chair, wearing a frivolous negligee, her shining hair combed loose and pushed back with a round comb.

"Mind if I come in?" She looked, over her shoulder, at Millicent twittering behind her and said, "Gail knows you're glad she's home. Shut the door as you go out."

Millicent shut the door.

"A pretty kettle of fish," commented Alexandria. "Bradford must have been out of his mind, taking you to dinner with a lunatic, and you in your condition!"

"He didn't know about my condition," said Gail, "and I didn't either. Besides, Erich Sturm isn't . . . I mean wasn't . . ."

"Of course he was. That girl must be an idiot, keeping him at home against everyone's advice, to say nothing of blowing herself up!"

"Well, really," Gail reminded her, "she didn't do it on purpose."

"Maybe not," admitted Alexandria grudgingly, "but she did it just the same. It could have had worse consequences. Working late, night after night, half dead with fatigue and worry herself. No wonder she grew careless. Suppose it *had* been worse? Suppose Bradford had been in the laboratory?"

Gail shivered. She had already supposed it, and turned her mind away.

"Well, she's gone," said Alexandria, "or will be soon."

"How do you mean, gone?" asked Gail.

"Away," said Alexandria. "California, for a long rest. Bradford insisted. She has friends there who will look after her and her aunt. She's been working the way some people drink . . . to get away from and to drug herself. She couldn't, of course, go on. And she can't help her husband, she can't even see him."

"I'm sorry," said Gail wearily.

Alexandria asked, and her thin fingers pleated and unpleated the folds of her handkerchief, "Gail, would you like to live elsewhere?" But before Gail could answer, she added, "Or have me do so? I haven't spoken to Bradford. I appreciate how he would feel, divided in his loyalty. But he needn't be. He must consider you first," she said firmly, but

317

her pointed chin quivered a little.

Gail thought a moment, and then spoke.

"Nothing is changed," she said, "because I'm going to have a baby." The truth of what she had just said reached her with great force, at the moment of its saying. Nothing was changed, she was herself, Brad himself, this old woman unaltered. It was not so easy as that. "Please don't look at me," she said earnestly, "as a — a sort of fragile vessel, a means of insuring the succession. You'd sacrifice your own comfort, your wishes, to that . . . of course. But don't. Whatever has to be solved between us can't be solved by the patter of little feet!"

"Asinine expression," said Alexandria crossly, but laughed, much to her own astonishment.

"There," said Gail, "that's better."

Alexandria said, "I haven't liked you nor approved of you. I haven't, I dare say, given myself a chance to do either. And you're quite right, I wasn't thinking of you nor of your happiness except as it might affect your pregnancy and the child."

"I told my father," Gail said, "that whether we ever liked each other or not, we could learn to respect each other. He said we had to respect ourselves first."

"It's enough to go on," said Alexandria.

She rose and remained standing. "Remember, you reminded me, this is your house," she said.

"My home," Gail corrected her. "Yes, I said it, but I didn't mean it. I was trying to get something of my own back. But when Brad told me I must go to the hospital I said I wanted to go home. Afterwards I realized it was the first time I had thought of this house as home." She looked up at Alexandria, and said, after a moment, "It's yours too, Gran."

"I'm selfish," said Alexandria, with a certain amount of complacency, "headstrong, and dominant, I had to be. You won't believe that, but it is so. I married a weak man; our son was his reflection. I didn't like their way, so I had mine. It gets to be a habit. You seemed a little — softened, just now. I suppose I am. We won't be, all the time. You can't change people with an offer . . . a refusal. But we'll get on better. I'll speak my mind, you speak yours. I don't think either of us was cut out to be a convert, but there are compromises. Most of life is a compromise I suppose, much as I hate to admit it." She smiled. "You get well," she said. "Maybe I'll like you that way, even better . . . spunky, knowing your own mind. But I don't count. You and Brad do."

Gail repeated the conversation to Brad

when he came home that afternoon. She said, "I think we have reached an understanding."

"It's more than most of us do, and certainly the first step. I saw your father today. Manners telephoned. It seems he's been worried. Not that he'd admit it. But he hadn't seen nor heard from you."

"I wasn't supposed to go for at least three weeks."

"I know. But he was watching the mail."

"How is he?"

"Well, he doesn't like the routine and he gripes continually. Still, he's behaving. He has considerable will power which, for most of his life, has been directed into the wrong channels. Now I think he's trying to prove something to himself and, possibly, you."

"If he succeeds," asked Gail, "then what?"

"Take it a step at a time," he suggested. "I don't think, for a moment, hearts and flowers, all is forgiven, and a yen to go out and be a missionary. No. If he succeeds he'll make his own life, and we'll help him. I can't picture him spending his final years at a daughter's fireside, bouncing a grandchild on his knee. I think he'll find something to do, and then do it. Whether he'll backslide or not, who knows? And it's too soon to be anything but hopeful. I told him, by the way, that you were ill, that you had been threatened with a miscarriage."

"What did he say?"

"He was appalled. He said he hated like hell to think of himself as a grandfather, that it was enough to drive a man to drink except that the circumstances were against that course. He said he didn't feel like a grandfather but hoped you were better and would soon be recovered. He said a man does the damnedest things, without thinking. He fathers a child and in no time at all finds he's an ancestor. Don't worry about him, Gail. He has to make his own way out of this. We can give him the opportunity, but no more."

"I've thought about him a lot during the last week," Gail said, "quite selfishly. I mean, I thought that if he were no longer a source of worry and uncertainty I might like him, as a person; he would infuriate me but also amuse me. I don't suppose that's the correct way to regard a parent."

"It's logical enough," said Brad, "besides, sober, and rid, eventually, of the long slow poisoning process, he's not going to be quite the same, you know. Just as astringent, perhaps, and with as much charm, but he'll have direction . . . I can't put it any other way. But I doubt if you two would get along under the same roof for more than an occasional long weekend. Which reminds me, there's no reason why you can't go to Ridgefield for the summer, in a little while."

"Is there any reason why I shouldn't stay here?"

"No, except when it gets hot you'll be uncomfortable."

"You'd like me to stay?"

"That has nothing to do with it."

She said, "Gran doesn't need me, she's happy up there with Millicent and her old cronies. Millicent told me there were always guests." She could call Alexandria Gran now, and without thinking about it at the time or after. "We could go up weekends. And if it gets awfully hot, and you insist . . ."

"I shall." He leaned to brush the hair back from her temple and to kiss her. He added, "But you're not to think of me."

"Isn't it about time?"

"No. And I must ask you something. Do you want to go on with me, Gail? I have thought about this, a great deal. I wish you would. I've tried to believe that you're reasonably content. Perhaps you have been. But should you be? Is that all you want . . . reasonable contentment? I was awake a good part of last night, thinking about this and about the baby. You asked me if I was glad and I evaded the honest answer by saying, 'If you are.' But I didn't go further; I didn't ask, How, exactly, do you feel about it? Do you feel that because you are going to have a child it obligates you to stay with me? Or do you feel that having a child is in itself in the nature of an obligation?"

She said, "I hadn't thought about it at all." She looked at him, troubled. "That is, in the ways you suggest."

He asked restlessly, "You're not resentful?"

"How could I be?"

"Very easily. That night, at Helena's, I went through all the automatic motions, calling Evans, carrying out his orders. But I found myself hoping that you would lose the child."

"Brad!"

He said, "A child would be one more confusing factor, something, someone else to consider."

"You don't mean that."

"Maybe not. I don't know what I mean." He sat back in his chair and drew a deep breath. "I wish I did."

She said quietly, "I am content. Not reasonably, Brad, but unreasonably. That's what I've been thinking about these past days. No, it's been like sitting in the sun and not consciously thinking. So much has, or will, resolve itself . . . Sam," she said steadily, "my father, and now Gran."

"I've been afraid of Sam all along."

"You didn't show it."

"I didn't dare. Sam's a symbol. Suppose he turns up again . . . oh, not as Sam, but as someone else?"

"Every husband takes that risk, doesn't he?"

"Of course, but not at the very beginning, as a rule."

"And every wife, for that matter, Brad, were you in love with Helena?"

His face, which had been somber, flashed into amazement. "Helena?" he said. "Why?"

"Every reason . . . I heard some gossip a while ago. And then there was all that Erich said; that she had loved you a long time; that he wouldn't have minded if she had had an affair. He understood those things, he said. But he couldn't endure to have her heart leave him. Something like that. He said he wanted to kill her, because he couldn't endure it, having her turn to you, finally. And then he confused me with her and —" She stopped and added painfully, "But I have no right to ask."

"I was never in love with her, Gail. She attracted me, which was natural. And I grew fond of her, I'll always be. She's a fine person, Gail."

"But if she loves you?"

"She loves Erich," he said obstinately, "and no one else. She isn't and never has been in love with me. I was someone at hand, to whom she could turn, on whom she became dependent. I was also a friend, and a coworker. Erich hasn't a long time, for which we should thank God. His is not one of the cases that must live on, mindless, to a great age. His constitution is too undermined, he is physically too depleted. He will die, and someday Helena will, I hope, remarry."

"And if I were not in the picture?"

He said, "Who knows? If I had never met you, if Erich died . . . How can anyone say, I would do this or that, under certain circumstances; or would not? There are no easy answers. You *are* in the picture, whether we go on together or not."

"You deserve so much," she began, but he broke in, roughly, more disturbed than ever she had seen him.

"Why? What sort of legend have you built up about me? I'm like any other man, fallible, jealous, afraid, dissatisfied . . . I married you because I was desperately in love with you, and you were willing to marry me.

I didn't care on what terms. I said, apparently, the right things, and didn't mean them all. What I wanted, I hoped to have eventually. I can be patient. I'm not by nature. I've had to learn. The sort of work I do teaches patience. Nothing comes out of the blue in my job. So you learn patience and plodding. You've told me that you're grateful to me. I was afraid of that, it's the last thing I want, to place you under a burden of gratitude. I remember you once said that I was . . . good. What did you mean? Good *to* you, good *for* you? Since we married, and before, I've walked with a conscious wariness. Do you think I was never impatient, angry, uncertain, moving from hope to hopelessness and back to hope again?"

"You never told me, or —"

He said, "I got you by being sweetly reasonable, didn't I? Would I be such a fool as to jeopardize what I had? The half loaf. You liked, you were fond of me, you responded to me, you were never cold or reluctant or unkind. I told myself few men had more, or as much, out of marriage, even those whose wives were in love with them, perhaps. Which was, naturally, supposition. I was not being good, but selfish. You see, I've always had my way, too, Gail, just as Gran told you

326

she had. I was not forced to earn a living. I could, I have a profession. But there was no need. I was never anxious as the majority of men are anxious . . . worrying because the job wasn't what they wanted. Mine was what I wanted. Worrying about hunger, and a roof and the cold, worrying about their families. I have never given a damn for the money, as money. I suppose I could get along on as little as most. But I haven't had to . . . Money's all right, it could buy the education I needed, the freedom from pressure, from influence, from anxiety. It could buy me what I found I most wanted, which was you. But although I was careful to point out this injustice to you, I didn't really consider it. I am now, I have been for a long time. I'm not asking you to make up your mind, here and now. I am trying to say that if you decide to go on with me, it must come from yourself, and not be entangled with any consideration for the Spencers, including the Spencer not yet born."

Andrews knocked, with her dinner tray, as the nurse had left a day or so before, and Gail said faintly, "Come in."

Brad rose and watched Andrews fussing about her. He said, when the old man had left the room:

"I should know better, of course. This

was hardly the time."

"I'm all right," she said. "Don't worry about me. Are you dining at home?"

"Yes. What I really wanted to ask you was, would you see Helena? She's leaving for California soon. She asked me today if she could see you this evening. If you'd rather not, she'll understand."

"I'd like to see her," said Gail, and he nodded and left the room.

The soup grew cold and the chop and the baked potato, the salad was untouched and the trifle, which Millicent, stirred to the depths of her sentimental heart, had made for the patient. Gail pushed the tray away and leaned back, trying to orient herself, for she had just encountered a stranger.

Helena came shortly before nine o'clock. Brad brought her upstairs, announced that he was playing Russian bank with Alexandria and went down again, leaving them together. Helena seemed shrunken, she had lost weight. The small face looked out of drawing, perhaps because of the way she had arranged her hair to conceal the place that had been burned. The burns had somewhat faded on her face, and above her eyebrows, but her hand was still bandaged.

She said, "I came to say good-bye and to

say how terribly sorry I shall always be that you were there. That you had to go through what you did. It was my fault. Not only the accident, which happened because I was careless, thinking of other things, while my mind should have been free to concentrate on what I was doing. Also I was more tired than I realized . . . Not just that, but because I would not consent to send Erich away long ago, when everyone, the doctors, Tante Elsa, Brad and even, in his clearsighted moments, Erich himself, begged me to. But I couldn't endure it for him. I thought we'd manage, somehow, during the time he had left. I knew it wasn't long."

"Please don't blame yourself," Gail said gently.

"I must. And you were very brave. Tante Elsa told me. Also she told me the things Erich said to you in his frenzy . . . about me . . . and Brad . . . I'm sorry for that, too."

"It doesn't matter," said Gail.

"I had hoped it would," said Helena, "after I thought about it. For Brad's sake, I suppose. Even though it wasn't true. Did you think it was true?"

"No," said Gail, "I didn't." And felt herself free and strong and convinced. "Perhaps," she added, "that's why — it doesn't matter."

"I don't understand you," Helena said, "I

never have. But I may not see you again. Brad wants me to come back again when I am rested but I think I shall find work to do elsewhere when the time comes. I can work anywhere, and there would be nothing to bring me back. Tante and I will find a place for ourselves. Brad has been very kind. And I have found him a new assistant, also a woman," she added, "an older woman, very clever, very dedicated."

"I'm sorry you aren't coming back," said Gail.

"Are you? Thank you," Helena said with her curious formality. "But it would only be painful. I must go on," she said half to herself, "to forget the unhappy things and remember only the good. Otherwise there's no advance, no growth. You see, my life was Erich and my work. When we were young, when we were happy, I could not divide one from the other just as he could not separate me from his work. We were very fortunate. Then there was the time of terror, of having no work, but still having each other. After that, the years of separation when I dreaded sleep because of what I must dream about him; yet knowing that it was worse than any dream. And after I was safe, and could work again, the waiting and the hope. And finally —"

She was silent a moment. Then she asked, "How was it *possible* that anyone could think I had anything to give another human being? Erich, in sanity, could not think that. When he thought it, he was not responsible. He had belonged to me, in his healthy body, his wonderful mind, his comprehension and tenderness. I tell you we were as one person. They destroyed his body and, eventually, his mind. But he was still mine, he is now. What we lost, we lost. I won't tell you I was easily resigned. I wasn't. I burned myself out, remembering, and suffering through remembering. I burned myself *free*," she said, "to love him, very much more. He knew it, for I told him over and over. It was only when he was not himself — when he was disturbed . . ."

"Don't try to tell me," Gail said, agonized for her, "don't . . ."

"I had to," Helena said, "otherwise you could not understand about Brad. I have such deep devotion for him," she said quietly, "but never the other . . . not even its shadow." She added, "And I am so grateful to him."

"Do you mind that?" Gail asked her.

Helena looked at her, bewildered. She asked, "Mind . . . being grateful? Why should I? I worked with and for him, I carried my share." She rose and looked down at Gail. "I am glad about the child," she said, "but sorry that because of my obsession, you, and the child with you, came into danger."

Helena had gone, and Andrews had come for the tray, clucking over its appearance, and departed, and Gail sat alone in the pleasant room, an unopened book on her lap. Helena had said, "No, don't ring, I will stop and say good night to Brad and Mrs. Spencer, on my way out." And Gail had waited for Brad to come upstairs.

He came, after what seemed a long time. "But I thought you'd be in bed," he told her.

"I'm hungry," she said plaintively.

"Good Lord, didn't you eat your dinner?"

"No. Don't ring for Andrews. Can't you find your way about your own kitchen?"

"I'll do my damnedest. What do you want?"

"Milk, crackers, fruit, if you find it . . . how about cheese?"

When he came back he brought a double portion. He said, "I didn't eat much either."

Presently she looked at him, a white rim of milk about her mouth.

"Helena was never in love with you," she said sedately.

"Wipe your mouth." He looked at her

quickly. "She wasn't?" he said. "Well, that's interesting. Who told you so besides me?"

"She did. Personally I think she's a fool."

"What?" said Brad incredulously.

"Well," said Gail, "she saw you every day. Not with company manners either. But probably stomping and swearing and throwing things . . ."

"Did she tell you that, too?"

"No. But you do, don't you?"

"I have on occasion. Now and then it's necessary to let off steam."

She asked, "Do you know why I didn't fall in love with you?"

"Gail, for heaven's sake!"

"I suppose you don't. I didn't until a little while ago. You made me feel inferior," she said. "You gave everything, asked for nothing. I felt humble. No one likes that. I thought you were perfection. I thought I could never live up to you. And I was so hideously grateful."

He moved the table aside and an apple bounced rosily along the rug. He lifted her feet out of his way and sat down on the end of the couch. "You were grateful," he repeated. "Past tense?"

She said, "I'm not, any more. Not in that — burdened sort of way. In quite another. Helena said *she* was grateful to you and I

333

asked her if she minded. She looked at me as if I were two years old. Why should she mind? she said, she did her share. It's that simple. Once I feel I'm doing my share."

"Here we go," he said helplessly, "right back to the baby again."

"Not the baby." She added thoughtfully, "I suppose I'll believe in the baby when I feel and look worse. Just at present I can't, quite. Have you forgotten that I married you for money?"

He grew white, he looked as if he'd like to shake her.

"Sometimes I try," he said.

"Don't, because I found I hadn't . . . I had just married you," she said, "*with* money. There's a difference. How can I detach you from it? I tried, while you were talking about it, before dinner. But I can't. It's as much a part of you as anything else; it's made your environment, it's part of your pattern. Yet if you lost it now, you'd be the same . . . You scared me a little tonight. I don't really know you. I'd like to, no matter how long it takes, the rest of our lives even."

He put his arms around her and held her. He said, "I don't know what's been eating me, really. I always believed some girl would marry me for the money."

"With," she corrected.

"With, then. I can look in a mirror, can't I? I'm the guy no one notices, remember? Mr. Average Man. My teeth and hair are my own, I have excellent health. But no glamour boy."

"Neither is Jimmy Stewart," she said dreamily, "and a couple of million women are crazy about him, including me."

"Now I'm to worry about Jimmy Stewart, who stands ten feet high and flew all hell out of an airplane? Gail, you've never been unkind to me. You wouldn't be now? You wouldn't let me hope —"

"Haven't you always, did you ever stop? Maybe I hoped too." She sighed and leaned heavily against him. "Happiness doesn't come in one piece like a prefabricated house," she said drowsily.

"They don't either."

"Don't split hairs, or houses. You have to build," Gail said.

Very soon she would be asleep, and he would put her to bed, he thought, and she only half waking. And then he would lie at a little distance from her, watching her across the dark space between, waiting for the day. He said, stroking her forehead, "Don't talk, darling, there's so much time for talking."

But she spoke, so low that he could not hear, close as he was to her now, and she herself did not know if she spoke aloud or only thought, fleetly, in a beginning dream. She said, "It's just as easy, after all, to fall from loving into love . . ."